ALSO BY CELESTA RIMINGTON

Tips for Magicians

THE ELEPHANT'S GIRL

CELESTA RIMINGTON

A YEARLING BOOK

Text copyright © 2020 by Celesta Rimington
Cover art copyright © 2020 by Ramona Kaulitzki

All rights reserved. Published in the United States by Yearling, an imprint of Random House Children's Books, a division of Penguin Random House LLC, New York. Originally published in hardcover in the United States by Crown Books for Young Readers, an imprint of Random House Children's Books, a division of Penguin Random House LLC, New York, in 2020.

Yearling and the jumping horse design are registered trademarks of Penguin Random House LLC.

Visit us on the Web! rhcbooks.com

Educators and librarians, for a variety of teaching tools,
visit us at RHTeachersLibrarians.com

The Library of Congress has cataloged the hardcover edition of this work as follows:
Names: Rimington, Celesta, author.
Title: The elephant's girl / Celesta Rimington.
Description: First edition. | New York : Crown Books for Young Readers, [2020] |
Audience: Ages 8–12. | Audience: Grades 4–6. | Summary: Twelve-year-old Lexington,
a foundling raised in a zoo, spends a summer cementing friendships, growing closer to
the elephant that saved her life, and learning about her family and herself.
Identifiers: LCCN 2019033391 | ISBN 978-0-593-12122-1 (hardcover) |
ISBN 978-0-593-12123-8 (library binding) | ISBN 978-0-593-12124-5 (ebook)
Subjects: CYAC: Elephants—Fiction. | Zoos—Fiction. | Foundlings—Fiction. |
Friendship—Fiction. | Family life—Fiction. | Ghosts—Fiction. | Winds—Fiction.
Classification: LCC PZ7.1.R565 Ele 2020 | DDC [Fic]—dc23

ISBN 978-0-593-12125-2 (paperback)

Printed in the United States of America
10 9 8 7 6 5 4 3 2 1
First Yearling Edition 2021

To my grandmother Jean Hays Russell,
who wrote her own stories and loved to read mine,
and to my mother, who has braved the fiercest of storms

Contents

1

The Wind and the Zoo

The wind and I have a complicated relationship.

Because of the wind, I'm the girl without a birthday, without a name, without a beginning to my story. See, the wind took my family away when I was small, and I don't remember them or where I came from.

I've tried asking the wind for my family back, but it isn't a very good listener. It does most of the talking. It whispers things only I can hear, reminding me that ghosts are real and elephants can speak. But even though I can hear the wind's words, and even though it follows me around and tries to give me advice, the wind can never make up for taking my family away. The way I figure it, the wind owes me big.

At least it left me in a place where I could have a home. Roger Marsh, the zoo's train engineer, found me in the Lexington Zoo after the biggest storm Nebraska had seen in nearly four decades. I've been here with Roger ever since.

A few things happen when I tell visitors that I live in the zoo. First, they laugh a little. It's usually one of those brief, explosive laughs. But after a while, they realize I'm not kidding. Then comes the following in this order:

1. They stop laughing.
2. They look me up and down.
3. Time passes like a snail while they consider whether or not I'm a rare breed of monkey.

I don't know who my parents are, but I'm definitely not a rare breed of monkey. And despite the "Elephant Girl" chant the kids at Lexington Elementary repeated when I used to go there, that's not who I am either.

Roger was checking the zoo's train tracks for damage when he found me. He had some help, though. He says a ghost saw me wander into the elephant habitat after the tornado hit the city, and the ghost showed him where to find me.

Roger, who clearly believes in ghosts, thinks I might have been five when I showed up at the zoo. And since I've lived here for seven years, we've decided I'm twelve.

He named me Lexington.

2

The Old County Bank

The zoo train is a genuine Union Pacific steam locomotive, so running it is a bigger job than you might think. Sometimes, I help Roger in the train shed when he maintains old Engine 109. He's taught me about the tools he uses. I even try to hand him what he needs, although the wrenches used to tighten bolts on a steam train are half as tall as me. I also help Roger by taking tickets, cleaning picnic tables, and sitting in the caboose to give the train speech. He has a fireman who shovels the coal and fills the boiler, and he has a part-time locomotive crew, but Roger says I give the best train speech.

Today is the first day of summer vacation for my friend Fisher, though, so I'm going to need the day off.

"Hey, Roger," I call to him from the staircase, waving my borrowed copy of *Island of the Blue Dolphins* at him. Roger looks up from his latest book and oatmeal. He's reading a psychology book this time, which is a weird change from his usual history choices. He has to shift in his chair to see me.

The living room between us is taller than it is wide, and Roger's place at the kitchen table is partly hidden behind what used to be a bank teller's counter. The engineer's residence at the Lexington Zoo was a county bank in 1907.

Roger's eyes widen when he sees the book in my hand. The constant creases across his suntanned forehead fold up in deeper lines when he does this, and his teeth flash white when he smiles. "You finished it?"

"Yep. This was my last assignment from Mrs. Leigh to finish my sixth-grade work. I'm done!"

Our voices echo in the center of the Old County Bank. The zoo paid to have the place fixed up like a house (preserving much of the historical stuff, of course). Roger did a lot of the work himself—more since I came to live here—but he couldn't upgrade the echo out of the place.

"Just in time, too," I say, weaving around the teller's counter and plopping into the chair across from Roger. "Fisher's vacation starts today."

Roger reaches across the table and pats my pale, freckled hand with his tan one. His hands are always warm, and he almost always knows what I'm thinking. "Ah yes," he says. "Elephant training."

4

Spending time with the elephants—one elephant in particular—is the thing that's going to make this summer great. Having my best friend finally out of school and in the zoo all day with me is going to make it even better.

"Yes. Mr. Leigh said we're old enough to help this summer, so long as we do it together."

"And so long as Thomas is there, right?"

I nod. Thomas O'Connell is the elephant manager. He handles all their training, which keeps the elephants busy and allows Thomas to check their health— especially their feet. The elephants can choose whether or not to come into the training barn, but since they get apples and sweet potatoes for rewards, they all seem to enjoy it.

Roger slides a bowl of oatmeal in front of me. "I know you're excited. But eat first."

I shove a spoonful of grayish-purple oatmeal into my mouth. Roger likes to put blueberries in it, and they dye the whole batch.

"I suppose you should take some time off from the station, then."

"Do you have enough people today without me?" I ask.

He smiles again and says, "I think we can make it work."

Roger taps *Island of the Blue Dolphins* on its cover. "Aren't you supposed to write a report on this?"

"Done. I finished it up this morning. I can give it to Mrs. Leigh when I go to see Fisher."

Roger scrapes the last of the oatmeal from his bowl and takes it to the sink. His overalls rustle when he moves, and his big work boots clomp on the tile floor. It's a good thing the Old County Bank has high ceilings, or Roger might be crowded.

"Fern and Gordon probably have some chores for Fisher," he says, scrubbing his bowl and the oatmeal pot. "So you help him if he does, okay?"

Fern and Gordon Leigh are Fisher's parents. They all live in the zookeeper's residence on a gravel road near the African Grasslands. Fisher's dad is in charge of all the keepers at the zoo, and that means he's the one who makes sure the animals have the best possible care. So they live in a residence on the property. Like Roger and me.

"Of course," I say. I always help Fisher with his chores. Helping the zookeeper's son with his chores is not exactly what I call work, especially since he's my best friend.

"Meet me for lunch, okay?"

"Of course," I say again. I always meet Roger at the Wild Eats Café for his noon lunch break.

I join him at the sink and fill a large water bottle for each of us. Nebraska is hot in June.

3

The Leighs

The walk to the Leighs' house is all uphill, since their house is halfway to the main entrance, which is the highest point of the zoo. The Old County Bank is near the main train station, which is the lowest point. I feel like I know every inch of the zoo, not only from hiking it every day but because of Roger's train speech. I've given it so many times, I have all the facts memorized. I can tell you that everything inside the perimeter fence is 130 acres. We have the third-largest aviary in the world, the second-largest indoor rainforest, and over 900 animal species. In seven years, I've never run out of new things to see.

If this were a school day and I didn't have Fisher here, I'd stop at the Swift Aviary to check on the flamingo babies and then head straight for the field behind the African Grasslands. A few years ago, Roger built a treehouse in a tall maple tree where I can watch the elephants. The treehouse was Roger's way of letting me see the elephants whenever I wanted, because until today, I wasn't allowed inside the training barn without Mr. Leigh. And Frank Bixly, General Manager, said I should stop distracting the keepers, but he didn't really like the idea of the treehouse. Frank Bixly has never seemed too happy about me living at the zoo. He likes things to be orderly and predictable, and I am neither of those things.

But since today is the first day of Fisher's summer vacation, I take a quick peek at the flamingo babies through the aviary netting and skip the treehouse altogether. I hike the paved road past the African Grasslands and take a swig from my water bottle. The wind checks in as a light breeze, whispering through my hair, tickling my ear.

"*Maybe she won't come into the barn today,*" says the wind. It knows the elephant I most want to see. It also knows Frank Bixly has kept Nyah and me apart since the night of the tornado. Sometimes I wonder whether Frank Bixly and the wind are friends.

"*She will. She'll come,*" I answer in my head. Ever since the incident at Lexington Elementary, I've chosen to answer the wind in silence rather than out loud.

I skip over the first two steps in front of Fisher's house and jump straight to the porch with a thud. Fisher hears me land by the door and opens it, propping the screen open with his foot. He's wearing a white-and-blue Omaha Storm Chasers jersey and holding a bowl of cereal.

"Hey, Lex," he says with a bright smile that says he knows how excited I am about today. "I'm almost finished." He takes a big spoonful of his Cap'n Crunch. He probably got a box from the guys on the grounds crew. His mom doesn't usually buy that stuff. I'm guessing by the amazing smell of curried onions in the Leighs' house that Fisher's mom already made him a warm breakfast.

Mrs. Leigh learned to cook from her Thai mother, Fisher's grandmother, who came to America when she married Mrs. Leigh's American father. You can't find anything as good as Mrs. Leigh's food.

"I don't know why you'd ever choose Cap'n Crunch when you have curried onions and omelets as an option," I say.

"Hey, just because my mom makes Thai food," he says with his mouth full, "doesn't mean I'm not going to want sugary cereal once in a while."

"Oh," I say.

"Do you want to come in?" Fisher asks.

"Yep," I say. "I have an assignment to turn in to your mom anyway." I wave my typed, double-spaced pages. I may have widened the margins a bit, to make my report look longer. Just a bit.

"I'm not hanging around for *that*," Fisher says,

raising an eyebrow. "She might get some ideas and make *me* write a paper. I've already had a list of chores from my dad this morning."

"I would have helped you," I say, stepping inside and catching the screen door before it slams. Mrs. Leigh always asks us not to track "the zoo" into her living room, so I pull off my tennis shoes by the pair of teakwood elephants facing the doorway. The statues are Asian elephants, so they have smaller ears and smaller tusks than Nyah. Their trunks are raised upward, and they face the door for luck and success. I think it's a good sign I'll see Nyah today.

Fisher swallows another bite and shrugs. "I'm finished, mostly. How about I meet you at the elephant barn when you're done?"

"Okay, but I really think it's just going to take a minute."

"Lexington?" Mrs. Leigh calls from her home office. "Come on in."

Fisher gives me a look that says he's glad his mom isn't his schoolteacher and disappears into the kitchen with his bowl.

4

Lexington

People at the zoo have asked why I have the same name as the town and the zoo. I know. Lexington is an odd name for a girl. But I had nothing to identify me when Roger found me. Roger tried everything he could to find my family—to find some clue about who I was and where I belonged—but he came up with nothing. Even the ghost couldn't help, and Roger hasn't seen her since that night.

The tornado tore into the town of Lexington several miles from the zoo. The weather experts labeled it an EF5 tornado, and that means it was the fiercest kind of storm, causing incredible damage. Imagine buildings yanked from their foundations and wind throwing cars through the air. Apparently, that is the sort of wind I survived. According to the newspaper articles, and what

Roger told me, the tornado tore through thirty miles of Nebraska farmland, nearly missing several farmhouses before destroying a small town called Haven Hills. Then it hit Lexington. It flattened the east section of the city, tearing up the concrete and everything. But as happens with tornadoes, even EF5-scale tornadoes, the funnel disappeared almost as quickly as it formed. It vanished before it could totally demolish the zoo. And even with an EF5, some things are unexplained—like why some buildings were left standing while everything around them was gone, and why no animals at the zoo were harmed, and why a little girl survived alone.

Roger filled out a lot of paperwork when I came to live with him. He had visits from people whose job it was to be concerned about where I should live and who I should live with. He bought me new clothes and fixed a room for me in the Old County Bank. It was a long time ago, but I remember how people visited and scratched notes on clipboards with their pens. Roger did whatever they asked so I could stay with him. And when it was all arranged, he had to give me a name. Since he found me in the Lexington Zoo, in Lexington, Nebraska, he decided to call me Lexington. I agree it's not that original. It wasn't a problem until he took me to Lexington Elementary, and the kids realized I was named after the school, the city, *and* the zoo. That didn't go well.

But Roger gets points in the naming department for also giving me the name Willow. Lexington Willow.

It has a rather satisfying sound. It sounds like Willow could be my last name, since we still haven't found out what that is, and Lexington can be shortened to simply Lex. I'll answer to any of it—just not to that name those kids called me at the school. That was one reason I left that place and never went back.

5

Summer Homework

Mrs. Leigh is sitting at her desk, typing on her computer. Her office is tidy and smells of the curried onions with a faint whiff of her vanilla lotion. A red, velvety chair sits in the corner, and next to the chair is a bookshelf full of the books Mrs. Leigh gives me to read. A framed photo on the bookshelf shows Mr. and Mrs. Leigh all dressed up at a fancy dinner. It was a special event where Mr. Leigh won an award for his time playing Cornhusker football a long time ago—which is what he did before he lived in Kenya and filmed a Discovery Channel documentary about Amboseli National Park. Mr. Leigh is something of a celebrity at the zoo. On the wall behind the desk hangs a glittery tapestry of sequined Asian elephants. Mrs. Leigh's mother gave her the wall hanging when she married Mr. Leigh.

Mrs. Leigh looks up from her computer and smiles. She always seems happy to see me, and she's like that with everyone. "Did you finish the book and write your report?"

"I did." I slide my double-spaced pages across the desk's smooth surface but hold on to the soft paperback copy of *Island of the Blue Dolphins*. I'm not sure why, but I'm not ready to return it to her.

"So—what did you like most in this book?" Mrs. Leigh asks. She glances at my report on the desk but leaves it untouched. "You liked it, right?"

"Yes."

Fisher peeks around the corner of the kitchen and rolls his eyes at me through the side door of his mom's office. He's trying to make me laugh. He lets his tongue hang out of his open mouth, as if to say, "Is *this* what you have to do for school?"

"Um . . . I think I liked how well Karana could take care of herself, even when she was alone."

Mrs. Leigh nods, so I keep talking.

"She notices things about the world, the animals. She can make weapons, hunt, make shelter. I'd feel pretty safe if I was stuck on an island with someone like her."

"Mm-hm. Very good."

Mrs. Leigh leans forward and looks over my paper. The clock on the wall ticks the day away while she takes longer to read it than I hoped.

Fisher pokes his head around the corner again. His

dark brown hair stands almost straight up at the top, yet he runs his fingers through it now like he wants it to do that. He tosses a backpack over his shoulder and points at the clock. He mouths, *I'll meet you there.*

"The trash, Fisher," Mrs. Leigh says cheerfully over her shoulder. Fisher slumps to the kitchen. His dad gives him a long list of chores, and Mrs. Leigh never forgets to remind him.

Finally, Mrs. Leigh sets down my paper. "This is well done, Lexington."

"Thank you."

"You've worked hard this year. Roger and I discussed it, and I believe you're right on track to be ready for seventh-grade material."

She's about to change directions on me. The wind does that kind of thing all the time, and I know Mrs. Leigh well enough to sense it coming. Mrs. Leigh left teaching to run the education program at the zoo. She also runs the zoo's special events and advertising, and it's here that she met Fisher's dad. She says she loves living in the zookeeper's residence and helping people understand what the Lexington Zoo does for animals and conservation, but I suspect she secretly misses teaching. She was more than happy to oversee my "homeschool at the zoo." And she takes it a little far sometimes. I can usually predict when it's about to happen.

"I have one more assignment for you," Mrs. Leigh

says. "This one doesn't have a deadline, though. You can work on it through the summer."

Through the summer?

"But if I did well on my assignments, and I'm on track . . . why . . ."

Mrs. Leigh laughs her signature laugh that means she wants you to lighten up. "Don't worry! It's a good one, I promise."

My insides are tight and squirmy at the idea of summer homework. I want to protest. I want to argue. But the sooner Mrs. Leigh gives me the details, the sooner I can leave to see Nyah. Thomas said he would start around eight-forty-five. I can't miss this.

The front-door latch clicks—the sound of Fisher's escape. He can thank me later for the distraction I always seem to provide for him to get out the door.

"It's an opportunity more than an assignment." Mrs. Leigh walks around the front of her desk and leans on it, partially sitting on the edge. Her smooth hair is the same rich dark brown as Fisher's, except hers doesn't stick straight up. Hers lies elegantly over her shoulders— not at all frizzy like my blond curls that can't choose a direction.

"I want you to determine how you are a survivor like Karana in the book. Like Karana, you lost your family in an unexpected way. Perhaps you'll find other similarities if you look for them."

I hadn't thought about that. Mostly, I thought of Karana as brave and tough and having long, beautiful hair like the picture on the cover. But it does kind of make sense. Karana's people sailed away and left her behind. She still had her brother on the island with her, but then the wild dogs killed her brother, and she was left completely alone. Boats and wild dogs, tornadoes and zoo animals . . . maybe Karana and I aren't that different.

The clock on the wall dings to signal the half hour. Eight-thirty a.m.

"Consider how Karana is a survivor at heart. What does that lead her to do? How does it help her? Once you know that, then decide what things you can do that apply to your life in a similar way."

I nod quickly. I have no idea how to do what she's asking me.

Just as I'm wondering how she's going to know if I've done this assignment, she says, "I'll check in with you once in a while, and you can report to me what you discover. Okay?"

I'll agree to anything at this point. Fisher's summer vacation has started, and elephant training is about to begin.

"Okay, Mrs. Leigh. I'll work on that."

She stands up from the desk with a satisfied smile and tells me I can go. I launch out of her office like a cat during Fourth of July fireworks.

I'm coming, Nyah.

6

The Gift of Memory

"Fisher!" I call into the wind as I round the turnoff from the Leighs' gravel road. It isn't very windy this morning, but even a small breath of a breeze will carry my words.

Fisher waves at me from the corner of the African Grasslands maintenance building, across the paved path and slightly down the hill. Morning in Nebraska smells like dew-moistened dirt and green plants all fat with humidity. I catch a swarm of gnats in the face as I run toward the Grasslands. Nebraska bugs are the gateway to summer.

"How'd you get out of there so fast?" Fisher asks.

"There is a trick to getting along with your mom, Fisher. One that you seriously need to learn."

"Oh yeah?" he asks, folding his arms and leaning against the maintenance door.

"Yeah," I say. "You gotta agree with her."

Fisher rolls his eyes, but he smiles his I-hit-a-home-run smile and knocks on the maintenance door. There's a keypad by the handle, but we don't have the code. Thomas, the elephant manager, is expecting us.

"So, what did you agree to this time?"

"It's a weird project," I say. "Kind of personal. She wants me to apply *Island of the Blue Dolphins* to my life."

Fisher wrinkles his nose and shakes his head. "You should just come to school with me next year."

It's my turn to roll my eyes. Fisher knows I prefer to stay in the zoo, and that's not going to change, no matter how much he bugs me about school.

The maintenance door opens.

"Just in time," Thomas says, his hat on backward as usual. "I was beginning to wonder where you were." He's speaking more to me than to Fisher. When I was younger, I used to follow Thomas everywhere, trying to get close to the elephants. He knows how excited I am for today.

"I had a little more . . . homework," I say. "I wouldn't miss this."

Thomas chuckles. He isn't tall like Roger, but he's strong. The sleeves of his khaki keeper's shirt are cuffed and stretched tight around his arms, as though his muscles got in the way. He pushes the door open wider and lets us inside.

We follow Thomas down the hallway toward the training gates, passing supply rooms and Thomas's office. Thomas has worked at the zoo longer than Mr. Leigh, and he was the elephant manager when Nyah, my Nyah, came to the zoo. He's lined the hallway walls with photos of each member of the African elephant herd. Their names, birth years, and relationships are printed on metal plates at the bottom of each frame. Although I have the information memorized, I read each one as I pass.

ASHA: ESTIMATED BIRTH YEAR 1989, SAVED FROM SWAZILAND DROUGHT IN 2008, HERD MATRIARCH, MOTHER OF ZAIRE.

ZAIRE: ESTIMATED BIRTH YEAR 2006, SAVED FROM SWAZILAND DROUGHT IN 2008, DAUGHTER OF ASHA.

JAZZ: BORN 2009, ACQUIRED FROM ARKANSAS FACILITY.

NYAH: BORN 1996, BORN IN CAPTIVITY, RETIRED FROM FENN CIRCUS WITH MOTHER, TENDAI.

TENDAI . . .

Thomas pauses at Tendai's photograph, places his hand on the glass over her image, and says, "Hey there, girl." Then he walks out into the open barn space toward the training gates. Fisher follows him, but I linger at Tendai's photograph a moment. The glass in the frame is covered with fingerprints, as though Thomas taps her photo every time he walks this hall. He hasn't taken her photo down after all these years. I'm glad, because Nyah would never forget her mother, so neither should we. Thomas did, however, update the details below Tendai's picture.

> **TENDAI:** BORN 1979, RETIRED FROM FENN CIRCUS IN 2011, MOTHER OF NYAH. PASSED AWAY IN 2013.

Tendai died in 2013.

The same year as the tornado.

The elephant barn is home to the best friend I have besides Fisher. She's a twenty-four-year-old African elephant named Nyah. And she took care of me the night I lost my family.

Fisher has doubled back to me and shifts the backpack on his shoulder.

"Wish you could've known her," Fisher says. "Tendai, I mean." Fisher was five years old when Tendai died in April, seven years ago. I showed up at the zoo a couple of months later. In June.

"I'm sorry that Nyah misses her mother," I say, more to myself than to Fisher.

"Maybe it's better not to have such a great memory," Fisher says.

I bite my lip and don't answer him. He means well, but only someone who knows who their parents are would say such a thing. I'd give anything to remember mine.

7

Nyah's Words

The hallway opens into a large barn space with a barrier fence separating us from the elephants. It smells of sweet apples and hay, soured only by a small tang of sadness. I can sense it from Nyah.

"I hate that we can't go into the Grasslands with them," I say to Fisher. After all, I *did* spend an entire night sleeping next to Nyah, and she never hurt me. But the Lexington Zoo is *compliant*. As far as the elephants and I are concerned, that's just a word that means the Association of Zoos and Aquariums—or the AZA—has rules, and humans can't share space with elephants without a barrier.

"Yeah," Fisher agrees.

To be honest, I wouldn't expect Fisher to care about Nyah and the Grasslands as much as I do. I mean, baseball does come first for him. But he knows how much Nyah means to me, and that's just one of the reasons Fisher and I are friends.

Thomas strides toward us from the other end of the barn carrying two large buckets brimming with chopped carrots, apples, and sweet potatoes—the elephants' reward food. I reach for one of the buckets. Thomas raises an eyebrow to go with his half smile. He gives me that same look every time he sees me on the observation deck.

Instead of handing over the bucket, he motions to the rack on the wall. "Why don't you get the target poles?"

I've watched the training through the windows on the deck above us enough times to know what he means. Fisher and I take three long poles with small rubber knobs on the end just as Jazz saunters into the left side of the barn from the Grasslands. We can see her between the railings of the barrier fence, but the rails are too close together for her to reach us unless we open a training gate.

"Hand me one of the targets and watch this first one," Thomas says. "Stay behind or to the side of me. No closer than that."

I hand him a target pole, and he opens a small gate in the barrier fence, just large enough for one jumbo elephant foot. He holds out the target, and Jazz moves closer. Jazz turns her massive body until her rear faces

Thomas, bends her wrinkled back leg at the knee, and lifts her rounded foot until it taps the target.

"Good girl, Jazz," Thomas says.

Fisher reaches into the bucket and grasps a sweet potato chunk.

"Not yet, Fisher," I whisper quickly as Thomas holds out his other hand to stop Fisher.

"The reward is for letting me inspect her foot," Thomas says in a low voice.

Fisher nods. Fisher enjoys the animals, but he doesn't pay close attention to these kinds of details. Instead, he remembers how many strikeouts the Dodgers' rookie had during the World Series.

With a large brush from the supply caddy, Thomas scrubs the dirt from Jazz's foot pad. Once it's clean, he inspects the foot and toenails.

"Good girl, Jazz," Thomas says when he finishes, nodding at me.

"Now," I whisper to Fisher.

Fisher rolls the sweet potato to Jazz. "Good girl, Jazz."

Jazz picks up her treat with the end of her trunk and curls it into her open mouth. I get an unexpected case of goose bumps all over my arms. Something fills me up inside, like a fast dose of hot chocolate, and it reminds me of being close to Nyah—being this close to Jazz, watching her think something through and make decisions and eat her snack. I think I understand them, even in their wildness. My heart feels like it's being squeezed from caring, as though I can't hold all the feelings in there.

It's the same with all the elephants, but especially Nyah. The keepers are constantly reminding me that she's wild—that I can't go into her enclosure. But Nyah never feels dangerous to me. She could've trampled me when I stumbled into the Grasslands during the storm. But she didn't. Instead, she wrapped her trunk gently around me and sheltered me from the winds with her body.

That's what I remember about that night. I don't remember anything before the tornado. Roger took me to some doctors, and they said that sometimes when people experience something traumatic, they forget what happened before the trauma. Sometimes they forget a little bit of what happens after, too. But I do remember feeling lost and confused and scrambling uphill through a terrible wind beneath a blackened sky. I remember hearing the wind speak to me for the first time. It said, *"They're all gone, but I'm still here."* I didn't know who was gone, but I knew I was alone except for the wind.

I remember tree limbs strewn in my way and the sting of debris pelting my skin and feeling like maybe I had been in this place before. I remember an opening in the fence and an invisible pull to find something I knew was there. My fingers finding Nyah standing tall and strong in the dark. The muddy and hay-sweet smell of her wrinkled skin. The feel of the muscles in her thick trunk, all 40,000 of them . . . not hurting me. And I wasn't alone anymore. The power of the storm was no match for the giant and gentle presence of Nyah. I was rooted to the ground behind the shelter of her body, and the wind couldn't touch me. Then, as if she knew how frightened I'd been, she rumbled a sound too deep for my ears to hear. I felt the rumble in calming waves, and my brain understood it.

It became a picture inside my head of two elephants in a field. They were entwining their trunks like a mother and baby. Nyah was telling me something important. And I knew she would keep me safe from the dark and the storm, safe in this place, just like a mama elephant protects her baby.

"If you don't pay attention, you'll miss what's right in front of you," Thomas says. His voice sounds a little stern, like going deep in my thoughts was somehow dangerous.

I never miss a thing, I think. *I notice everything.*

Jazz is turning to tap Thomas's outstretched target pole with her front leg. She's on the left side of the fence, and now Nyah ambles in on the right. She sways with each step. Her trunk, powerful yet gentle, bobs up and down as the two "fingers" at the tip sense the air and feel the earth. She comes straight for me, her tail swinging behind her. Her soft eyes look only at me. My heartbeat changes with her approach—a stronger, longer beat that roots me to the earth yet makes me feel like I have wings.

Fisher hands me the target pole that I somehow dropped.

I open the lower gate for her foot and hold out the target. Her trunk bounces and twists near my feet, feeling the ground on the other side of the barrier just inches from where I stand. Her eyelashes are so long, they shadow her eyes, but I can still see the color—a perfect mix of light brown and gold. She lowers her head slightly and then moves closer, presenting her front left foot at the gate and tapping the target.

"Good girl," I say. Somehow, I feel it more inside my chest than in my throat.

"Good girl, Nyah," Fisher says.

Nyah holds still, patient, while Thomas inspects her foot. I plunge my arm into the bucket and curl my fingers around a cool piece of apple, waiting. When Thomas finishes, I gently toss the apple along the barn floor to Nyah. She finds it with the "fingers" of her trunk, grabs it, and presses it into her open mouth. Her lower lip flops loose as she chews, her eyelids closing as her mouth fills with the juice.

I want to talk to her more. But Thomas says we must stick to words and commands the elephants are used to hearing. I want to tell her she's magnificent, she's beautiful, she's my rescuer. I want to tell her I'm sorry she misses her mama. I feel her heart. We have so much in common, Nyah and I, and talking to her from the top of my treehouse where only the wind can hear is just not enough.

And then Nyah steps closer to the training gate again and feels for me with her trunk, as though she is seeking something more.

"Not too close, Lex," Thomas warns, doing his job.

I look into Nyah's light brown eyes.

Suddenly, an image of trees in a wild-looking forest comes into my head through a low rumble that my ears didn't hear. It's been seven years since my brain has felt this rumbling. Somehow, and I have no idea how, Nyah is speaking to me.

I look around at Fisher and Thomas. They are saying, "Good girl, Nyah." Thomas is inspecting her front right foot and trimming her toenails, and Fisher is digging through the bucket of chunky carrots and sweet potatoes for Nyah's next treat. They don't seem to feel this rumbling or see an image from her. Only I do. And Thomas thinks I don't pay attention.

"Do you kids feel that?" Thomas asks without pausing in his work.

I'm speechless.

"Feel what?" asks Fisher.

"The rumble," says Thomas. "It seems Nyah has something to say."

"I don't hear anything," Fisher says.

"Not everything elephants communicate is something you can hear." Thomas's voice is soft and soothing, as though he doesn't want to interrupt Nyah.

And I want to tell Thomas I feel the rumbling, but then Nyah turns her head toward me, and I look into her eyes again.

My mind fills with images—of a woman I don't know and an unfamiliar place. The woman is thin and wears fancy, flowing fabrics. She's in a place I don't recognize, surrounded by fields and crowds of people in colorful outfits. And before I can study any more details, I see another image. This is a place I do know. It's the trees and the wild-looking forest again, and I know where it is. It's the undeveloped land outside the zoo's perimeter fence. I've seen it from the road when I've waited for Fisher at the bus stop near the zoo parking lot.

The image of this place comes with a feeling. Something urgent, something lost, something that will change everything. This seems to be Nyah's feeling about the place. It's a place she would go if she could leave her habitat. Perhaps she wants me to go there for her—to learn something, to search for the lost something. Whatever it is, Nyah thinks it's urgent.

Nyah's eyes go all lazy and half closed. She swishes her tail from side to side, a sign that she's calm and relaxed. Her eyes open wider again, and another image rumbles into my thoughts.

This image is of three elephants standing together. I'm pretty sure one of them is Tendai, Nyah's mother. I don't know the other two. They aren't the elephants in the Lexington Zoo.

"Lex?" Fisher holds out the bucket to me, and the sweet and tart smell sets my brain straight again. Fisher looks hard at my face, as though I have something written there. Did he see the images from Nyah? Did Thomas see them?

"What are you doing?" Fisher asks me.

Nyah has turned around and taps the target with her back foot. Thomas moves in to inspect it.

I shake my head at Fisher. If he didn't see what I saw, I can't explain this. Not right here and right now. Fisher knows I talk to the wind, but it's not something we discuss in front of anyone else. I think talking to elephants goes in that same category.

I grab a chunky carrot as Thomas finishes with Nyah's foot, and I roll it through the gate. "Good girl." My voice sounds like someone else's in my ears.

I'm back to listening with my ears like a normal human, and it's like waking up from a nap you didn't plan to take. I can't feel the low rumblings anymore, and Nyah's images are gone. Before, it was like clips of a movie were playing in my head, and now, those images are only a memory—less vivid. And Fisher and Thomas are looking at me like they're waiting for me to transform into a moth, so I can't focus on it more.

Nyah bobs her head a little as she chews her carrot and then, without another glance at me or any of us, she turns on her clean, newly trimmed feet and trundles out of the barn and into the sun.

8

Things That Are Old

Roger likes things that are old. Steam trains, of course, is the first thing. He knows how steam engines work, how to fix them, and how to keep them running. The steam engine he runs at the zoo, Engine 109, was donated by the Union Pacific Railroad. Most zoos don't have anything like our train, except maybe Omaha's Henry Doorly Zoo and Aquarium. They have a Union Pacific train, too. Anyone who spends any time in Nebraska will probably notice that Union Pacific is a big deal here.

Roger likes books. Real books. He won't read anything on a screen or a device. The only reason we have a computer in the Old County Bank is because Mrs. Leigh insisted I needed one for my schoolwork. The living room bookshelves in the Old County Bank are full of books, and Roger has read every one. He reads about other people and places, about historic events, wars, presidents, inventors, and countries. He rarely reads made-up stories. He sort of disapproved of me reading *Island of the Blue Dolphins* unless I promised to read the epilogue that talked about the real woman Karana was based on—the Lone Woman of San Nicolas Island.

Roger likes radios. He thinks they're much better than cell phones, especially for emergencies. He gave me my own radio to carry with me, but it's big and awkward. I usually keep it in my treehouse. Zoo employees use radios to communicate across the zoo, but most of them also have cell phones. Not Roger. The radio is enough for us, he says.

All these old things that Roger likes sometimes make me wonder whether he was born in the wrong century. Once, I had to write a paper for Mrs. Leigh about the Middle Ages. People believed in spirits and ghosts. They believed you could lose your soul if you sneezed and someone didn't say "God bless you." They believed in jinxes and curses and, sometimes, even magic. I don't think many people believe in stuff like that anymore. But Roger does. Roger believes in ghosts. He believes that a ghost showed him where to find me the night I came to the zoo. And he believes I can talk to the wind.

I wonder if he'll also believe that I can see Nyah's thoughts in my head.

9

Fisher's Plans

"So, what happened in there?" Fisher asks when we leave the barn. "You kinda went all zombie-like."

"Uh . . ." I don't know where to start.

"I mean, elephant training is all you've talked about for a long time, and then when we finally get to do it . . ." Fisher hitches his backpack strap over his shoulder. "It just seems like you weren't having fun is all."

"Secret," says the wind. I'm not sure whether it means I should keep Nyah's communication with me a secret or whether Fisher has a secret. The wind often knows things I don't.

"I had fun," I say. Without talking about what we're going to do next, we've both started walking up the main path toward the entrance gates, and we pass the turnoff to Fisher's house. I'm walking toward the gates because that's the way out . . . and I'm thinking I *might,* just maybe, go out and search the woods that Nyah seemed so anxious about. That is, if Fisher will come with me. I don't want to get lost in the acres of wild growth beyond the zoo's west fences, with no idea why I'm there except that Nyah thinks it's urgent, without Fisher.

And suddenly I realize that Fisher is also walking to the main gates, without knowing that's where I'm headed.

"I had fun, Fisher, I just . . . something happened that surprised me. It sort of threw me off."

"You mean what Thomas was talking about? You didn't hear Nyah speaking to you like the wind, did you?" Fisher doesn't laugh one bit when he says this. He's not making fun of me. He's not like the kids at school. But Fisher does like a good laugh, and he's the master of the serious face that turns funny at just the right moment.

I stop walking, and he stops, too. I stare at him— watching for his mouth to turn upward, or any sign that he's kidding. But he only stares back with his dark brown eyes, waiting for my answer.

"Why . . . why would you say that?" I ask.

Fisher inches closer. "So you did, huh?"

"Well . . . not exactly. I didn't *hear* her speak. I looked in her eyes and . . . I saw images in my head as though she sent me her thoughts. They were like scenes in a movie. How did you know?"

He shifts his backpack strap again and smiles at some of the bronze-badged members of the grounds crew heading down the hill. The voice coming from their radios is talking about a delivery of fish for Harbor Reef.

When they've passed us, he says, "Well, Nyah hasn't been this close to you since the tornado. It makes sense she'd have something to say as soon as she saw you on the other side of that fence."

"Oh." Maybe Fisher notices more about the animals than I give him credit for. "But . . . *you* didn't see anything . . . or feel anything?"

"Nah." Fisher sounds a little disappointed, but he shrugs and keeps walking up the hill toward the main gates. He seems to be in a bit of a hurry. "So you saw pictures in your head when you looked into her eyes?"

"Yeah. It seemed like those two things were connected. I felt a deep rumbling first, exactly what Thomas was talking about. It was like a bass speaker playing really loud right next to me, except without sound. And then came the movie scenes."

"What did you see?"

"The trees beyond the fences," I say, pointing.

"The undeveloped property the zoo owns?"

"Yeah. And it seemed like Nyah was anxious about it. I could feel that she wanted to go there, or that she wanted *me* to go there." I didn't realize how much keeping this to myself made it heavy. Nyah didn't just show me images, she handed them off like an elephant-sized suitcase that she no longer wanted to carry. Telling Fisher makes all of it less heavy. I'm so glad I can talk to him about these things, and that he believes me.

Fisher keeps walking with a purpose up the main gate hill. It's only nine-thirty in the morning, but the summer sun is already sending thick waves of moisture into the air from the nearby Platte River. It's an invisible soup that makes walking up the zoo hill a major effort. But we keep going.

"Fisher . . ." I pause for a breath. "Where are you going?"

He ignores my question. "So did she show you anything else? Like something to tell you *why* this is important? Why, after all these years, the first time she's close enough to communicate with you, would she try to tell you something about the woods?"

Good question. "I . . . I don't know. But she showed me a lady in fancy clothes, someone I've never seen before. And she showed me a herd of elephants."

"Seriously?"

People are swarming down the hill from the ticket stands and the entrance gate. The zoo is open for the day. Fisher and I are heading the "wrong" way. We are like those salmon that swim upstream, but instead of leaping over boulders like the salmon, Fisher and I must skirt around giant double strollers.

"A fancy lady and a herd of elephants," Fisher repeats. "You don't think she means you'll find those things out there in the woods, do you? I mean . . ."

"I don't know what she meant, I . . . Fisher, where are you going?" I ask again. I'm breathless from trying to keep up with him and his new Omaha Storm Chasers backpack that matches his jersey.

Fisher glances quickly at me and then looks straight ahead again. "I was worried about telling you, but you're gonna know soon, so . . ."

"Worried about telling me what?"

"This backpack is part of the gear for the baseball camp I'm doing this summer."

Fisher stops walking and turns. He looks up at the tree branches overhanging the main path, avoiding my eyes. "I'm going away to a baseball camp in Kansas City. Some of the Royals will be there. It's an amazing opportunity. . . ." He runs his fingers through his hair and spikes it higher. "I would've told you about it sooner, but I didn't think I was going to get to go until my grandma offered to pay for it. She's really supportive about this kind of thing."

"With the Royals? Fisher! You love that team!" I've never seen Fisher play in an official game, but he talks about baseball almost as much as I talk about elephants.

". . . but I'll be gone for three weeks."

"Three weeks?" I didn't mean to repeat that, and I didn't mean for it to come out all high-pitched.

"Yeah, three weeks. I leave in July."

"Okay." I steady my voice. "But that's not for almost a month. We have lots of time before then."

"If I'm going to be ready for this camp, I have to practice. More than just playing in the city league like last summer. My grandma thinks I'm going to be the family claim to fame, her American grandson she can tell all the cousins in Thailand about, so she's offered to pay for special lessons."

"Wow. That's cool, Fisher."

"Every day."

I nod again and chew on my lip. Fisher has big ideas for big things that aren't in the zoo. I've known this about him for years, but today it hurts a little.

The thing is, I like staying at the zoo and not going to school. I have friends here, and no one calls me Elephant Girl or makes up stupid rhymes or throws mud at me. I get to be with the animals and watch flamingo eggs hatch and see everything when it's most active in the morning. Most of all, I can be near Nyah. But I still wait for the city bus to drop Fisher off when he gets home every day at three-thirty. And I still count down the days to summer vacation, when we can hang out all day and he can catch up on all the things he misses when he's at school.

"Starting today?" I ask, already knowing the answer. Why else would he have packed his special new backpack? He wasn't planning to spend the day exploring the zoo with me and hanging out at the treehouse like last summer. He was planning to leave.

"Yeah. Lessons start at ten, so I have to get on the next bus. But you know, it's not like it's all day. I'll be home on the one-twenty bus. We can still have a fun summer."

I chew my lip some more and nod. "Yeah. It'll be fine." I force a smile. "It just means this summer will be different, that's all."

"Yeah, but still good," Fisher says, looking a little relieved. "You're still my best friend, Lex."

My heart squeezes a little—like when I watched Jazz work so hard to get her snack. It's a good kind of squeeze, but it hurts a tiny bit. "And don't you forget it," I say, elbowing him in the ribs.

"Ow!" He grabs his water flask from the mesh pocket of his backpack and pours ice water on my head.

"Fisher Leigh!" I squeal, running from him as the glacial cold rolls down my neck and the back of my shirt.

He runs to catch up, but he's done throwing water on me. He needs all that water for his practice in this jungle heat.

"Are we good?" he asks, laughing a little at my wet hair.

"Well . . ." We've reached the top of the hill, where the path turns and opens into what I think of as the zoo town square. A large bronze statue of a lion pride sits in the center, surrounded by the main gates, ticket booths, gift shop, and food carts. My favorite cart is open for business.

I point at the frozen chocolate banana cart and give Fisher a look to tell him he's got it coming. "We're good . . . *if* . . ."

Fisher glances at the frozen banana cart. "Oh no! My brain freeze with those things is the worst! Come on, Lex!"

"You just dumped ice water on my head." I give him my best innocent face. "I think you can handle it."

I march over to the food cart, plunk down my zoo ID card that gives me employee discounts, and pull out one of the five-dollar bills from my pocket. Roger gives me five dollars a day for snacks, but sometimes Mrs. Leigh feeds me and I don't always use Roger's money. Roger says I can keep it and share with Fisher.

"Two bananas, please," I say to the girl. She looks new. The zoo hires a lot of high school and college kids for the summer season. They always start with the food carts.

Fisher joins me at the cart. "Okay, but if I get a frozen banana headache, you have to help me with my chores tomorrow."

"Are you kidding? I help you with your chores anyway. What does your dad have you doing this week? Chopping carrots for the orangutans or shoveling hay for the giraffes?"

"Garbage duty," Fisher says flatly with a devilish look. He may have planned this all along.

The new girl squints at my ID card. "This says *Roger* Marsh."

I must've grabbed Roger's card off the counter instead of my own by mistake.

"That's her da—" Fisher stops himself from saying "dad" and looks at me all stiff.

"He's my guardian," I say. Fisher forgets sometimes that Roger never adopted me. Roger asked me a long time ago if he could adopt me, and I think I kind of ruined it. I was little. And I couldn't stop crying about my lost family. I feel the memory creeping back, and I shove it down.

The girl hands me a dollar in change and two frozen chocolate bananas on a stick. She looks thoroughly confused. "You two kids . . . *work* here?"

Fisher and I smile. We get this a lot.

"We *live* here," we say together.

Someone forgot to tell the new girl about the resident kids. It's something every new employee learns eventually.

"I'm Lexington Willow, but you can call me Lex if you want."

"And I'm Fisher." Fisher immediately starts on his frozen banana. I think his appetite is stronger than his fear of brain freeze.

The girl is still speechless, trying to figure us out, but

Fisher doesn't have time to stick around if he's going to catch the next city bus. I glance at her purple food services name tag. "Nice to meet you DaLoris."

I pocket the dollar and Roger's ID card, and Fisher and I take off toward the main gates.

"Nice to meet you, too!" DaLoris calls after us.

The parking lot is already more than half full of cars. We walk the length of the parking lot toward the bus stop on Wild Kingdom Avenue, scarfing down our frozen bananas, laughing, and moaning when the cold sends spiking pain to our heads.

But even Fisher's squished-up, brain-freeze expression can't stop me thinking about Nyah and the pictures she put in my head.

"Earth to Lex."

"Huh?"

"I said are you going to check out the woods while I'm at baseball? Are you going to try to figure out what Nyah meant?"

I glance over at the undeveloped land—the wild acres of tangled trees and unruly bushes. It flanks the west side of the zoo fences and would at least double the size of the zoo if someone had the money to do the work.

"Um . . ." Fisher and I have always gone exploring in the zoo together, but we've never ventured out in the undeveloped land. This will be a first for me, if I go into the woods alone. "Maybe."

We've reached the bus stop, and the growl of the city

bus approaches from the other end of Wild Kingdom Avenue.

Fisher pulls a Kansas City Royals baseball hat from his backpack and settles it over his spiky hair to shield his face from the sun. He scans the wild woods for a moment and then points at the blue metal roof that towers higher than the other buildings inside the zoo fences.

"If you lose your way, use the Giraffe Encounter roof to get back and then follow the fences to the parking lot."

I nod. I wish Fisher could go with me, but I also don't want to wait. Nyah's message felt urgent, and the longer I think about it, the more urgent it seems.

"Okay," I say, swallowing a lump. "I will."

The bus creaks and groans as it pulls up to the curb. This feels just like the school year, not like summer vacation. The day is just getting started, and Fisher is leaving.

"Thanks for the banana . . . and the brain freeze," he says.

I watch him climb the bus steps and wave at him until I can no longer see his baseball cap through the windows.

10

Frank Bixly, General Manager

Frank Bixly wasn't too thrilled when I showed up inside the African Grasslands the morning after Lexington's EF5 tornado.

According to Roger, Frank Bixly was *especially* not thrilled when the Channel 5 News arrived to do a story on my appearance and my missing family following the storm. The reporters called it "a human-interest piece." They said it had "a lot of heart." Frank Bixly didn't want bad publicity for the zoo. He said people already protest keeping animals, especially elephants, in captivity. Mr. Bixly didn't want anyone getting ideas that the animals were unsafe or that the zoo didn't have a good handle on the cleanup and repairs after the storm.

Roger didn't want the news station to do the story either. Not the way the reporters planned it. He wanted them to make the story about my missing family, because he promised me he'd do everything he could to find them. But the reporters were much more interested in the sensational stuff—that I survived a tornado, that I tamed an African elephant. Which is ridiculous.

But as General Manager, Mr. Bixly agreed to let them film the story inside the zoo if they included information that would sell more tickets. He announced a short-term closure while they assessed the damage and assured animal health and safety. Then he announced that the reopening would include a free day at the zoo for all children with paying adults. The reopening would feature limited tickets to view elephant training and a chance to see Nyah, the heroic elephant who saved the little girl.

It seems like he would've sold tickets to see *me* if someone had let him.

I'm much older now, so I know that Mr. Bixly and the reporters never meant for what happened next. But it did. Somehow, people and the other reporters heard "the elephant who saved the girl" and turned it into "the elephant girl."

And that didn't go well when I got to school.

Despite the publicity, no one claimed to be my family.

But I'm fairly certain, after all these years, that they would've come if they could have.

11

The Trees

I stride through the weed grass, some of it thorny and flowering, and my steps send up little clouds of plant dust mixed with bug swarms. Some of the bugs are light green like the grass, smaller than a seed, and they settle on my clothes and in my hair. I swat them off, but they're replaced by more. I finally give up swatting and aim for the denser part of the trees where the branches shade the earth. The trees are far apart at first, and the sun beats on my head in the rising humidity until my curly hair is thicker than a wool blanket. Sharp dead branches litter the ground from past storms.

No one ever goes in here. At least I don't think they do. Maybe I should go back to the Old County Bank, put on some boots, and change my shorts for long pants before wading any farther. Suddenly, though, the tangle of bushes and dead wood is replaced by softer dirt and an easier path. The thick weeds don't grow in the shade.

I've reached a spot where the trees are more dense, where the long-reaching branches nearly touch each other and only scattered sunlight makes it all the way to the ground. I've stayed close enough to the zoo's west fence that I can still see part of it beyond the trees. The gray roof of the Ape House and the chimps' tall climbing poles are barely visible here, but I can easily see the Giraffe Encounter's blue roof.

Exploring this side of the zoo fence by myself wasn't what I thought I'd be doing today. But I also didn't think I'd hear Nyah's low rumble and see her thoughts again. I was so young when I wandered into Nyah's enclosure, looked into her eyes, and saw the image of a mama elephant and her baby that I've sometimes wondered whether it really happened. But now I know it did.

I wish I could've talked it over more with Fisher. And suddenly I picture myself standing on the sidewalk as Fisher rode away in that city bus, and I feel like Karana from *Island of the Blue Dolphins* as she watched her people sail away from her island. The zoo is like my island. I stay here because it feels safer than leaving. My family is gone, but the zoo is my home. This tangled wood outside the fences is a weird middle place between my island and the outside, a waiting zone where nothing good or bad happens.

The wind kicks up the leaves around my feet. Unlike Nyah's low rumble that passes through me like invisible waves, the wind speaks in ticklish whispers.

"You shouldn't be here," the wind says.

"What do you care?" I answer in my head. Whether I speak out loud or in my head, the wind never directly answers my questions. If it did, I would've had the answer about my family a long time ago.

"You should listen to me." For something that owes me big, the wind sure tells me what to do a lot.

"I'd rather listen to Nyah," I answer. It's true. Although I'm not sure yet what Nyah was trying to tell me, exactly, I prefer her rumblings and pictures to the wind's words.

I think Nyah hopes I will find something out here where the wind doesn't want me to be, and I'm too curious not to keep trying. Besides, Fisher left on the nine-forty bus, so I'm pretty sure I have a little more than two hours before I need to be at Wild Eats to meet Roger for lunch.

I've never been outside the zoo entirely alone and without a way to tell time. I don't have a watch, because I've never needed one inside the zoo. Clocks in every building and train whistles at the station keep everything inside the zoo on schedule. I suppose I could listen for the train whistle out here, too, but it won't tell me which hour or half hour we're on. I look up through the canopy of branches overhead and try to notice where the sun is. Who am I kidding? I have no idea how to tell time by the sun. I'm not much like Karana with that outdoor survival kind of thing.

Well, I figure I can head back when my water runs out and I get thirsty. That won't take too long in this heat. I continue deeper into the shade, angling slightly away from the fence.

A breeze rustles the branches, and at the exact same time, my skin prickles all over my arms and on the back of my neck like something just snuck up behind me. I turn around, but everything looks the same as it did before. I turn again and see something long and blue fluttering between two trees. The blue something is thin and wispy and lets the sunlight through it. With goose bumps still rising on my skin, I move closer to the fluttering thing.

It's fabric.

It's some kind of a fancy scarf.

And it's attached to a lady.

I'm pretty sure it's the lady I saw in Nyah's images.

She's sitting at a patio table beneath the awning of what looks like a giant silver can of ham—an old-fashioned trailer. She's wearing a light blue business suit and a tilted hat that makes her look like one of those movie stars from the black-and-white films Roger likes to watch. She sips something from a teacup, sees me, and sets the teacup gently on a saucer. It makes a satisfying clinking sound.

"Well now," she calls out, "don't you look worn-out." She speaks Southern. Big-time. "Why don't you come and set a spell?"

12

Something Lost

I'm used to meeting new people inside the zoo, but outside the zoo, it's different. I feel . . . exposed. I'm not attached to the ground enough. I might blow away like my family. The wind rustles the branches, and my skin prickles into goose bumps again, even though it is so hot that my forearms are sweating.

The lady waves me over, like she's telling me it's normal for me to visit her at this tin can trailer that probably has no business being parked on this property. I don't mind about her trailer—it's just that if Mr. Bixly learns someone is camping out here, he'll have her out before she can pack up her patio furniture.

"Who are you?" I call to her as I step over another fallen log toward the lady and her trailer. It's not the politest way to greet someone, I realize after I've said it.

"I'm Miss Amanda Holtz," the lady answers. "But you may call me Miss Amanda, darlin'."

I'm near her table now, but I don't step close enough to be under the striped pink awning just yet. "Hello, Miss Amanda. What are you doing here?" Again, not very polite, but people can't just decide they live in the woods outside the zoo fence.

"Oh, come set down, child. I don't bite." Miss Amanda taps the chair next to her at the table. She has some biscuits set out on a plate. A fat little teapot in the center of the table drips with condensation. It smells like cranberries and mint. It might be the tea, or it might be the biscuits, or it might be Miss Amanda. Perhaps all three.

I sit, but not beside her. She has four chairs at this picnic table, and I choose the one across from her.

"I'm here because I have some *business* at the zoo," Miss Amanda says once I've sat down.

"Oh?" Immediately, I imagine this small, skinny woman pulling off her long scarf and tossing it over a branch, hoisting herself above the zoo fence, and climbing inside under cover of darkness.

"What sort of business?" I ask.

"None of your *business,"* the wind says, tossing one of my frizzy curls into my face.

"I need to speak with Frank Bixly," answers Miss Amanda. She moves her hands and arms a lot when she speaks. It's like her movements need to make up for how small she is.

"Does Mr. Bixly know you have this trailer set up out here?"

Miss Amanda Holtz laughs. "My heavens," she says finally. "You sure know how to make one feel welcome. Tea?"

She lifts the teapot and holds it over an empty cup, waiting for my answer. The thing is, I'm not sure she's actually holding the teapot. It's almost like the pot moved a millisecond before she touched it. I think I can see a tiny space between the handle and her fingers. Or maybe it's the weird shadows in the woods.

I nod, if only to watch her pour the tea and set the pot down. I don't think I'd actually pick up a cup and drink something offered to me by a perfect stranger, alone in the woods, outside the zoo.

Miss Amanda smiles and pours a purplish red tea from the pot. A sweet, cranberry spice smell rises into the air. "It's not your usual sweet tea, but I've come to like teas with a little gumption. Don't you worry about me or Mr. Bixly. It'll all work out."

Something about the combination of Miss Amanda's small body and big gestures, or her cheerful tone, or the cranberry spice and the lingering mint, is encouraging.

Encouraging enough to trust her.

A little.

I came into the woods because Nyah's rumblings and pictures showed me these trees and showed me a lady in a fancy dress. And I'm pretty sure that lady is Miss

Amanda. So maybe that's another reason I can trust her. Because I trust Nyah.

Miss Amanda pushes the teacup and saucer across the table, and I set it in front of me.

"Thank you," I say.

"If you don't want to drink it, that's fine. You don't know me, and you're a smart girl to be cautious," says Miss Amanda, adjusting the angle of her elegant gray hat and leaning back in her chair. A key on a small chain around her neck settles on the top button of her business suit. "It's just a habit of mine to offer tea and biscuits to visitors. You can leave the South, but Southern hospitality follows."

"Um . . . where are you from?"

The wind swirls my hair into my eyes. *"Go home,"* it nags.

"Get off!" I tell the wind, wishing I had Nyah's strength to shut it out.

"Alabama. Beautiful place," Miss Amanda says. "Ever been there?"

"No. I . . . I've never been anywhere but here." I really have no idea where I was before I showed up at the zoo. I bite my lip. I'm thinking of the last image I saw from Nyah, the one with the three elephants. The next question I want to ask is going to sound strange.

I'm just going to go for it.

"Miss Amanda, do you know any elephants? I mean, have you worked with elephants or been around them?"

Miss Amanda, who's been holding her teacup to her lips, sits perfectly still for a moment. Then she moves the cup from her mouth and slowly lowers it to the saucer with another tiny *clink*. She presses her berry-colored lips together in a line, which smooths out the wrinkles around her mouth. Her eyes, which I notice now are very blue, look like they're trying to see through to the back of me.

"When you say you've never been anywhere but here, do you mean this town, or . . . this zoo?"

"Um . . . both."

"And what is your name?"

Maybe she knows me. If she knows Mr. Bixly, then maybe she's been to the Lexington Zoo before. Maybe she worked here when I was young, and I just don't remember her.

"I'm Lexington Willow. Many people just call me Lex."

Miss Amanda's expression doesn't change. My name doesn't seem to mean anything to her.

"I live with Roger Marsh." Now I don't know if I've said too much. I'm giving personal details to a stranger—a sort-of stranger who knows Frank Bixly.

"Roger Marsh," Miss Amanda repeats as though she's trying to find a memory. "The train engineer?"

"Yes."

"He lives in the old bank building at the corner near the aviary and the main station?"

"Yes," I say again. Somehow, Miss Amanda knows Roger. I feel a little better knowing this.

Miss Amanda smiles. She picks up her teacup with a satisfied sigh, and again I think I see the cup move slightly independent of her fingers, almost like she coaxed it to her hand. The sun slants through the tree branches that shade this spot, but it's blocked by the trailer's striped pink awning. The light rays behind Miss Amanda, who sits in shadow, must be playing tricks with my eyes.

"So you live with Roger Marsh."

"Yes."

"But he's not your family?"

"Not exactly. I mean, he sort of . . . found me." It sounds like I was a lost puppy.

Miss Amanda wrinkles up her forehead like she's either confused or concentrating really hard. She stares at my face and then at my hair, which is surely even more wild and frizzy thanks to the humidity and the wind. Suddenly, her eyes go wide like she's just realized something.

"Did he happen to find you after a storm?"

"A tornado," I say.

"I remember!" Miss Amanda exclaims, and I jump in my seat, nearly knocking over the teacup in front of me.

"How can you remember that? Were you here at the zoo then?"

"As a matter of fact, I was. My goodness, I'm a mess these days, and I can't seem to remember anything better than my own name unless someone reminds me. But you reminded me of something, and now I remember!"

"Do you remember *me*?"

Miss Amanda leans closer, and her necklace clinks against the table. "You were such a little pint back then, and I didn't get a good look at your face, but if Roger found you after a tornado, it has to be you. I *was* there that night. I was the one who showed Roger where you were."

"But . . ." Even the cicadas pause their incessant chirping. The wind keeps silent. It stops playing with the tree branches and the leaves. Everything in these woods is listening. Everything seems to know the very same detail that I feel taking shape in my brain as I realize the light and shadows have not been playing tricks on me. "Roger says the person who led him to me was a . . . ghost."

13

The Misplaced Spirit

"Who says I'm a ghost?" Miss Amanda folds her arms, and her bangle bracelets jingle together. "*Ghost* is a right terrible word."

"Why?" I didn't know a ghost would have a preference for what they were called.

She tilts her head, considering. "*Ghost* sounds so . . . haunting."

"But isn't that what you're doing here? Haunting the woods?"

"Now, would you really call this *haunting*?" Miss Amanda sweeps her arms wide and refers to the tea and biscuits, the patio furniture, the shiny silver trailer.

It's actually the nicest little spot of color and pleasant smells that I could imagine. There's nothing particularly haunting about any of it, except for the way Miss Amanda moves things without quite touching them.

"No, I guess not," I say.

I tap my fingers against my bare knee. Now that I know Miss Amanda is the ghost from the night of the storm, I have questions. Several very important questions, in fact. Maybe she can tell me who I am and what happened to my family.

"Well, I'm not a ghost in my estimation," Miss Amanda says. "I'm a misplaced spirit with some business to attend to."

"The business with Mr. Bixly?" I ask.

"Well . . . I've lost something that I need to find."

She's lost something? I've lost a family, and that's a pretty big thing to lose. All my questions begin spilling out, and I can't stop them. "If you were here that night, did you see how I came to the zoo? Do you know who my family is? Do you know what happened to them?"

It feels like the wind, only a light breeze now, snatches every one of my questions and suspends them all in midair. Miss Amanda's blue eyes are calm and clear and young-looking if I stare straight into them, but as soon as I do, I look away. I'm afraid I will see that confused look of hers again, and that it will mean she can't remember. I focus on her hands, which are long and slender with wrinkles as soft as her flowing scarf.

"I'm sorry, Lexington Willow. I remember seeing the

elephant wrap you up like a baby, protecting you from the wind and the rain and hiding you from view, but I didn't see anyone with you. If you had family with you that night, they weren't here when I saw you."

I inhale a sharp breath of the green-scented air. I've known for a long time that my family is probably dead because of that tornado. Deep inside, I know I'll probably never find out who they were. The wind's silence on the subject has hinted at that.

I wonder what will happen if I take a sip of that cranberry spice tea from the cup in front of me. Can you drink tea prepared by a ghost? Can you trust a ghost you just met to tell the truth about what they saw seven years ago after a storm?

I half expect her tea to be impossible to drink. But I try it anyway. It's real and cold, and the fruity spice tastes as good as it smells. It doesn't take away my disappointment, but it's sweet. Sweet and sour go well together sometimes.

"You know what, though?" Miss Amanda adds. "You sparked a memory by coming here and talking to me. Maybe if we keep talking, I can remember something else. I think my memories are all still in here somewhere, you see." She taps the side of her head with her finger.

I take another sip and set the teacup back onto its saucer. I like this idea that I might be able to wake up her memories and set them loose.

"Does Frank Bixly know he's doing business with a

misplaced spirit?" I ask, lifting one of the biscuits from the plate. It may be ghost food, but I'm not worried about it anymore. I was clearly supposed to meet Miss Amanda. I bite into the biscuit. It is buttery soft, and it flakes apart in my mouth.

"Oh, Frank." Miss Amanda sighs. "He's a lonely one, now isn't he?"

Frank Bixly? Lonely? I haven't ever thought of Mr. Bixly as anything but the General Manager with lots of rules and lots to say. He lives in the only other residence on the zoo property—in a small house at the top of the zoo hill and west of the gift shop.

"I used to work at the Lexington Zoo before I . . . be-came *misplaced*," she adds. "Frank knew me back then."

It's weird she doesn't just say that Frank knew her when she was alive. But maybe ghosts who don't like to be called ghosts also don't like to be called dead.

"And did you live out here in the woods then?" I ask, imagining a version of Miss Amanda in life, watering flowers in the flower box and riding the bright red bi-cycle that's leaning against the trailer.

Miss Amanda tilts her head like she's considering, although I can't understand why she would have to re-member whether or not she lived here. I mean, we're sitting on her patio furniture and drinking from her tea-cups, for heaven's sake. Of course she lived here. The wind blows the striped pink awning overhead, and rosy hues flicker across Miss Amanda's face.

"Darn if that awning didn't weigh a ton when I tried to put it down in that dreadful storm." Miss Amanda waves her arm at the poles supporting the awning.

"Wait . . ." I swallow a mouthful of buttery biscuit. "You were alive when the storm came?"

"I guess I must've been. Why would a misplaced spirit need to take down an awning?"

"But . . . you were a ghost when you showed Roger where to find me."

"Misplaced spirit," Miss Amanda corrects me.

"Sorry," I say. "You were a misplaced spirit after the storm, when Roger was checking the railroad tracks and saw you."

Miss Amanda nods. "I suppose that's because the wind caught the canopy and the whole thing slammed down fast. Hit me on the head." She straightens her hat again as if the memory knocked it crooked.

"So"—I try to avoid the words Miss Amanda seems to dislike so much—"you became a misplaced spirit that night?" I've often wondered if people can choose what they do and where they go after they die. If Miss Amanda stayed around the zoo, could my parents have done the same thing? "Then you hung around here so you could show Roger where I was?"

"Well . . ." Miss Amanda narrows her eyes in concentration. "I suppose."

She presses her lips together and taps one finger

against them. Her bracelets jingle in rhythm with the motion.

I look more carefully at the awning and the trailer and everything. It all looks new and undamaged. The trailer's silver shines in the slanted sunlight as if someone has just washed and polished it. The awning isn't broken or torn. How can this have been here for seven years and look so clean and new?

"I may have stayed around here for another reason," Miss Amanda says. "Don't get me wrong, darlin'. Of course I'd want to help find someone to take care of you and get you out of the elephant habitat. But that's not why I'm still here."

"It's that business you have with Mr. Bixly?" I ask. "The something lost you need to find?"

She nods. "I hid something here that needs to be returned to someone. At least I think I hid it here."

"Miss Amanda, that's not very specific." If there's one thing I've learned well from Mrs. Leigh's writing skills lessons, it's the importance of being specific.

"Yes, well, I'm missing some important details. I don't know about ghosts, and I don't know about souls who have gone on to wherever it is they're supposed to be. But for me, it's like the creek rose too high and I can't get across. I don't have all the pieces, but I sure have to fix it. And I could use some help, if you're willing." She offers me the plate of biscuits, and I take another.

My head is spinning with thoughts of helping a ghost with scattered memories to remember things she forgot. Maybe she'll remember seeing me with my family. Maybe she'll know something about who I am.

The real reason I want to help her, though, the very real reason, is a 6,000-pound pachyderm who somehow reached into my mind and showed me Miss Amanda, these woods, and some elephants. And because I think it mattered a lot to Nyah that I come here to find Miss Amanda.

"I'll help you," I say.

Miss Amanda reaches across the table as if to pat my hand, but she stops, and I pull back at the same time. Maybe she knows her hand will go right through mine. I don't want to find out if it will.

She smiles anyway. "Since you've been here, asking me about Frank Bixly, I remembered something I couldn't before. We need to start with the gift shop. I think I hid it in the gift shop behind a loose board."

"Hid what? What are we looking for?"

Miss Amanda's eyes widen as the wind moves the branches, creating an opening for an angle of sunlight beneath the awning. It catches the blue from her scarf and her eyes at the same time.

"We're looking for a lost treasure."

14

Lost Time

I missed lunch with Roger at the Wild Eats Café. I never miss lunch with Roger. But it seems you don't know how much time is passing when you have your first conversation with an actual ghost. Apparently, the odd shadows traveling over Miss Amanda's striped pink awning happened because the sun was moving in its path across the sky, and I didn't feel the time passing.

I left Miss Amanda at her silver trailer, promising to return soon, and promising to bring Fisher. I headed straight for the Giraffe Encounter's blue roof to follow the fence line back to the parking lot, and that's when I heard it—the music for the Birds of Prey show. The show is new, but I already know the schedule. The first show is at one o'clock. Somehow I sat and had tea and biscuits with Miss Amanda for more than three hours.

I don't know what Roger will say about me missing our lunch. I mean, Roger doesn't get mad, so I'm not worried about that. I think he'll understand when I explain that I met *the ghost*. This will be big news. And I plan to tell him. I'll explain what happened with the time and why I never showed up for lunch, just as soon as I take Fisher to see Miss Amanda. I'll be extra careful not to stay so long this time.

I'm not very hungry after tea and biscuits with a ghost, but as I wait for the city bus's one-twenty arrival, I buy two frozen lemonades with the six dollars I have left in my pocket. Vendors on the street corner don't offer zoo staff discounts. At least I didn't miss Fisher's return when I was stuck in some weird time pocket at Miss Amanda's trailer.

I am pretty lucky I ended up at the zoo where Fisher lives. We pretend we are the same age, Fisher and I. Since we have no idea when my birthday is or how old I am exactly, we decided I was born the same year as Fisher. That way, we can do things at the same time—like learning the same things for school (sort of), and being old enough to help with elephant training. Since I arrived at the zoo on June 9, that's the day I chose for my birthday—it's sort of an anniversary anyway. And that means I will be twelve next week.

Sometimes it feels like Fisher is older than me. It felt like he was the older one when he told those girls at Lexington Elementary to lay off or he'd bring the meanest baboon to their houses so it could eat their heads. Fisher and I both got sent home, but he'd shut those girls down. Other times it feels like I'm the older one— like when Fisher doesn't know how to talk to his own mom or when he says he could never stay in the zoo all day like I do. It really sounds like whining.

Right now I feel like the older one. Because I know something Fisher doesn't know, and I'm on a first-name basis with the zoo ghost.

The bus approaches from the other end of Wild Kingdom Avenue, and I step toward the curb, stretching myself as tall as I can for a glimpse of Fisher's hat in the bus windows. The condensation from the no-longer-frozen lemonades drips icy water down my arms. The lemonades are still cold, though, and I think Fisher will appreciate that after playing baseball in this humid heat. The bus pulls up to the stop.

Suddenly, I wonder whether Fisher will believe me. Maybe it's best to just take him into the woods and let him see this for himself.

"See you tomorrow, Slugger," says the bus driver, chuckling, as Fisher appears at the front of the bus and starts down the steps. He's covered in red baseball-diamond dirt, he's carrying his soiled Kansas City Royals hat, and his hair is plastered to his head with sweat. He moves like he's walking through something heavy. But he's smiling.

Fisher waves at the bus driver, who waves back and

pulls the doors shut. The bus creaks and growls and drives away.

"You look like you could use these," I say, holding out the dripping lemonades.

"Wow, thanks." Fisher takes one from me, removes the lid, and drinks for a long time.

"Did you have fun?"

"Mm-hmm," he answers as he drinks. His eyes are closed and a drop of sweat carves a path from his forehead down the side of his face to his jaw, where it pauses and then drops to the ground.

"So you're doing this every morning, huh?"

Fisher lowers the cup and wipes his forehead. "Yeah. Well, Monday through Friday anyway."

"I guess it's a good thing you like it." I wait while Fisher has another drink.

Finally he says, "You know, it's not the heat that's the problem. It's the air-conditioned bus. If you never felt the air-conditioning, the outside wouldn't seem so bad. Your body gets used to one climate or the other. It's the going back and forth that gets you."

"Yeah."

He points at the other lemonade in my hand. "Are you going to drink that?"

"No. It's for you, if you want it."

"Oh, I do."

I hand it to him.

"Thanks!" He stacks the full cup into the empty one

and starts walking in the direction of the long zoo parking lot and the front gate.

I stop at the edge of the grass. Fisher walks ahead toward the first row of cars until he realizes I'm not walking alongside him. He turns around. His backpack has slid off his shoulder, and he hasn't bothered to pull it up again. It bangs awkwardly against his legs.

I smile. "Do you want to see something cool?"

His eyes widen. "Did you go into the woods? Did you figure out what Nyah was telling you?"

"I figured out *something*," I say, still smiling. "But it's better if I show you."

"Now?"

"You got another baseball lesson to get to?"

Fisher bobs his head a little and shrugs, admitting that I've got a point. He may be tired and dirty from playing baseball all morning, but we both know if he goes home, his mom is going to give him work to do or send him to help his dad—which will result in Fisher taking out a lot of garbage from a lot of maintenance sheds.

Fisher follows me through the long grasses toward the trees. He coughs as our movement stirs up fresh clouds of bugs and weed dust.

"Please tell me it's in the shade," Fisher calls.

"It is."

I stay within view of the fence line until we're even with the Ape House roof and the chimps' climbing poles. From there, we angle away from the zoo, deeper into the trees. I take Fisher past the fallen logs to the place where I noticed Miss Amanda's scarf flowing in the breeze. My breath catches as we get closer. It's still amazing and dreamlike to think of seeing and talking with a ghost. She's not sitting outside this time, but as I step over the last fallen tree toward the spot where I had tea and biscuits only a half hour ago, I stop suddenly.

"Wow," Fisher breathes. "Cool. What a wreck. How long do you think this has been here?"

My mouth is all cottony, and it's hard to form words, but I manage. "About seven years."

The silver trailer and its awning are not what I saw a half hour ago. The trailer is dented where something big, perhaps a tree trunk, long ago slammed into its side. The poles that held up the awning have been yanked from their holes and are twisted and rusty. The fabric that once was a striped pink awning dangles from the poles in shreds. It is now more brown and yellow than it is pink. The table and chairs where Miss Amanda and I sat are scattered around the clearing, upside down or on their sides. Most of the furniture is broken with bits of the wood missing.

"I don't understand," I whisper.

"*Don't you?*" taunts the wind.

"Is this not what you wanted to show me?" Fisher is walking through the wreckage and lifts a piece of awning fabric off the rusted red bicycle.

"I . . . I don't think we should touch this," I say.

"Why not? What about inside this old trailer? Did you go in here?" Fisher's eager face looks like I just gave him the best present in the world.

"No, Fisher. Stop." My voice isn't projecting right. It's coming out all airy. Fisher doesn't hear me, or else he doesn't listen. He's climbing the trailer steps and trying the door. I feel that flying-away feeling again, like the wind could take me at any moment and I don't have anything to hold me down.

"Fisher! Stop!"

He stops, his hand frozen on the trailer door handle.

"This isn't what I wanted to show you. Please don't touch any of it."

"Lex . . ." Fisher has that look he gets when he thinks I'm not making sense. He tilts his head slightly to the side, and his dark eyes reflect a blend of laughter with concern—how I imagine an older brother might look at a silly little sister who is about to cry.

"Lex, what's wrong?" He drops his backpack to the ground. It settles into the mass of leaves and sticks with a *crunch*. He sits on the trailer step and stares at me, waiting for an explanation.

I don't know how to explain, but I sit on the step next to him.

I think of Nyah and how when she wanted to tell me something, she just did it.

And so I start at the beginning. I tell Fisher about

my search in the trees and the wind nagging at me and saying I shouldn't be here, and about the light blue scarf rippling through the trees. I tell him about Miss Amanda—her Southern accent and her fancy clothes, and how she looked like the woman Nyah showed me.

Fisher is a good listener.

"And all of this"—he points at the wreck in front of us and the damaged trailer behind us—"this was . . ."

"It was perfect," I say. "It was shiny and new, and the table was set up"—I wade through the blanket of dead leaves to the exact spot—"over here. She had tea—spicy tea in a little fat teapot! I drank her tea and ate her buttery biscuits until I was full!"

Fisher's face is surprisingly still. He hardly moves at all except to blink his eyelids. Then he nods very small, as though he's realizing something, and waits for me to continue.

I tell him what Miss Amanda said about knowing Frank Bixly, about Roger, about working at the zoo and showing Roger where to find me.

About the storm.

About her death.

Fisher turns very slowly to look at the trailer door behind him. "She died in the storm that brought you here?"

I swallow my cottony spit and sit next to him again. "Seven years ago."

"Wow." Fisher's eyes widen. He's looking at the wreckage.

"She said she died when the awning fell and hit her on the head," I almost whisper. I close my eyes, hoping that somehow all this will transform to the way it looked before. Shutting out the sight of Miss Amanda's broken furniture makes the hum and chatter from beyond the distant zoo fence louder in my ears. The low growl of the howler monkeys isn't usual for this time of day, yet they howl as if they know something strange is happening. The whooping cranes let loose a bugle call as Fisher taps me on the shoulder.

My eyelids fly open.

"I'm surprised at you, Lex," Fisher says with a mischievous grin.

"What do you mean?" Does he think I'm making this up?

Fisher raises his eyebrows. "You brought me here to meet a ghost and didn't even think to warn me?"

"Well . . ."

Fisher reaches to the ground beneath the step, grabs a handful of wild grass, and tosses it at me. "I'm kidding," he says, laughing. "Seriously, this is really cool. You met the ghost. *The* ghost. Roger used to talk about it all the time. The ghost who appeared while he was inspecting the railroad tracks after the storm and told him he needed to rescue a little girl. You met her!"

The wind rustles the branches, but I don't fear blowing away anymore. I'm solid. Stuck to the ground. Safe.

"So you believe me?"

Fisher pauses, turning over a single blade of grass in his fingers and rolling it into a little ball. "It doesn't surprise me that you saw a ghost. Just because I haven't seen a ghost doesn't mean they aren't out there."

I want to hug him. Instead, I elbow him in the ribs, but not hard. "She says she prefers to be called a misplaced spirit."

"Oh really?"

"And she said she's stuck here because she has something she needs to finish. I told her I'd help her."

Fisher flicks away the little blade of grass and looks into my eyes with his deep brown ones. "Help her do what?"

"She says she hid a treasure and needs help finding it and returning it to the rightful owner. I think it might be stolen or something."

Fisher looks as though he may never need to play baseball again to be happy.

"What else did she say?" He's leaning forward on the step, like he might launch out of the woods and over the zoo fence to the Ape House.

"She says her memories are a mess. The longer she's a ghost, the less of her life she remembers. But she remembers things when I get her talking, and she remembers the treasure because it's the thing she needs to fix.

That's why she needs my help—our help." I add that last bit at the end—hopeful that Fisher will take the bait. He's never turned down a possible adventure as long as I've known him.

Fisher nods, waiting for the rest.

"She says to try the gift shop." Miss Amanda recalled a single detail before I left her sipping her tea in the woods. "She remembers she hid the treasure behind a loose board."

"In the gift shop," Fisher repeats. He actually launches off the step, not all the way out of the woods as I imagined, but his pre–baseball-practice energy is definitely back. He clasps his hands together and holds them on top of his head like he's keeping his thoughts together. "Lex! There is definitely a loose board in the gift shop. At least there was. I don't know if Mr. Bixly has had it fixed after all these years, but I remember where it was."

"You do?"

Fisher's enthusiasm changes everything. He believes what I'm telling him without needing any proof. It melts away my disappointment in finding the real, destroyed state of Miss Amanda's abandoned property. We leave her trailer and the wreckage behind, swatting away rising clouds of gnat swarms as we run, not even caring that afternoon storm clouds with the smell of rain are rolling in from the south.

We have a treasure to find.

15

The Gift Shop

It's raining by the time we reach the front gates and slip through the turnstiles with our employee passes. Normally, afternoon rain just means Fisher and I hang out in the treehouse behind the African Grasslands. But today it means we have a crowd of zoo patrons filling the main gift shop, just when we were hoping for a chance to yank up a loose floorboard unnoticed.

Fisher and I shove our way inside the double doors. The gift shop staff, with their bright turquoise shirts, skillfully herd rain-soaked people to various displays, trying to show kids the polished rocks, the animal figurines, and the wall of science experiments. I notice they try to steer the kids around the piles of plush animals. Rain-soaked kids with muddy shoes aren't a good combination for the white tiger and polar bear plush toys.

"There used to be a loose floorboard where they had the puppet stage, remember?" Fisher points to the clothing racks that now occupy the old puppet show space. When we were much younger, Fisher and I used to sit and watch Isabel Acosta, the gift shop manager, put on puppet shows for the kids featuring zoo animal puppets speaking English and Spanish.

"Oh yeah!" I wriggle between two enormous strollers taking up valuable real estate inside the crowded shop. The rain pattering on the roof and its steady tapping against the windows seems enough to keep all the people inside for a while. However, a small line has formed at the cash registers, and a few people have the yellow Lexington Zoo rain ponchos and umbrellas in their hands.

Outside the gift shop windows, some people still walk the main path leading to the Wild Kingdom Education Center and Bear Country on the left and the African Grasslands on the right. If more people would dare to get wet, Fisher and I would have room to breathe.

"Lex," Fisher calls up to me from the floor. He's down on his knees, knocking on the floorboards beneath a rack of Lexington Zoo seasonal jackets. So far, no one has noticed, or if they have, they don't care.

I dodge a couple of girls looking at gold-dipped animal earrings and join him on the floor, careful to keep my feet out of the path of people.

"This actually works out better for us," he says,

leaning in close and keeping his voice low. "So long as the gift shop is full of people, and the staff is busy selling rain ponchos, no one is going to notice what we're doing."

I hadn't thought of that. Without all these people around, Isabel and her sales clerks were sure to notice Fisher and me yanking up a piece of the wood floor.

I kneel across from Fisher. The loose board I remember had a little notch on its edge, and it would make a wooden *thunk* when I stepped or sat on it.

"I think it was over here more," Fisher says, crawling behind a clothing rack.

A pair of black tennis shoes stops right next to my hands, and I glance up. A blond guy is looking down at me. He's wearing one of the bright turquoise shirts and a name tag that says Cory. "You need some help?" he asks.

"Uh, no." I stand up. Since he clearly doesn't recognize Fisher and me, he must be one of the new summer employees. "Thought I dropped a quarter, but I can't find it."

"I found it, Lex!" Fisher says a bit too loud. Several people in the store, including the helpful Cory, turn to look at him.

"You found my quarter?" I say, giving him a wide-eyed look so he'll play along.

"Uh, yeah."

I turn to Cory and smile. "I guess he found it."

Fisher hands me something from the floor. It feels like one of the polished rocks from the big barrel. "We're good," I say, waving my other hand at Cory. If he sees I'm holding a polished rock, he'll think we're trying to steal. And then we'll have to explain that we live here and that we weren't stealing, and then Mr. and Mrs. Leigh and Roger will have to come over and bail us out, and then we'll never hear the end of it.

Cory nods. "Okay, well, let me know if you need any help finding what you want."

Haha, right. "Sure, thanks."

It's so weird when the new employees think Fisher and I are visitors at the zoo. We know more about this place than almost anyone. I could tell Cory where to find the secret stash of candy Isabel keeps in the back storeroom. He walks away, looking for more people to help.

When Cory is far enough away from us, I quickly slide the polished rock into the barrel and whisper to Fisher, "Don't hand me store merchandise like it's my quarter from the floor. What if he saw it and thought we were trying to steal? We're acting suspicious enough already."

"Yeah, sorry. I just thought I'd better hand you something." Fisher taps his foot on the board where he stands and smiles. His tapping makes that familiar hollow *thunk* sound.

My heart thunks in my chest along with it. All the

times Fisher and I sat in here and laughed at Isabel's puppet shows, all those times I noticed the hollow sound of this board, and there could have been a treasure under here all along.

I nearly forget that the gift shop is packed with people. I almost don't care. Fisher and I are going to find Miss Amanda's missing treasure. Right now.

"Lexington Willow." Mrs. Leigh hurries toward us from the other side of the gift shop. Isabel is with her, pointing at Fisher and me. They're both holding their zoo radios. Mrs. Leigh doesn't take long to get through the crowd. She reaches us before Fisher and I have time to plan.

"Hi, Mrs. Leigh," I say politely, trying to sound calm. I haven't done anything wrong . . . yet. It's not like Fisher and I pried up that floorboard . . . yet.

Mrs. Leigh looks relieved to see me, but the smile she usually greets me with is missing. "Where have you been?"

"I've been here. I walked Fisher to the bus and . . ." I trail off because I'm not sure what I should say. There's plenty I probably shouldn't say with all these people here. A few nosy patrons are standing close enough to eavesdrop. They pretend to look at T-shirt sizes.

"Roger asked me to help him find you," she says when I don't finish my sentence. "He's been so worried. We've radioed him to let him know you're safe, but I think you should go to the station and talk to him yourself."

Oh, this is about lunch at Wild Eats—that I didn't show up. With taking Fisher to see Miss Amanda's wrecked trailer and then searching for this loose board, I completely forgot.

"Am I in trouble?" I didn't expect this. Fisher gets in trouble for not doing his chores sometimes, and he used to get in trouble for fighting mean kids when I went to school with him. But I never get in trouble. I'm a little confused.

"That's between you and Roger," Mrs. Leigh says. "Come on. I'll drive you down there." She looks Fisher up and down. He's filthy. Mrs. Leigh raises an eyebrow and smiles a little. "You look like you had a good practice."

Fisher nods and gives me a look that says he's sorry we can't look under the loose floorboard right now.

And with nothing more we can do, we follow Mrs. Leigh past Isabel, who hands me a piece of candy like she always does and gives me an I'm-sorry smile. Isabel has a good imagination. And I'll bet she can imagine what it's like to have people report on your whereabouts with radios. We follow Mrs. Leigh through the crowd and into the rain—away from the loose board and Miss Amanda's lost treasure.

I just hope someone else hasn't already found it.

16

The Train Station

Fisher and I follow Mrs. Leigh into the rain-soaked plaza, shielding our eyes from the slant of the rain. Mrs. Leigh slides into the driver's seat of a large covered golf cart parked outside the gift shop. Fisher and I climb into the back.

The zoo has several of these carts. The keepers use the small ones to speed around the zoo paths from one maintenance building to another. Mrs. Leigh uses the larger ones like this, with the forward-facing back seats, to give tours to the zoo donors. Frank Bixly uses the carts more than anyone, though. He doesn't really need to speed around to do his job. I think he likes to feel important.

Despite the small roof over the cart, the seats are wet. My shorts and T-shirt are instantly soaked. A light wind is slanting the downpour, but this still isn't one of those worrisome storms. The sky is just gray, not black. The air is only misty, not pre-tornado green.

Mrs. Leigh drives us down the hill to the left, toward Bear Country. Fisher leans over to me and whispers, "We can go to the gift shop tonight, if you aren't in trouble."

"Oh, I'm not in trouble," I say. I do feel an odd twinge inside that I don't recognize, but I think it's because today has been very weird. I saw an elephant's thoughts, and I had a ghost's tea and biscuits for lunch. It makes sense my stomach would be a little unsettled.

"Well, I might be in trouble," Fisher says. "Who knows." He doesn't look worried—he's just stating the facts. "I'm not sure why, but it probably has to do with taking out some garbage." He rolls his eyes. His dad grew up on a ranch and gives Fisher chores to teach him to work. I giggle and quickly clap my hand over my mouth to silence it.

The girl we met earlier, DaLoris, is now working at the hot dog stand in front of Bear Country. We wave at her as the golf cart zips past. DaLoris has a little hut with a decent roof to sit under, so she's reading a book as the rain pours down around her. She waves back.

"I hope someone didn't already find Miss Amanda's treasure," I whisper. "The board is still loose after all these years, so that probably means no one has tried to fix it."

"And if it's not there?" Fisher asks.

"We go back to Miss Amanda's trailer and hope she shows up again."

Fisher's eyes widen when I say the words *Miss Amanda's trailer,* and he puts a finger to his lips, even though I'm already whispering.

"I hope I don't miss it if she does," he whispers, looking sideways at his mom in the front seat and shielding his mouth with his hand. "But don't tell my mom."

I wasn't planning on telling Mrs. Leigh. I remember a concerned look she gave to Roger when he mentioned the ghost once. Like she thought he was crazy.

"I won't," I say.

We pass the Birds of Prey Amphitheater on the right. The soggy seats are empty, but a few zoo patrons have clustered together underneath the small pavilion where people stand in line for tickets to the Birds of Prey show. Water runs in small streams off the banner at the entrance. One of the bird handlers, a guy named Javier who wears khaki shorts even in winter, is covering some of the platforms and gathering wet props from the set.

The path turns and we head north, parallel to Miss Amanda's woods. I stretch to see if I can make out any part of her trailer beyond the boundary fence, but the Ape House and maintenance buildings mostly block my view. Whenever a space opens between the buildings for a moment, all I see are tree branches blurred by slanting rain.

"Why do you think no one ever cleaned up out there?"

I ask Fisher, jerking my head toward Miss Amanda's woods and watching Mrs. Leigh in the rearview mirror. Her lips are pressed together in a line, not in an angry way, but more like she's working something out. I don't think she can hear what we're saying in the back seat with the rain pelting overhead and the whir of the golf cart's motor.

"Maybe no one realized it's there," Fisher guesses. "Or maybe they just forgot about it."

The weird twinge in my stomach twists a little tighter. *Someone* should have realized Miss Amanda's things were out there. She was a person with a life, and she died. That matters. The things she left behind matter. Her memory matters.

I wonder, as I have a million times, what else happened the night I came to the zoo. And then it hits me.

"Fisher!" My enthusiastic whisper comes out as a hiss. "I have that old newspaper article from the *Lexington Herald* about the tornado, remember?"

"Yeah." Fisher wipes the rain spray from his face and shields his eyes toward me. The wind is blowing from his side of the cart now. He tucks his backpack on the other side of his legs, protecting it.

"The article said that several people died and some others were reported missing after the storm. I wonder if someone reported about Miss Amanda."

"You mean . . ." The idea spreads across his face.

"We could search for her name."

"You could see if anyone wrote anything about her and who she was."

"It's perfect," I say. I'm about to tell him Miss Amanda's last name again, so he can help me search, but Mrs. Leigh stops the cart and turns around. We're at the main station, as close as the golf cart can get to the train without driving across the long stretch of grass.

Mrs. Leigh's face glistens with rain, making her look even more radiant than usual. Her dark hair is sleek and shiny. Her skin is all one smooth color, unlike my own that gets more freckled with each summer day.

Mrs. Leigh reaches over the seat and settles her hand gently over mine. "You shouldn't do this kind of thing to Roger, Lexington," she says.

What kind of thing?

"You're very important to him. You know that, right?"

I nod.

"I hope the things I said to you this morning have nothing to do with you disappearing on Roger today."

"What things?"

"The assignment I gave you."

"Oh," I say.

"I don't want it to make things difficult between you and him."

Difficult? That's not a word I would ever choose to describe Roger, or me and Roger, or things between me and Roger. Maybe that weird feeling in my stomach isn't from Miss Amanda's tea and biscuits. It's probably something else, but I'm not sure what to call it. It's not right, though.

"That assignment I gave you is to help you grow. I intended for you to learn something new about yourself, as well as to more deeply evaluate the book you read."

Fisher squirms and shifts in the seat so he can look out the other side of the cart. He doesn't like listening to my school lessons. He says he gets enough of it when he's at school. But this time feels different. I get plenty of school lectures from Mrs. Leigh, so this one shouldn't bother me. But it does, a little.

"You need to do this assignment and still respect what Roger asks you to do," she continues. "Does that make sense?"

I swallow. "Yes."

"Okay." Mrs. Leigh smiles. "And I'm going to want you to write something for me about what you discover about Karana and yourself."

I hope she's not about to give me a deadline, because I've been doing school assignments since last September, and this treasure of Miss Amanda's should get to come first. Mrs. Leigh turns back around.

Across the grass from our golf cart, Engine 109 idles on the tracks. Pop-off valves by the whistle shoot clouds of creamy-looking steam into the air with a loud hiss, releasing the extra pressure from the boiler. The rhythmic clank of the steam-powered compressor sounds like the locomotive's metallic heartbeat. Roger's assistant engineer, J. P. Felt, looks out from inside the red-and-gold-painted cab. He sees me and waves his gloved hand out the window and then down the tracks at Roger, who is doing his pre-run inspection and hasn't noticed us yet.

"Thanks for the ride," I say to Mrs. Leigh. Then, thinking that Fisher and I have some planning to do, I add, "Can Fisher come on the train for a while?"

Mrs. Leigh doesn't answer but instead glances over at the train. Roger is now striding toward us with his long legs and work boots. He waves his engineer's cap at us, not looking upset with me at all. I knew he wouldn't be mad about lunch. That's just not Roger.

"I think you need a little time with Roger," Mrs. Leigh says, "but you and Roger are invited to our house for dinner tonight." Her voice lifts almost like she's singing whenever she invites us to dinner. "So you and Fisher can make your plans then."

Fisher looks at me. How his mom always knows when we're up to something is a mystery. Luckily, she doesn't always know *what* we're up to.

I step out of the cart just as Roger reaches us.

"Thanks for bringing her, Fern," Roger says. He puts his arm around my shoulders. It feels like it weighs more than me, even though he doesn't rest its full weight. Roger shovels coal, lifts heavy machinery, and can fix nearly anything. His arm feels safe, but it's not enough to keep me from feeling like I might blow away sometimes. Even Roger's strong arms couldn't have kept my family on the ground in the tornado. Sometimes I wish he could've been there to try.

"It was no trouble," Mrs. Leigh says, holding up her radio and waving it.

The zoo staff radios are set to the same channel, so everyone hears all the messages. Heat spreads in my cheeks when I think of Roger sending that message on the radio for everyone at the zoo to find me.

"You and Lexington are invited to dinner at our place," Mrs. Leigh calls out happily. "Come over any time after closing."

Roger glances down at me and raises one bushy eyebrow. He's asking my opinion about dinner with the Leighs. He knows I already spend a lot of time with Mrs. Leigh, and not as much as I would like with Fisher. I nod and smile. Dinner with the Leighs is perfect—especially today, when Fisher and I have work to do.

Roger smiles. His eyes are kinder than most. "We'll be there."

I watch as Mrs. Leigh drives Fisher away in the golf cart and then look up at Roger. The rain has streaked the coal dust on his face and has completely soaked us both, but a few minutes inside the steam engine's hot cab will dry us off.

"So . . . ," Roger says, drawing the word out long with the deep rumble of his voice. He takes his arm from my shoulders and rubs his neck like he does when he's thinking. We slog through the wet grass toward the main station pavilion. "What happened with lunch today?"

I'm not sure if now is the right moment to tell him I met the ghost from the night of the storm. I want to tell him, but not here, at the station, in the rain, after being brought here like a fugitive.

"I went out of the zoo—to the woods. I lost track of time."

Roger's eyebrows lift so high that his forehead wrinkles.

"I'm sorry. Are you angry?" I have to ask, because I've never seen Roger angry. I don't know what that would be like.

"I'm not angry. Just surprised. *You* went out of the zoo and into the woods? Didn't Fisher have baseball this morning?"

"Yes. I went in the woods by myself."

Roger presses his lips together, still rubbing his neck. We reach the pavilion. It's full of people waiting for the train's next run. A train ride is always a good option for the guests when it's raining. Roger walks around the side of the pavilion to the gate that leads to the tracks. He leans one arm against the metal railing and bends at the waist, lowering his head a little closer to mine and keeping this conversation just between the two of us.

"I expected you were with Fisher, but when no one could find either of you for a while, I got worried."

Why would Roger worry? I've been roaming free in

this zoo for a long time. I know every inch of this place. I know where I'm allowed to go, and I never get lost. Roger rubs his hand over his hair and sighs. Suddenly, I think of Roger bent over his food, sitting all alone at a table for two at the Wild Eats Café. I think of him waiting for his entire lunchtime, possibly not eating because he wants me to get there so we can eat together. I think of how he didn't know what happened to me and that I've never made him worry like that before.

I put my hand on top of his where it rests on the gate holding his engineer's cap. "I'm sorry I didn't come. I'm sorry I worried you."

Roger gives me a slight smile. "I gave you a radio to use. I know it's kind of bulky, but I want you to take it with you when you go out for the day. Do you know where it is?"

"Yes. It's in the treehouse. On the charger." My radio is set to a different channel than the main zoo communication. It uses the same channel as the second radio Roger keeps with him on his train runs. Basically, it's just for us. And I think about that as I realize I haven't really used it all that much.

He stands up straight and places his engineer's cap on his head. "Get it, keep it charged, and keep it with you. Okay?"

"Okay."

Roger pats my hand gently. My hand nearly disappears underneath his. Then he steps into the pavilion and speaks to the people waiting on the benches. His deep voice carries easily across the crowd. "The train will leave for another round trip of the zoo in five minutes. If you take a ride and want something to do to wait out the rain, we have a station stop just beyond the African Grasslands at the Wild Kingdom Education Center. You can check out the displays in there, watch a movie about the zoo conservation programs, and stay dry."

Roger knows everything there is to know about the steam train—its history, how to maintain it, how to keep it running even though it's an antique. He also knows almost everything about the zoo's schedule and activities. He makes sure we mention those things in the train ride speech.

But now, I realize, Roger knows how to take care of people. I think people sense it, because they like his ideas. Moms and dads with baby strollers, kids, older people—they get up from their seats after he finishes talking. Either they line up to show their tickets to J. P. Felt at the gate, or they buy tickets from the girl running the booth.

"Come on the run with me, Lexington," Roger says.

"Of course." I never get tired of the train. "Roger?" I say as I climb the metal steps into the cab.

"Yes?"

"I'm sorry again that you waited for me and I didn't come."

Roger helps me up the last step—it's a tall one.

The cab smells of grease and coal and hot metal. It's a good smell. "Well"—he tilts his head to the side and checks the gauges, monitoring the water level and the pressure—"I suppose it was bound to happen at some point. What were you doing out in the woods?"

I don't mean to say it, but it's just me and Roger in the cab, and it bursts out of my mouth. "I met the ghost you told me about. Miss Amanda Holtz."

Roger's coal-streaked face suddenly looks like it's made of clay that was left out in the sun.

17

Fisher Tells Mrs. Leigh's Tale

"She never talks about it anymore, but my mom knew a ghost once," Fisher says quietly. I settle into the soft cushions on the Leighs' living room sofa and hug my knees.

Roger wouldn't tell me what was so bad about me seeing our ghost. He just got quiet for the rest of the day. He only spoke when necessary—to give me things to do at the station. Then, as he drove the engine into the train shed for the night, he asked me if Fisher saw Miss Amanda's ghost. I told him Fisher hadn't been with me when I saw her, and that when we went looking for her again, she wasn't there. All Roger said was "Well, that's good."

Fisher watches the kitchen carefully through the

doorway that joins the two rooms, making sure our conversation is private. The grown-ups are still at the dinner table. Roger and Mr. Leigh are on their second and third helpings of Mrs. Leigh's delicious green chicken curry. They're discussing some trouble Mr. Leigh is having with the new habitats in the reptile house and about a keeper at the Harbor Reef who's been missing shifts.

"They can't hear us," I say. "Tell me about the ghost."

Fisher picks up a stack of his baseball cards from the teakwood table near the couch. Beneath the protective glass top, a hand-carved scene depicts a busy Thai village full of trees and people carrying baskets. The carvings are so detailed that I've always wanted to touch the texture on the ferns and coconut palms.

Fisher passes his baseball cards back and forth from one hand to the other. "When my mom was a girl living in California, her dad still had business in Thailand sometimes. My grandpa's business in Thailand is how he met my grandma, you know."

I nod. I did know that Mrs. Leigh's American dad was in Thailand on business when he met her mom. They were married and moved to California after that.

"When my mom was ten, my grandparents took her to Thailand for a few months while my grandpa was working there. That summer"—Fisher pauses to glance at the kitchen doorway again—"my mom's best friend back home in California died in an accident."

The air feels heavy as I hear this. I hug my knees tighter. I didn't expect the conversation to go this direction.

"Fisher, that's awful." Fisher is *my* best friend. I can't imagine what I would do if he died in an accident. It hurts to even consider it. I suddenly want to go into the kitchen and hug Mrs. Leigh really tight.

"When they got home to California, my mom kept running away and disappearing. My grandparents would search for hours with no idea where she went, and when they would find her, she would say she'd been with her friend—her friend who died."

I feel a chill that's not from the ceiling fan spinning overhead.

Fisher keeps shuffling through his baseball cards, not looking at them. "Pretty soon my grandparents couldn't keep her from running off. She would say she needed to visit her friend. People kept an eye on the place the girl was buried, but my mom was never there."

Goose bumps prickle over my arms and neck.

"She was with her best friend's ghost. My mom says they would go to the park or down to the beach and talk like they had when her friend was alive. The problem was, the longer her friend was a ghost, the more forgetful she got. My mom had to reteach her things every time they were together."

"Hey, Fisher!" Mr. Leigh has stepped into the living room, startling us so much I nearly fall off the couch and Fisher drops half of his baseball card stack. "Do you two want dessert?"

I sometimes forget that Mr. Leigh is completely bald underneath the Indiana Jones–style hat he wears for work. He shaves his head because he was losing his hair anyway, and Fisher says Mr. Leigh didn't like being partially bald.

"Bixly sent me home with leftover brownies and ice cream from the AZA meeting today," he says. "You're welcome to it."

Mr. Leigh meets with people from the Association of Zoos and Aquariums to be sure the zoo stays compliant. It seems Mr. Bixly provides the treats.

Mr. Leigh fills up doorways much like Roger does. Besides working on a Wyoming ranch when he was a boy and playing football in college, he was a wildlife ranger in Nairobi, Kenya, and in a documentary movie before becoming the wildlife expert he is for the zoo. Mr. Leigh is the zoo's very own superstar, but to us he's just Fisher's dad.

Fisher takes a deep breath and gives me a look of relief. "Yeah, we'll be right there." We don't eat in the living room at the Leighs' house—only the kitchen.

Mr. Leigh starts to head back to the kitchen and then quickly turns around. "Oh, how was your first day of baseball lessons, son? Are you going to be the next Johnny Damon?"

"Who?" I ask.

"He's a Major League Baseball player," Fisher tells me. "I found out his mother is Thai, so we kinda have that in common. He also played for the Kansas City Royals."

"Fisher gets to go to Kansas City to train with the pros this summer," Mr. Leigh says, sounding super proud. "Did he tell you?"

"Yes!" I say, trying hard to sound excited. I can't imagine wanting to play baseball for three solid weeks. It seems like that would get boring. But I do think it's cool that Mr. Leigh has a football trophy sitting in a display case in the living room, yet he's happy for Fisher, who wants to play a different sport.

"The lessons were great, Dad," Fisher says. "Coach says I'm doing really well throwing to the corner of the strike zone. My velocity isn't as good as some my age, but he says that command is always better."

I have no idea what he's talking about. Fisher and I haven't talked baseball in this sort of detail.

"That's good news," Mr. Leigh says. "Be sure to let Grandma know how much you're enjoying the lessons."

"I will," Fisher says.

Mr. Leigh returns to the kitchen and continues a conversation with Roger and Mrs. Leigh about the AZA and the recent cooperation between the Lexington Zoo and the Denver Zoo.

Fisher picks up the cards he dropped and says, "So . . . where was I?"

"Your mom had to help her friend remember things," I prompt.

"Oh yeah. Pretty soon, my mom spent every moment she could with her friend's ghost to teach her all the things she couldn't remember. I heard my mom tell Roger once that spending time with ghosts makes you forget how to live. She and Roger had an argument about ghosts and whether they can be trusted."

So that's why Roger seemed upset after I told him I saw Miss Amanda today, and that's why he was glad Fisher didn't see her. Because of Mrs. Leigh.

"How did she ever stop seeing her friend? What happened?"

Fisher fidgets with his baseball cards some more. "Well, my mom disappeared again, only this time no one could find her for two days. The police were looking and everything. Everyone was afraid she'd been kidnapped or drowned in the ocean. When they finally found her, my mom said she'd been with her ghost friend."

"Two days? That's really bad!"

"Yeah. My grandparents decided they had to get her away from the ghost for good, so they all moved to Omaha, where my grandpa had a business opportunity. My mom knew it wouldn't be long before her ghost friend would forget her and all their memories together. It takes three days to drive from Los Angeles to Omaha, did you know that? And my grandma says my mom cried almost the whole way."

"Poor Mrs. Leigh," I whisper under my breath, thinking of a little-girl version of Fern Leigh, crying about losing her friend. It makes my throat tighten up.

I lean over the teakwood table and imagine the scene in the Thai village coming to life. These beautiful things in the Leighs' house have always reminded me that everyone has a piece of their life that's different from what we know. But I never really thought about the feelings attached to that life before. Maybe Mrs. Leigh and her parents visited a village in Thailand like the one carved into this table. Maybe this is similar to where her mother grew up. I think the wooden scene probably reminds Mrs. Leigh of good things, a place that's special to her and her family, as well as the sadness of coming home from Thailand as a girl to find out her friend had died. A sort of happy-sad table.

"And *that's* why you *can't* say anything to my mom about Miss Amanda. She will absolutely lose it. She believes in ghosts, but she doesn't like the idea of them."

"I won't tell her about Miss Amanda," I say. "What do you think, though? Should we be worried about talking to Miss Amanda? She's losing her memories, just like your mom's friend."

"Nah," Fisher says, stacking his baseball cards with his favorite Kansas City Royals pitcher on top. "It's not the same at all. You didn't know her before. She isn't going to trap you into reminding her about her life, because you don't *know* anything about her life, right?"

"Right." I think so. A tiny gnat of a thought buzzes in my brain, and I sort of wish I could swat it away. I completely lost track of time when I was with Miss Amanda's ghost. I forgot about lunch with Roger, and I never forget that. I wonder if this losing track of time is how it started with Mrs. Leigh and her ghost friend.

18

Wind Immersion

"Let's have dessert and then go," Fisher whispers. "While my mom was cooking dinner, I went back to the gift shop and propped open the employee entrance. Isabel was closing up and she didn't notice."

"Nice work, Fisher!" I say with as much enthusiasm as I dare without drawing attention. I'd rather leave now, but Fisher never passes up food, and if we leave without dessert, everyone will be suspicious.

The brownies and ice cream look good, but I prefer Mrs. Leigh's green curry with chicken and red peppers to the ultra-sweet stuff, so I ask for dinner leftovers instead. Roger and Mr. Leigh change the subject from AZA elephant regulations and move on to paper lanterns, of all things.

"No, I told them absolutely no balloons," Mr. Leigh

tells Roger. His arm is resting on the back of Mrs. Leigh's chair, and she relaxes against him. "They want to do a special tribute and release a bunch of balloons, and we can't have balloons near the animals."

"But isn't there a risk with the paper lanterns as well?" Roger asks.

Mr. Leigh finishes off his coffee and nods. "We're working on the details. These are high-profile zoo donors who want to rent out the zoo for a family reunion, and we want to keep them happy while not putting animals at risk. Mrs. Ashby is one donor we definitely don't want to offend, and she thinks she's found biodegradable sky lanterns. The paper completely burns up and so does the fuel cell. All that's left behind is a bit of cardboard when it's finished."

Mrs. Leigh joins in. "We bought a box of them and thought we could try out a few, follow them, and see what's left when they land. Honestly, I think we'll be telling the Ashby family they can plant seeds of indigenous flowers for their special tribute."

"Well," Roger says, nodding, "that might work."

Fisher finishes his ice cream and announces, "I think I left one of my baseball cards up by the gift shop. Is it okay if Lex goes with me to find it?"

Brilliant.

"It's okay with me," Roger says.

Mrs. Leigh nods. "Clear your dishes and take out the trash first."

We take the trash to the dumpster behind the zoo-keeper's residence and pull the lid down. Although most of our animals are inside enclosures, the many birds and squirrels will make a disaster with open garbage.

It's dark now, and the screeching hum of the cicadas has quieted. Without the constant mumble of the zoo crowds, the crickets have the nighttime stage and sing out strong. The air smells of rain-soaked concrete and the sour, earthy scent of layered damp leaves.

We leave the gravel road and turn onto the main path up the hill. The African Grasslands are not far in the other direction, and I ache to see Nyah, but we'd be breaking about ten zoo rules if we went to the elephant barn. I'm not sure how many we're going to break at the gift shop.

"That was a good excuse you made in there," I say.

"Well, it wasn't a lie," Fisher says. "I really did leave one of my baseball cards at the gift shop. It gave us an actual reason. With how much my mom checks up on things, I figured I'd better make it real."

"Good plan," I say, still wishing we could sneak inside the elephant barn first. I want to tell Nyah what I found in the trees today. I want to see what else she might show me if I can feel her low rumble and look into her eyes again. But in a few hours it will be morning, and Fisher and I can return to the barn when Thomas is there. I hope Nyah will come to the training gates.

"Do you think Nyah knew about Miss Amanda and

the treasure?" I ask, mostly to myself but loud enough that Fisher can hear.

Fisher, who is ahead of me on the hill, turns around and holds his arms out like a great big I-don't-know. "Lex, I'm still trying to figure out why you hear the wind and elephants speak at all."

"Elephant," I correct him. "Only one."

"True. But that may change. Who knows?"

"I have a theory about the wind and Nyah, if you want to hear it."

Fisher raises his eyebrows and waits for me to continue.

"Well, I really met them both on the same night. I escaped one and found the other. So . . . maybe . . ."

The crickets quiet for a moment as if they need to hear what I have to say. The wind is completely still.

"Maybe losing my family and being alone taught me I had to stand up to the wind and find a friend. And it all just kind of stuck with me."

The lamppost light angles across Fisher's face. He nods. "That actually makes a lot of sense."

And my heart squeezes a little as I realize how much I'm going to miss him when he goes to baseball camp. Even with all the animals and other people in the zoo, I'll feel like Karana on her island when he leaves.

I shake all that off for the moment.

"I mean, I did survive the biggest tornado in

Nebraska's history in like forty years. That kind of thing could teach a person a few things."

"That's true." Fisher picks up a loose rock from the path and rolls it around in his fingers.

An even bigger idea starts to take shape in my mind. I'm thinking of Karana in my book, and how she didn't understand the language of the Aleuts, the strangers who came to her island to hunt. They didn't understand her either.

"Your mom speaks two languages because she had parents who spoke both Thai and English to her, right?"

"Yeah. She still speaks Thai to my grandma sometimes."

"When your grandparents took all of you to visit Thailand a few years ago, you said you didn't understand the language when you were there."

"Right. My mom didn't teach me Thai when I was little. Only a few phrases."

"Okay, so I was thinking about how people learn to communicate when they're young. Maybe I learned the wind's language and Nyah's language so easily because I was so close to it, and I was young when I heard it."

Fisher stops walking as we reach the top where the path curves in front of the main gates. His eyes widen. "It's like the kids who go to Spanish immersion at school. The kindergartners pick it up really fast, because they're young and they're hearing a lot of Spanish. It's like concentrated orange juice."

"Concentrated orange juice?"

"Yeah!" Fisher looks like he's discovered some secret of the universe. "A lot of strong stuff in a small container."

"Fisher, I'm still not . . ." I shake my head, not understanding him.

Fisher drops the rock he's been holding and gestures at the sky. "What is the strongest, most concentrated form of the wind?" His voice grows more intense and excited with every word. "A tornado, right? You were so close to wind in its most concentrated form that you barely escaped it. And you were young and really small. It was like . . . *wind immersion*." A proud smile spreads across his face. "Instead of Spanish immersion—you had wind immersion."

"And elephant immersion," I add.

The lampposts cast yellow light over the entrance building, and a bluish glow illuminates the inside of the gift shop. A single light is on in the upstairs office. Frank Bixly's office.

19

Loose Board

"What is Mr. Bixly doing at work so late?" Fisher asks.

"If he catches us yanking up a floorboard . . . ," I begin, not sure how to finish. I'm not scared of Frank Bixly. I'm not scared of Roger hearing from Mr. Bixly that I pulled up a piece of the gift shop floor. I'm a little worried that Mr. Leigh might heap enough chores onto Fisher that he won't have time to do much of anything with me. I'm worried Mrs. Leigh might give me a research paper about the history of wood floors in Nebraska.

"He won't catch us," Fisher says. "Come on."

The employee entrance is propped open just as Fisher said. He left a small stick in the frame that kept the door from latching. He also left a baseball card tucked behind the door, making the story he told his mom true. I pick up the card. It's not one of the Royals or the Dodgers. Fisher wouldn't have left behind any of those. I hold it out to him.

"Found it," I say with a grin.

We close the door behind us, holding the handle until the latch clicks softly. The last thing we need is for Mr. Bixly to come down from his office to investigate a noise.

We navigate around the racks and displays by the dim glow of the blue security lights. Isabel and her team have cleaned things up nicely. The shirts on the round display tables are folded in uniform piles, organized by size and color. All the plush animals have been returned to their proper shelves. The floor is swept and mopped, erasing all the muddy stroller tracks and footprints. The whole place smells of pine and ammonia glass cleaner.

Our loose floorboard thunks when I tap on it with my shoe. I get down on my hands and knees and feel around its edges. It lines up evenly against the other boards except where there's a small chunk missing on one side, like a knothole. I can't quite fit my finger all the way in it, and trying to pull it up without a good grip doesn't work. Fisher tries with no luck.

"Well," Fisher says, rubbing his finger after pinching it in the knothole, "I thought about how to get in here, but I didn't figure how to get the board out."

I stand up. "Isabel's storeroom probably has a lot of things we could use." I sneak to the back of the shop with Fisher behind me. Inside the storeroom, with the door closed behind us and the regular lights on overhead, we look through Isabel's supply closet, careful not to move things around in a way she'll notice. We find a screwdriver and a removable broom handle that could work but might be too big around. I grab one of the feather dusters with a skinny plastic handle that comes to a point.

"Turn the lights off," I tell Fisher before we leave the storeroom. This building has giant windows on every wall, and people can see inside from Bear Country to the Reptile House if they simply look up.

I try using the end of the feather duster first. I place the end of the handle inside the knothole and lever it against the floor. It's the right idea, but the plastic handle is not going to withstand the pressure. I remove it before I break it and try the screwdriver next. I place one end in the small hole and make another lever. The wood creaks, and bits of sealant around the floorboard crack along its edges, but the floorboard is stuck.

Fisher and I look at each other, and I know he's thinking the same thing. I had thought this board was loose enough that someone could simply lift it and hide something beneath it. If Miss Amanda ever hid something in here, the floor must've been resealed since then.

Roger refinished the wood floor in the Old County Bank a few years ago. I still remember how bad it smelled and how smooth and shiny the top coat was. I should've known better when this board didn't want to come up.

Someone is going to discover damage to this floor. Even if we pound the board back down, it's not going to look the same. I didn't think it would be this hard to check underneath what felt and sounded like a very loose board. I imagined lifting the board out, retrieving Miss Amanda's treasure, and replacing the board so that it looked undisturbed. This isn't going right at all.

"Maybe this isn't what Miss Amanda meant." I'm going over my conversation with her in my head. She definitely said *loose board,* and she said she'd hidden it in the gift shop. "Maybe we should walk around and see if it could be another board."

"We've gone this far with it," Fisher says. "I say we keep at it."

"Okay." I hand him the screwdriver. "But if we get caught and you get grounded from baseball camp, don't say I didn't warn you."

Fisher jams the end of the screwdriver into the half-moon knothole and pushes down at an angle, shaking his head. "My grandma paid too much for that camp for my parents to not let me go. They won't waste her money like that."

And suddenly, the board breaks free of the floor with a loud clatter as it flies up and tumbles sideways. The screwdriver also goes flying, but not before smashing down on Fisher's fingers. He stifles a yell and falls into me, nearly knocking me over. I grab the board and the screwdriver and hold very still. I've no doubt that Mr.

Bixly has heard us. The floor in the office above creaks with movement. Mr. Bixly's desk chair rolls on its wheels and then stops. Then footsteps thump overhead with the weight of Frank Bixly.

I give Fisher a we're-dead look and point at the ceiling, mouthing, *Bixly!*

Fisher shakes out his wounded hand and points at the hole we just made in the floor. I slide over to it on my stomach and plunge my hand into the opening without pausing to think what might be down there. We don't have a flashlight, we can't turn the overhead lights on, and Mr. Bixly is surely on his way to the stairs. So I drag my hand through years of dust and the sticky feel of what must be several spiderwebs. I find a few small things with my fingers, grab them in my fist, and yank them out. I have no idea what I'm pulling out of the floor, but I grab everything I touch and drop it into the bottom of my T-shirt, which I hold out from my body with my other hand.

Mr. Bixly's footsteps are near the top of the stairs now. If he comes down, he'll end up by the cash registers. There's no way Fisher and I can get to the employee door from here without running directly in front of the sales counter.

Fisher is watching me grab things and drop them in the bottom of my T-shirt. He points at the side doors, the ones that are deadbolted and will set off an alarm if we open them. It might be our only option if we don't want Mr. Bixly to see us. I'd rather get out without setting off the alarm, but I'd also like to avoid a visit to Mr. Bixly's office with Roger and the Leighs. Mr. Bixly is their boss. He's everybody's boss.

I pinch the last item I can feel through the opening. It's paper. That's the last thing. I'm sure I have everything there is to find. Fisher replaces the board, fitting it into the floor like the final piece of a puzzle. I brush the crumbly pieces of sealant away with the feather duster, and Fisher grabs the screwdriver. We tiptoe to the side doors. Fisher holds his hand poised over the deadbolt, ready to turn it. As soon as we push on these doors, the alarm will sound.

But Mr. Bixly isn't coming down the stairs. I hold up a finger to Fisher, telling him to wait. We watch the bottom of the staircase like it's going to tell us what to do, but if we see Mr. Bixly step off that last step, it'll be too late. I still don't hear any footsteps, though.

I'm holding the bottom of my T-shirt in my fist. Who knows what I have in here? I hope it isn't a bunch of dead spiders. I'm sweating and cold at the same time. The pine and ammonia smell is now mixed with dust in my nose, and I'm going to sneeze. The miserable prickling in my nose moves higher and higher. My eyes water until Fisher is just a blur. He's waving his hand at me, begging me not to sneeze. If only Mr. Bixly would just go back to his office. If only we could sneak across the front of the cash registers without him seeing us. If only we could go out the back doors. If only I could stop myself.

I can't.

I smash my nose and mouth into the crook of my arm, but the sneeze still comes out like a squeaky explosion. I swallow some of the sneeze in my effort to silence it, and the air fills my throat and makes me cough.

"Who's down there?" Mr. Bixly grumbles, and he starts down the stairs.

Fisher flips the deadbolt, slams into the doors, and we run out of them with the alarm blaring.

20

Fugitives

Fisher and I run like prey animals. The police are surely coming, because they respond to security alarms. We go back the way we came, but just off the path in the dark spots where the lamppost light doesn't reach. Those gift shop windows can see all. We scramble through the bushes and down the hill toward Fisher's house. Before we reach the gravel road that leads to the zookeeper's residence, Fisher turns into the surrounding trees. I have a hard time keeping up with him. All that practice running bases has paid off.

The wind whirs in my ears. *"Too bad you're not as fast as me."*

I run faster. I think of Nyah and what image she might show me if I could visit her in the barn. I think of the trees in the woods, and that makes me think of *my* tree. My treehouse.

Fisher turns to look for me, but I'm right beside him now. Under cover of the trees and their shadows, we sneak around the zookeeper's residence from behind. Roger and the Leighs might see us through the large living room windows if we go across the front. Once we're past the house, we angle over the main path toward the African Grasslands. I can feel Fisher running beside me. He knows where I'm headed.

My chest feels like it's going to burst, but the wind pushes me from behind, and that makes it easier for a moment. I don't know whether the wind means to help me or not. I think it's just showing off. When we reach the clearing behind the Grasslands' lower boundary, Fisher bolts ahead. He laughs as he passes me, his chest out, his shoes barely touching the earth.

I slow to a jog when the treehouse comes into view. My legs are rubber and don't seem attached to my body. Somehow, they hold me up enough for me to make it to the ladder at the base of the cottonwood tree. I'm breathing so hard that my throat crackles like a dusty riverbed when I try to swallow. I reach for the ladder and step onto the first rung. My foot doesn't feel solid, and I slide off, dropping Isabel's feather duster. I land in the grass beside the tree, still holding my shirt tight in my fist and laughing.

Fisher laughs, too. He laughs so hard, his legs seem to give out. He rolls onto the ground, landing like one of the penguins when they slip on the ice.

"Why . . . why are . . . we laughing?" I gasp between aching breaths.

Fisher shakes his head. "That . . . was . . . awesome."

I sit up, the unknown objects balled together at the bottom of my shirt. I can't believe I ran that fast and that far and didn't lose my grip on any of it.

Fisher holds out the screwdriver. "I'm kind of surprised I didn't hurt myself running with this."

"How are your fingers?" I ask.

He holds them out and wiggles them. "A little sore, but fine."

It's too dark in this part of the zoo, away from all the lampposts and security lights, for us to investigate the objects we found. And I don't want to dump it all out here in the grass and risk losing something. I must move my legs. They feel less like rubber now but tremble as I put weight on them.

"Let's get up there and radio Roger," I say, still a little out of breath. "If he gets a message from us soon, maybe they won't think we could have been inside the gift shop when the alarm went off."

"Good idea," Fisher says.

This treehouse is my private space inside this very public zoo. When Roger built it, he said it was good for me to have a place I could go where I could see the animals and enjoy the zoo without all the crowds. Mostly, he wanted me to be able to be close to Nyah in the Grasslands without breaking rules.

Fisher and I climb the ladder to the platform. We each grab one of the solar-charged lanterns hanging on the nails by the front door and take them with us. Inside my treehouse, Roger put an old table and chairs from the Wild Eats Café. When the café went through a remodel, Mr. Bixly sold off the old tables and chairs, and Roger bought a set for $10. Fisher and I set the lanterns on the table and switch them on. The small space is filled with LED brilliance. I grab the radio and turn it on.

"Willow to Hostler," I say into the radio, using our code names. Roger likes to use railroad terms. A hostler is someone who services train engines.

My hand is in a stiff, sweaty grip around the clump inside my T-shirt. Everything I pulled out from the gift shop floor feels heavier with the weight of not knowing. I don't dare drop any of it out until Fisher and I can really examine it.

"Hostler here," says Roger's voice over the radio. "Go ahead."

"Slugger and I are in the nest," I say.

The radio is silent for a moment.

I lift my finger off the radio talk button and ask

Fisher, "Do you think they've heard about the gift shop alarm going off?"

"I don't know. If Bixly doesn't notice what we did to the floor, and he doesn't think anything is missing, maybe he won't notify everyone."

"Yeah, but he's going to know someone went out that side door," I say.

"Hostler to Willow," Roger's voice says.

I give Fisher a worried look. "Willow here."

"Slugger needs to be home in ten minutes."

"Got it. Willow out." I set down the radio. "Okay." I breathe out a long sigh. Away from Mr. Bixly and the screaming alarm, and having created what I hope will be an alibi to keep us out of trouble, we can now focus on what we found.

"Let's see it, Lex," Fisher says eagerly.

Carefully, I unclench my fist from around my T-shirt. By the LED lanterns, I notice how dirty I am. My left arm is streaked with dirt and the rest is even paler than usual from a coating of dust. My shirt and pants are muddy from falling in the damp clearing. I hold my shirt over the café table, gently let go of the fabric, and shake out the contents.

A button

A hairpin

A few pennies

A quarter, three dimes, and an arcade token

Two polished rocks
An old ticket to the zoo train
Some pebbles—unpolished
We've messed up part of the gift shop floor, risked getting caught doing it, set off an alarm that likely caused a visit from the police . . . all for some garbage.

21

In the News

Either we had the wrong loose board, someone got the treasure already, or Miss Amanda is forgetting an important detail. Considering what I now know about ghosts, I think the last thing is pretty likely.

Luckily, Roger assumed my dirty clothes were from being out in the clearing after a rainstorm, which is partly true. He didn't want to talk about Miss Amanda when we got back to the Old County Bank. Maybe he had his fill of talking after dinner with the Leighs. The only thing he said to me about it was "Just keep this between me and you. She's the reason we have each other, but it's really no one else's business."

Now that Roger is asleep upstairs, and I think about the look in his eyes when I mentioned Miss Amanda, I realize he may have known her non-ghost version. If she died the night of the tornado, and she worked at the zoo, they should have known each other. Maybe he's sad she died. Maybe that's why he doesn't want to talk about it.

When I was little, I asked Roger what he thought happened to my parents if they died. He didn't seem to want to talk about that either. But he wrapped his strong arms around me and said they probably went to live in the sky right over the zoo, where they could watch over me all the time. It made me feel even more that the zoo was a safe place.

The clock in the Old County Bank ticks a rhythm that echoes through the main floor. I sit at the desk with the computer screen and my newspaper article in front of me. I've read the article so many times, I have it nearly memorized.

CATEGORY FIVE TORNADO DESTROYS FARMLAND, HAVEN HILLS, AND LEXINGTON NEIGHBORHOODS

Leaves Many Without Homes
Eight Reported Deaths
June 9, 2013

On Saturday, June 8, the dark skies above eastern Nebraska brewed a particularly rare kind of storm, the kind that hasn't hit the state since 1964. A supercell thunderstorm first appeared over farmland 30 miles northwest of Lexington. It grew to an EF5-level funnel cloud—

on the 1–5 Enhanced Fujita scale—and destroyed the small farming community of Haven Hills. The twister traveled 10 more miles and crossed the Lexington city limits behind Lilian Park at approximately 10:15 p.m., with winds estimated to have exceeded 220 miles per hour. The section of the city between Lexington Way and Telegraph Road was completely destroyed, with no structures remaining and much of the debris launched like missiles into other parts of the city. Only a few minutes after entering the city, the tornado dissipated one mile south of the Lexington Zoo. The zoo sustained damage to fences and structures; however, the zoo has reported that they've had no losses among the animals.

As emergency response teams joined the citizens of Haven Hills and Lexington in relief efforts, eight people have been found dead. Many have been left injured and homeless, and dozens have been reported missing. An unidentified young girl was found after the storm inside the elephant enclosure at the Lexington Zoo. She was alone and dirty but otherwise unharmed. Authorities are making every effort to locate her family. If you know of any possible leads, please contact the Lexington Police Department or Child Welfare Services.

I scan the article, and my eyes hover over the words "eight people have been found dead." Was Miss Amanda among the eight?

I type in a search window: *Amanda Holtz.*

I get 3,472 results.

I add the words: *Lexington Zoo.*

The top of the results screen shows a row of images. Some of the pictures are of the Lexington Zoo—the advertising images Mrs. Leigh posts online. Some show the gift shop with the bronze lion pride statue, some show the African Grasslands' grand opening, and others advertise educational programs at the Wild Kingdom Education Center. I scroll through the images, past all the zoo pictures, until I find people in the pictures.

Two pictures catch my eye. One is of a very thin, very elegant-looking woman shaking hands with what looks like a younger, less round Frank Bixly. The woman is in high heels, unusual for the zoo, and she's wearing a red dress with a navy belt around her waist. She looks like she should be on the entertainment news, except that she's wearing one of the old Lexington Zoo uniform hats—the wide-brimmed safari style. It's Miss Amanda Holtz. I'm sure of it.

The second picture is even more striking. It's a close-up of her face in black and white. She's younger-looking than the ghost I saw in the woods—less wrinkles around the eyes and fuller lips. She's absolutely beautiful. I click on the photo, and it takes me to a website about the Fenn Circus, a North American traveling circus that has gone out of business.

I know something about the Fenn Circus. It's written on the plaques below the photographs on the elephant barn walls. Nyah and her mother, Tendai, came from the Fenn Circus. I scroll down the page and find the photograph of Amanda Holtz, finance manager for Angus Fenn. According to the website, Miss Amanda had worked for the circus for almost thirty years.

I return to my search results and click on the first photograph of Miss Amanda—the one with the younger Frank Bixly in front of the zoo gift shop. The photo links to a newspaper article printed by the *Lexington Herald*.

LEXINGTON ZOO WELCOMES NEW RETAIL MANAGER

September 24, 2009

Just after completing a successful protocol inspection with the Association of Zoos and Aquariums (AZA), the Lexington Zoo has acquired a new face. Amanda Holtz, experienced finance manager for the Fenn Circus, says she's ready for a change from life on the road and has consented to join the ranks of Lexington Zoo employees. Ms. Holtz will oversee the zoo's retail operations and assist in fundraising efforts. Frank Bixly, Lexington Zoo General Manager, says the zoo is still searching for the right candidate to train with Joe Tredwell, head keeper, with the aim of taking Tredwell's post when he retires.

In smaller letters, the caption below the photograph says:

Frank Bixly, General Manager, with new retail manager
Amanda Holtz in front of the Lexington Zoo gift shop.

So Miss Amanda *did* work for the zoo. She knew Mr. Bixly. She worked here before I came to the zoo, before Fisher's dad got the head keeper job. And before that she worked at the very same circus that Nyah and her mother came from.

The wind picks up suddenly, something it often does late at night. It rattles the windows of the Old County Bank and clanks the metal cover over the chimney. I don't hear its words unless it's blowing in my ears, but suddenly I'm not interested in what it has to say. I have enough to think about for now.

I save the websites about Amanda Holtz in my Favorites tab and shut down the computer. Roger dislikes the whirring sound it makes when we leave it on. He says technology makes the whole house hum with an unnatural buzz. I switch off the downstairs lights and take my newspaper article upstairs to my bedroom.

It's a tiny room—barely large enough for the bed, a smallish dresser, a nightstand, and a lamp. But Roger and I hung a mirror on one wall and a map of the world on another, and both are enough to make the room just right for me. Roger said that every time I look into the mirror and see my blue eyes looking back at me, I can remember that I'll always have a piece of my family with me. He said that when I wonder where I came from and what my parents were like, I can look at my face, my rounded nose, my crazy curly hair, and know a little something about them.

I must resemble them in some way. I wonder if I do things they did, like how some people crack their knuckles and some people always drink the milk left in the bowl from their breakfast cereal. I don't know if I'm left-handed because my dad was or if I chew on my lip when I'm concentrating because my mom did that.

I like to think so.

The map of the world on my other wall is covered with stickers Roger and I use to identify the original homes of the various animal species we have at the zoo. Stickers on the African continent say *sand boa* over Kenya and *elephant* over Tanzania and Swaziland. I don't know where my sticker should go, since no one found evidence of a family for me in Lexington—or in Nebraska at all.

I've laid out the collection of junk I found from beneath the gift shop floorboard. I flop down on the bed and pick up the old, crinkled train ticket. The zoo train tickets aren't small like carnival tickets. They're more like the size of a skinny postcard. It doesn't seem possible that this ticket slid into the space beneath the floor. Besides being fairly wrinkled, the ticket's edges curl up like it was once rolled into a tight cylinder—like maybe someone rolled it up and pushed it through the half-moon knothole.

I smooth the ticket as best I can, feeling sorry that I didn't find something valuable under that board, sorry I didn't find Miss Amanda's treasure. And as I unfold a creased corner on the ticket, I notice something I didn't before. I'm not sure what it means, if anything, but it's too weird not to mean *something*. This ticket was printed on June 8, 2013.

The day of the tornado.

22

Caught

The next morning, no one answers at the Leighs' house. Fisher couldn't have forgotten about elephant training, but maybe his chores took him longer than usual. I head to the maintenance shed at the African Grasslands and knock on the door. Thomas doesn't come, so I knock again. A little louder this time.

Thomas finally opens the door, his hat on backward. He takes one glance at me and asks, "Where is Fisher?"

"I can't find Fisher this morning, but I was hoping you'd let me help with training anyway?" I give Thomas a pleading look that shows I know the rules but I'm asking him to overlook this small detail. Mr. Leigh said Fisher and I could help with the elephants if we went *together*. But I don't know where Fisher is, and I *really* need to see Nyah.

Thomas thinks for a minute. He rubs his hand over his mouth and chin like he's working out long division. He sighs.

"I know elephants well enough to see that Nyah has a connection with you," he says. He glances over my shoulder, toward the veterinary headquarters and Mr. Leigh's office. His muscled arm holds the metal door open all the way, and he waves me inside. "Keep it quiet, okay?"

"Thanks, Thomas," I say.

Nyah is waiting several feet from the training gate, her trunk bobbing and twisting in the air as though she's searching for something invisible to grab. Her big feet look too soft to support something so large. She lets her ankle joint relax as she lifts her front foot, and it looks almost too flimsy to hold her, but then she steps on it, and the baggy skin stretches as the foot spreads under her weight. There's a reason Thomas invites them to have their feet inspected every day. Their feet must stay healthy.

"She was here at sunrise," Thomas says, a hint of a question in his voice as he unwinds the hose from its tether. He knows something is going on.

"She must've really liked her training session yesterday," I say, picking up two target poles from the rack.

"Or something like that." Thomas carries a pile of foot-care tools to the training area. "I've been working with elephants a long time, you know. I've observed them in the wild and in captivity. Sometimes, if you pay attention around elephants, you can notice a pulsing feeling—as though the air is thumping against your head. Have you noticed something like that?"

"I've noticed that," I say eagerly. "It's a rumbling with no sound."

Thomas smiles and nods. "You noticed it in here yesterday, didn't you?"

"Yes," I say, wondering what else Thomas knows.

Thomas joins me at the barrier fence and watches Nyah with a calmness in his eyes that tells me Thomas is one of those special people elephants can trust. Nyah walks toward him with her tail swishing from side to side. "Researchers have recorded the sounds of elephants for long periods of time," he continues, his eyes still on Nyah, "and they've taken those recordings and sped them up. At a higher frequency, we can hear the elephants speak to each other with sounds we couldn't hear before. Isn't that something?"

"Yes," I say softly, wondering what Thomas would think if I told him I could see images from those rumblings. But then Nyah takes a few steps closer, and I feel the thumping of invisible sound waves, just like Thomas described it. Except the thumping and rumbling come through the earth as well. Nyah bobs her head lower, and I look into her beautiful eyes.

Images flood my mind like those pictures that change as you move them in the light.

Elephants.

A large circus arena.

The elephants are in a line, rearing up on their hind legs, following the arm motions of a trainer.

Crowds of people.

A circus man with a brown beard and a long coat in the center of it all.

A blond woman in overalls, leading the elephants away from the show and the crowds. They follow her without ropes or prodding. They walk together like friends.

And just as I knew Nyah's urgent feeling about the woods, I feel an emotion with this image, too.

She misses them—the elephants and the blond woman.

"I went to the trees, Nyah." I think the words the way I talk to the wind. *"I found Amanda Holtz. I found a train ticket from the day of the tornado. I don't know what that means."*

Nyah grabs a clump of dirt with the two fingers on the end of her trunk and tosses the dirt in a cloud of dust over her massive shoulders, something she does to protect her skin from insects and the sun. She sways a little, bobbing her head and swinging her trunk from left to right. It looks like she's dancing to the rhythmic African music playing from the Grasslands' speakers, or else she understands me. But this is actually a rocking habit she developed because there wasn't enough space for her to roam at the circus. I've heard Mr. Leigh talk about the behavior and how elephants have to move. He says her swaying has lessened since coming to the zoo, because now she has more space.

I try to think the way Nyah does—in pictures. I think hard about the woods, about Miss Amanda and her trailer in the trees, about the gift shop and what I found there. I focus on Nyah and the scenes in my mind, hoping that somehow she will know what I want to tell her.

Nyah stops bobbing and swinging her trunk. Another slow, calm rumble comes through the earth and the air and into me. And I see another image.

Three elephants standing together with trainers beside them, and since I see this through Nyah's eyes, Nyah makes four.

Elephants with circus adornments on their heads and backs.

One looks like Tendai.

But Nyah's mother has died, so that leaves Nyah plus two.

These pictures in my head come with feelings so familiar that they might as well be my own. Nyah wants me to find her family.

"Lex," Thomas says, breaking the silence. I realize he's been leaning against the barrier fence—watching me and Nyah. I completely forgot Nyah and I weren't alone.

I blink, feeling a little like I just woke up, like I can't remember how I got into the elephant barn for a few seconds. And then my brain defrosts, and Thomas is waving at me with a frantic expression.

"Frank and Gordon are coming," Thomas says.

He means Mr. Bixly and Mr. Leigh.

"You've got to go. You're not supposed to be here. Go out the side door." He points around the corner from the supply shelf and walks that direction with me a few paces. "That was interesting to watch," he says quickly under his breath, "and I've seen a lot of things and a *lot* of elephants. Please come back tomorrow and explain to me what's going on with you and Nyah. I'd really like to know."

I nod and head out the side door before Mr. Bixly and Mr. Leigh find me breaking the rule about elephant training. I wouldn't want Thomas to get in trouble or lose his job because of me. He's very good with the elephants—especially Nyah.

The side door puts me out onto a smaller walkway— one of many that lead to the Wild Kingdom Education Center. I make sure the door latches completely; then I spin around and run right into Roger.

"Whoa there," Roger says.

He's usually preparing the steam train in the morning before the zoo opens.

"Roger, what . . . ?"

"I've just been talking with Mr. Bixly," Roger says. He looks really uncomfortable—not angry, but not happy either.

I know where this is going, even though I hope it's nothing.

But it's not nothing for Roger to leave the train thirty minutes before the zoo opens. It's not nothing for him to be waiting at the barn doors to catch me coming out of them.

"Lexington, did you know Frank Bixly installed security cameras in the gift shop?"

My heartbeat is like a hummingbird in my chest. I stare at him, waiting to find out what else he knows.

Roger rests his hands on his waist like he can't decide whether to fold his arms or what. "Did you know the alarms went off at the gift shop last night, and Frank watched those security tapes?"

The air feels heavy and prickly.

"Too bad," whispers the wind.

I think of how I tried to cover up what Fisher and I did in the gift shop by calling Roger on the radio, like we'd been in the treehouse all along. Like a lie. A lie in the treehouse Roger built for me.

"He knows what you and Fisher did in the gift shop last night."

Roger never frowns at me like this. He never fidgets—folding his arms, unfolding them, putting his hands back at his waist—like he doesn't know what to do. I don't like it. I want Roger and me to be back to normal.

"I've decided that you will help Isabel do chores in the gift shop until she says you've worked enough to make up for the damage."

That's okay. I like Isabel. I did damage the gift shop floor. I can do chores for Isabel.

"And Mr. Bixly has decided that no employees' kids are allowed inside the maintenance buildings"—he stuffs his hands into the pockets of his overalls—"including the elephant barn."

"What? Because of the gift shop floor?" The words are launched from my mouth like rockets, and they keep coming. "That doesn't have anything to do with Nyah. I haven't done anything to the elephant barn or to Nyah. And when he says 'employees' kids,' he really just means Fisher and me. *Why* is Mr. Bixly so—"

"Shhh," Roger hushes me with unaffected calm. "We both know how Mr. Bixly can be. He wants to show you he's in charge, and he's serious about the zoo. The zoo is—well, I guess it's like his property. That's the way he thinks of it, anyway, and anything like what you and Fisher did he takes very personally."

The cicadas rev up their vibrating buzz in the trees. The sound makes me feel itchy and angry. Hot tears burn the corners of my eyes. Mr. Bixly's precious gift shop floor is nothing compared to my friendship with Nyah. It's not fair for him to keep me from visiting her.

I think of Nyah coming to the training gates to look for me. And I won't be there.

"The Leighs and I are paying to have the floor repaired, and we think you and Fisher can work off the cost of the damage—you working with Isabel, and Fisher with his dad. I will talk to Mr. Bixly in a few days when he's had a chance to cool off."

"Okay," I say quietly. "You'll talk to him?"

"Yes." Roger puts an arm around my shoulders, and it holds me together. I'm suddenly very sorry for Fisher. I hope Mr. Leigh will let me help him with his chores.

"Lexington, I just want you to tell me one thing."

"Yes?"

"What in the world set that idea in motion?" Roger's deep voice stays smooth and steady, but he still sounds very serious. "Why would you break into the gift shop and do that to the floor?"

This just got tricky. I don't lie to Roger. I've never had a reason to. But if I tell him that the ghost of Amanda Holtz started all this, or that it was Nyah who sent me into the woods in the first place, I'm risking a whole lot here. What if Roger tells me I can't go see Miss Amanda either? I can't lose Nyah and Miss Amanda all at once, and Miss Amanda may know something about Nyah's family.

So I take a page from Fisher's book. And I tell Roger just enough of something true.

"Fisher and I knew that floorboard had been loose

for a long time, and we thought it might be a place people could have been hiding things."

A tiny smile starts at the corner of Roger's mouth. "Buried treasure, huh?" He sounds amused.

"Yeah."

"Did you find anything good?"

"Not really. Just a bunch of stuff that would fall through a crack." I pull the ticket out of my pocket. "Except for this. Look at the date."

Roger takes the ticket and turns it over in his hands. He finds the date and stares at it for longer than it takes to read it. "You found this beneath the floorboard, huh?"

"Yeah. It was for the day that . . ." I don't need to finish. Roger knows what day it was.

He takes a deep breath and hands the ticket back to me. "That's a weird coincidence," he says, raising his eyebrows.

He pats me on the shoulder and points out a monarch butterfly about to land on the purple flowers of a butterfly bush. We watch it flit about until it chooses one.

"I want you to start helping Isabel this morning, meet me for lunch at noon, and take the radio with you," Roger says when the monarch flies away. "Do you have it?"

I unhook the cumbersome thing from the waistband of my shorts. "Right here. Fully charged."

"Good." Roger turns and starts toward the main path. His engine needs attention or it won't be ready for the first run of the day. It takes more than one skilled person to get a steam train going, and I'm guessing Roger has left J. P. Felt alone at the station.

As we part ways, me going uphill to the gift shop and Roger going downhill, he says, "No more destroying zoo property looking for buried treasure."

And from the look in his eyes, I think Roger knows there is more going on here than what I've told him.

23

What Isabel Knows

I spray another mist of glass cleaner over the sawdust-covered display shelf and wipe it with a microfiber cloth. Isabel assigned me to polish all the surfaces after the wood-floor guy finished sanding. We covered everything with plastic before he started, and we did it before the zoo opened. But even with the plastic, the sanding left a layer of powdery-soft wood dust all over the place.

It's been four days since Fisher and I triggered the gift shop alarm. The shop's new security camera recorded everything Fisher and I did to the floor. I used to think Fisher and I knew everything about the zoo and the way it runs, but Mr. Bixly has been installing security cameras, and we didn't even know about it.

I've helped Isabel move display tables, refold T-shirts, and find new places to shelve the books and games while the damaged section of floor has been blocked off with orange cones and yellow caution tape. I've always liked helping Isabel, so I don't mind this part of my consequence. It's not being allowed to be close to Nyah that's driving me crazy. I haven't dared to ask Thomas to sneak me in again, not after he had a visit from Mr. Bixly and Mr. Leigh. But Roger says he's going to talk to Mr. Bixly after the floor is fixed, and it's nearly done.

Fisher hasn't gotten off so easy. As he predicted, his parents told him he could still go to his baseball lessons and his camp, but the minute he gets home from baseball, he's stuck helping his dad with everything from sweeping floors to chopping the orangutans' vegetables. Fisher hasn't been able to go anywhere or do anything else. So he still hasn't been to the woods with me to find Miss Amanda.

I've searched the woods twice but found only the old wreckage and no Miss Amanda. I'm starting to worry she's lost all her memory and has wandered away and can't find her trailer. I don't know how ghosts keep track of anything if their memories disappear.

"Lexita," Isabel calls from the jewelry counter. She means me. "Come over here."

I gather up the cleaner and the dirty cloths and join her behind the cash register.

"Look at these," she says, showing me the box of turquoise-and-silver rings from her recent shipment. "¿Son bellos, no?"

I'm pretty sure she means these are pretty. Isabel speaks Spanish to Fisher and me sometimes, hoping we'll learn it. I like that.

"Want to help me set these out?"

"Sure," I say, smiling at her. Isabel has never seemed the slightest bit upset with me for breaking into the gift shop. I start unwrapping rings from their plastic bags and set them one at a time into the foam trays, organizing them by price and size.

Isabel leans closer and whispers, "You know, Lexita, you really did me a favor getting Mr. Bixly to fix that floorboard. Garbage was getting dropped down there, and the floor is going to look so much nicer now."

"Oh," I say, a little surprised. "Well, that's good, I guess."

"I have a rather strange question for you," she continues, rubbing a small cleaning cloth around a ring until the sterling silver shines.

"Yes?"

"What did you find under that board?"

I turn sharply to look at her. Could she possibly know something? Then I realize she probably saw the security tape. She would've noticed that I reached into the hole several times before Fisher and I replaced the board and left.

"Just an odd bunch of . . . well, garbage . . . as you said." I try not to sound like I expected anything else.

"The kinds of things people would drop down a little space. Some polished rocks—which I can definitely return to you—some loose change, pebbles . . . um . . . an old train ticket."

Isabel nods, her face flat and her eyes distant. I wonder what she expected.

"Why?" I ask.

She sets the finished tray of rings into the case under the glass counter and tucks a brunette curl behind her ear. "People have said some interesting things about the woman who ran this shop before me." Isabel opens her mouth as though she's going to say something else, but she pauses and takes a breath. "I just wondered. That's all."

"Oh."

Isabel starts to walk me to the front doors, her way of letting me know I don't have to work for her anymore today. "Just promise me that if you want to come in here looking for something, or digging for something, again, you'll talk to me first. Okay?"

"Okay."

The big hand on the giant zoo clock outside points to the rhino, and the little hand points to the sea lion. It's nine a.m. The public is starting through the front gates and curving around the lion pride statue. Most hurry down the hill to the right or the left, but some trickle straight ahead into the gift shop. This probably isn't the best time for me to ask this question, but I can't help it.

"Is there something I should be looking for—or digging for—that you know of?"

"Well . . . maybe." Isabel shakes her head like she shouldn't have said that. "But I don't want you getting into more trouble!"

"I promise I'll be careful," I say. "*Please* tell me."

Isabel has a young face, but if you look closely, she has some wrinkles that give her away as someone old enough to have grown kids. She smiles at a family walking into the shop.

"¡Buenos días! Welcome!" she calls to them. Her retail clerks in their turquoise shirts fan out to talk to the customers. When it seems she is satisfied the customers are taken care of, Isabel says to me, "I found a letter when I came to work here, and I think it was written by *her*. The woman who used to run this shop."

"Miss Amanda Holtz?" I ask.

"You know who she is?" Isabel looks surprised. She shouldn't be *that* surprised.

"I know a lot of things about the zoo."

"Well"—she nods like I'm not quite correct—"there are some things I'm not going to tell you. I mean, Roger should . . ."

"I know that she died the night of the tornado," I say. "Amanda Holtz died in the woods outside the zoo."

Isabel looks around like she's worried someone could

have heard me. She leans in closer and whispers, "You know about that?"

"Yes."

Adults sometimes think they must keep secrets from me. It's a pain. I have a lot of questions, and it doesn't do me any good when they make me work extra hard for information.

"Oh." She nods to tell me I'm right. "I didn't think I should be the one to tell you about that, but since you already know something about her, do you want to read the letter? It's rather . . . well, I know you like a bit of adventure . . ."

"Yes, please, Isabel!"

She holds up a finger at me. "¡Ah! En español."

She knows I can do this much. "¡Sí, por favor!" I give her a look that says that's all I've got. "Please may I see the letter?" It's too good to be true. I'm dying for more information about Miss Amanda.

"Come with me," she says.

Isabel leads me to the back of the store, past the Employees Only sign, and through the doors where Fisher and I went during our "break-in." I follow her to the desk opposite the supply closet. Isabel has pictures of her family in frames on the desk. She has a husband, three grown kids, and a little terrier. I look at the photos as she opens the bottom desk drawer, and I realize I sort of invaded Isabel's privacy coming in here the other night. It sometimes just feels like the whole zoo is, well . . . mine. And I didn't think about this storeroom as Isabel's space.

"I'm sorry I came in here without your permission," I say. Fisher and I already returned the screwdriver and the feather duster we took, and I said sorry then, but I feel like I need to say it again.

"I know you are." Isabel stops digging in her files and looks at me. She tries to give me a serious expression, but it's not convincing, and a smile breaks through. "And you won't do it again, right?"

"Not without asking you."

"Muy bien." Isabel looks in her drawer again, fingering through some loose papers in a file. "That's what I told Mr. Bixly. I told him you wouldn't do it again. Do you know he wanted to ban you from the gift shop? You *and* Fisher? I'm not allowing it."

Angry heat boils in my stomach at Frank Bixly, General Manager. He's banned me from visiting Nyah at the training gates, and he tried to ban me from the one place everyone goes in the zoo. That's like telling someone they can't go into their own living room. I'm grateful to Isabel for standing up to him.

I'm about to tell her so when she says, "Miss Holtz worked for a very rich man. Did you know that? She left working for him and came here—from a traveling circus to a zoo. I think maybe there's a story about that rich man and why she left."

She holds out a small, yellow piece of paper in front of my face. "And here it is." She lays the paper faceup on the desk between us so we can both have a look. I lean in.

It's a letter written in tidy but very slanted cursive. Good thing Mrs. Leigh insists I do handwriting worksheets—otherwise this letter would be nearly impossible to read. Even so, the slant of the words makes it a little tricky, and many parts have been crossed out and rewritten.

> Dear Eden,
>
> I'm not sure how to say this or how to make it truly right, but I have a good deal of your father's fortune that I didn't return to him while he was alive. I'm truly sorry to hear of his passing. ~~Since it is now your money,~~ I want to return ~~it~~ the money to you with my deepest apologies and sympathies for your loss.
>
> ~~The money is here, but it's hidden away. I'll retrieve it as soon as I am able~~
>
> Please contact me so we can arrange the best way for me to get ~~the box~~ it to you.

There's no more to the letter.
Isabel raises her eyebrows at me. "Strange, no?"
"Yeah."

"You see all those crossed-out words?" Isabel runs her finger over them. " 'Since it is now your money.' . . . 'The money is here, but it's hidden away.' . . . "

My heart is beating fast, and I realize I haven't swallowed for a while.

"Are you sure you weren't looking for buried treasure when you pulled up that floorboard?"

I don't want to tell Isabel this. It's not my story—it's Miss Amanda's—and what if Isabel tells Roger, and I'm not allowed to go to the woods anymore?

Isabel suddenly bursts out laughing. "I'm only teasing you."

I nearly choke on my spit, but I laugh, too.

"So"—I try to keep my voice calm—"where did you find this?"

Miss Amanda didn't sign the letter at the bottom, but this has to be her writing. Maybe, if I can show this letter to her, it will help her remember things.

"In this desk."

"Was there anything else?" This isn't only about finding a lost fortune and finishing Miss Amanda's unfinished business; it's also about Nyah. I can almost feel Nyah's rumbling if I concentrate on the images she showed me. They move through me with my breath and my heartbeat.

The trees, a younger Miss Amanda, the circus man, the blond girl in the overalls, the elephants—Nyah's herd. This matters, and I don't know why, but I have to figure it out for Nyah *and* for Miss Amanda.

Miss Amanda was at the Fenn Circus with Nyah and her family. I need her to remember the circus and what happened to Nyah's herd. I need her to show up at her trailer again and remember.

Isabel straightens some supply order forms on top of her desk. "Only the paperwork for the gift shop—you know, orders, shipping receipts, employee records—and an old train ticket, which I don't have anymore."

My skin prickles. We see old train tickets all over the zoo. We're constantly picking them off the ground. They're as plentiful as the zoo maps and the show schedules, which people rudely leave behind, allowing the wind to scatter them. But I have an old train ticket in my pocket, which I found under the floor, and that's not far from Isabel's storeroom. That's a little weird.

"What happened to the train ticket?" My voice comes out a little scratchy.

Isabel shrugs. "I never noticed when it disappeared. It probably blew off the desk when one of my staff let the storeroom door slam. They do that sometimes. It sends papers flying. So now I try not to leave loose papers out on the desk." As if to demonstrate, Isabel gathers a few papers and files them in the drawer.

"May I have this letter?" I ask her.

Isabel hands me the yellow paper. "I haven't been

able to figure out what it means, so . . ." She holds up a finger at me. "No more digging around in the gift shop, though, okay?"

"Okay." I smile at her. I fold up the letter and put it in my pocket with the train ticket. We go back into the store, and Isabel hands me a piece of candy before I leave. I exit the main gate in time to see Fisher in the parking lot.

"He's leaving without you again," the wind says.

24

The Bus

I run the length of the parking lot to catch up to Fisher.

"How's it going?" I ask, gasping for breath.

"Hey, Lex," Fisher says, smiling and snickering a little, as he's done every time we've seen each other since we vandalized the gift shop. No matter how much Mr. Bixly blusters about it, or how much work Fisher has to do for the keepers, he still thinks the whole thing is hilarious. It's like seeing me brings it all back, and he starts laughing again. That's okay with me. I'm very glad he isn't grumpy that my visit with Miss Amanda resulted in a botched treasure hunt that got him in trouble.

"What are they having you do today?" I ask.

"Thomas made me wash the elephant grooming tools. It's so gross." He holds up one hand at me. "And before you ask, no, I did not get to see Nyah."

"Oh." Some of those grooming tools are used to shave calluses off the elephants' foot pads. That is probably gross, but it can't be much worse than things Fisher has cleaned in the Ape House. "Sorry."

Fisher shrugs. "I think everyone is getting tired of finding things I can do without supervision. The AZA is working in my favor. All the rules and regulations limit what I can do, and having me around is starting to drive the keepers crazy." He hitches his backpack higher up his shoulder by the strap. "Yesterday, my dad kept sending me to Thomas to give me more chores. Thomas rolled his eyes and told me to shake out the entrance rugs and sweep again. But the maintenance crew does that every day, so it was kind of pointless."

"Poor Thomas," I say, thinking of how he let me see Nyah that day. Even against Mr. Leigh's instructions that Fisher and I go together. He didn't have to do that. I've wanted to go back to the barn and tell him what I see when Nyah communicates in rumbles, but he might have gotten in trouble because of me. I don't want to make things worse. "We should do something nice for him. Cookies . . . or something."

"Yeah."

"Hey, did you ask your dad about Miss Amanda? Did he know her?" I already told Fisher what I found on the internet—the pictures and the articles about Amanda Holtz. He said he'd try to get more information. But he warned me to keep his mom out of it.

"I did ask him." We reach the bus stop and wait beneath a tree for shade. "He said Amanda was the gift shop manager when he was hired here. He and my mom both knew her. He thought she was good at her job and a little eccentric—you know, she lived by herself in a ham-shaped trailer in the woods. He didn't know much else. Most of the time Amanda was here, my dad was busy training with the head keeper he replaced. He didn't have much to do with anyone in the other divisions, even Roger, at first."

That makes sense, but it doesn't help us much.

"Then," Fisher continues, "he asked me where I'd heard about Amanda."

"What did you tell him?"

"I said we heard her name at the zoo and wondered who she was."

"Good one, Fisher."

"He didn't want to talk about it after that. I think maybe it's because she died here, and he doesn't want to upset my mom with talking about the ghost thing."

"Yeah, probably. Isabel didn't want to tell me about her death either. They're trying to protect us." I reach into my pocket for the folded letter Miss Amanda never sent. "But I told Isabel I already knew about Miss Amanda, and she showed me something."

Just as I pull out the letter, the city bus growls its way down the street to the stop. I wish Fisher didn't have to go. I don't want to show him the letter in a hurry. We need more time.

Fisher looks at the bus and then at me. His eyes sparkle with excitement. "You should come with me today."

"What?" He's crazy. I don't play baseball.

"I'm serious. We're going to play a mock game with the coach's other students. You can watch. You've never really seen me play, Lex."

"Well, I . . . I have to meet Roger for lunch. . . ." I don't want to leave the zoo. At least I have a good excuse.

"The game won't be as long as regular practice. We can be back in time."

"But what about . . . ?" I'm still holding the letter, and I point toward the woods.

"We can talk about it on the bus," he says, "and we can look for Amanda together when we get back. Besides, I have something else I want to tell you."

"More secrets," the wind taunts.

The bus rumbles and hisses to a stop in front of us. The bus driver opens the folding door. Fisher points at the radio hooked on the waistband of my shorts. "You've got your radio. Get a message out to Roger, and you can tell him where you're going."

My feet are stuck to the ground. The zoo is my island, and I don't leave—except sometimes with Roger to get food or to find supplies for the train shed. And then there were those few days I tried going to school.

"Are you in or out, kids?" asks the bus driver.

Fisher has one foot on the bus steps and a hand on

the railing, like he's showing me how to get on a bus. I'm not stupid, Fisher. I just don't like the feeling I will blow away if I leave.

As if it knows my thoughts, the wind whispers, "*Stay. You're not strong enough out there.*"

It's one thing to worry. It's another to be told you're not strong.

"*You wanna bet?*" I shoot back at the wind. And then, without pausing to think, I leap up the bus steps, grabbing the handrail tight.

Fisher's smile goes from here to Omaha. He shows the bus driver his city bus pass, and I dig in my pocket for the five-dollar bill Roger gave me this morning. I hold it out to the driver.

"Exact change, missy," says the driver, rolling his eyes. "It's a dollar twenty-five."

I look at Fisher. He turns his pockets inside out. "I'm sorry, Lex. I always use my city pass. I didn't realize you had to have exact change."

A couple of ladies sit together near the front. Their floral perfume reaches all the way to the fare box and tickles my throat. It's the kind that will bring bees from every direction if someone wears it inside the zoo. I ask them, "Do either of you have change for five dollars?"

"I do," says the one with dark red lipstick. She unsnaps the latch on her purse and digs out dollar bills and quarters from her wallet. She reaches across the aisle with four one-dollar bills and four quarters.

I hand her my five in exchange. "Thank you."

I drop $1.25 in the fare box. *"I'm strong enough,"* I say to the wind. The wind probably didn't hear me from inside the bus, but it feels good to think the words anyway.

"Willow to Hostler," I say into the radio as I follow Fisher down the center of the bus. The radio crackles as I wait for Roger to respond. We walk past a guy hunched over his smartphone, another guy who looks like he's asleep, and three girls chattering about someone they thought they saw at the mall.

"Willow to Hostler," I try again.

Fisher chooses some empty seats at the rear, and we sit down. The three girls turn around and watch us. One of them looks at me, at my hair, at the radio in my hand, and then at Fisher. She smiles at Fisher and then turns back to her friends. They whisper to each other and start giggling.

"Hostler here." Roger's voice comes through the radio. It's staticky, but I can make out the steam engine's metallic heartbeat in the background.

"I'm going with Slugger to his lessons," I say. "I'm with him now. On the bus."

The bus has whirred to life and pulls away from the curb. Every movable joint in the big, hollow vehicle creaks and complains as the bus turns and picks up speed. I much prefer the train.

"Thanks for the heads-up," answers Roger. "Back for lunch?"

"Yes," I say.

"Hostler to Willow." Roger's voice is breaking up. The radios can reach a long way, but sometimes things interfere with the signal. I've never tried to use one away from the zoo.

"Willow here."

"Have fun." Maybe it's the steam engine interfering with the sound, but Roger's voice seems more enthusiastic than usual.

"I will. Willow out."

The girls in the middle of the bus keep turning around and watching us. I look away and shift sideways in my seat. In the zoo, I'm sure of myself. I can direct people to any place they want to go, answer questions about the train and show schedules, and talk to anyone without wondering what they're thinking. The staring and whispering and occasional giggles from the middle of the bus feel very different. I'm not in charge here. It's unpredictable like the wind. I wedge my shoulder against the seat in front of us, so I don't feel quite so much like I'm going to go sailing into the bus's wide-open space when it stops.

"So—do you want to go first or should I?" I ask Fisher. The air-conditioning clicks on from somewhere in the back, sending condensed, cold air down on us. It smells like a mixture of stale water and tire rubber.

"You go," Fisher says.

I show him the letter. "Isabel found this in Miss Amanda's old desk in the gift shop."

Fisher takes the paper and reads for a minute. "It isn't signed," he says.

"I know. But it has to be from her. Isabel said Miss Amanda used to work for a very rich man, and here she says she has money that belongs to someone else."

"It doesn't say who Eden is, who her father is, or where the money came from. That's not a lot to go on."

Without realizing it, I've assumed a lot from these few handwritten lines. I assumed, because Isabel assumed. I still think I'm right, though.

"True, but it's definitely something we could ask Miss Amanda about when she shows up again," I say.

The girls in the middle of the bus giggle. I think they're giggling at us, but Fisher ignores them. He looks over the letter again. He runs his fingers over the crossed-out words. "Did you notice this? *The money is here, but it's hidden away,*" he reads, and then scans farther down. "And then this: the person changed *the box* to the word *it*."

"Yeah. I wonder if that's because the money is no longer in a box, or because she didn't want Eden to know it was in a box. If that's true, then this is probably a draft she never planned to send, and she rewrote the letter without the crossed-out words. If this is Miss Amanda's writing, it would have helped to have this the other night. I didn't know we might be looking for a box."

"Well, this is pretty cool. Maybe your ghost is a

thief—or someone at the zoo is." Fisher combs his fingers into the front of his hair and ruffles it so it sticks up.

"She's not *my* ghost," I say, wrinkling my nose at him.

"Well, you're the only one who's seen her."

"Other than Roger, you mean," I point out.

"Well, I meant lately. You're the only one who's seen her *lately*."

Miss Amanda did say she needed to discuss something with Mr. Bixly. I wonder if she found him and if he saw her like I did. Maybe I'm *not* the only one who has seen her lately.

Fisher looks out the windows to check the bus's location.

I have no idea where we are. The bus turns left at a traffic light with a street sign labeled Telegraph Road. This street was mentioned in the newspaper article about the tornado. The street name makes me think of Roger—because telegraphs kind of fit with the railroad and all the old-fashioned things he likes.

"And *that's* what I wanted to tell you," Fisher continues.

"Has anyone else seen her?"

"Last night, when my parents thought I had gone to sleep, I got up to get something to eat. I was pretty hungry."

"You're always hungry."

"I know. I went into the kitchen to get a snack, and my mom and dad were talking in my mom's office. They didn't know I was there. I heard your name, and Roger's, so I stayed quiet and tried not to make any noise."

My heart starts pounding a heavy beat, and I lean in closer.

"My mom was saying something about Roger's concerns."

"Roger is concerned?"

"I guess. They were talking about a book he's been reading."

Roger has been reading a psychology book lately. I don't know why. But Roger being concerned about something to do with psychology doesn't sound very good.

"And *then* my mom said she told Roger to just come out and ask you and that you might surprise him. I don't know what that's about."

"Ask me? Ask me what?"

"I don't know."

I groan at him. "Fisher! This isn't exactly helpful. None of this means anything if you don't know what they were talking about."

"Yeah, sorry. I'm just telling you all of it. What I *did* hear was that my mom saw Amanda's ghost the night she died, which she said was the night Roger found you asleep next to Nyah. No one knew Amanda had died yet, but my mom was the first to realize it. After the storm, she saw Amanda walking in front of the aviary, along the stretch of tracks that goes to the train shed and the main station."

"How did she know Miss Amanda walking along the tracks was a ghost?"

"Because ghosts aren't affected by weather. My mom said it was raining, and Amanda wasn't wet." Fisher stops for a moment. "Lex, are you okay?"

I remember the rain. I remember hearing the rain falling around me and Nyah shielding me from it. "Uh, yeah." My voice sounds scratchy. "I've always wanted to know more about that night, but it's strange to actually hear it. Is there more?"

Fisher checks out the windows again. A sign up ahead says Allen Sport Park.

"Yeah," he says, sounding hurried. "My mom saw Roger follow Amanda's ghost to the Grasslands. That's why my dad got there so quickly to help get you out. My mom has always said Roger 'thought' he saw a ghost, but I never knew *she* saw the ghost, *too*. And while my dad and Roger got you out of Nyah's enclosure, my mom went looking for Amanda."

"But couldn't she see her there at the Grasslands?"

"No. I mean, she went looking for Amanda's *body*." Fisher says the last word like the voice in a horror-movie trailer. I elbow him. "She's the one who found Amanda dead outside her trailer."

"Oh." My insides feel suddenly squirmy and then

hollow—like I have nothing in there. The emptiness hurts. It hurts for Miss Amanda. It hurts because I've always thought of my family as living, breathing people, even though I know they're probably dead. I may not remember them, but it hurts to think of them as bodies.

Fisher suddenly starts fidgeting with his hands. "Sorry."

"What are you sorry for?"

"Was it rude for me to tell you that?"

"No." I try swallowing to get rid of the hollow feeling, but it doesn't really work. "Well . . . maybe you could have left out the horror-movie voice."

"Yeah, I'm sorry. I uh . . . I just forgot about . . . well . . . that we're talking about the night you lost your family." Fisher squirms in his seat and grabs his backpack, unzipping the main pocket and pulling out his baseball glove. The bus is slowing to a stop at the edge of a parking lot. The baseball field sits just beyond it.

"Don't worry about it, Fisher," I say. "I want to know these things." People are afraid of talking about my parents or the night I lost them. They are afraid of talking about death in front of me. But the thing is, it's worse to not talk about it, because burying it hurts more.

25

Sinking Canoe

The giggling girls from the bus get off at the ball field, too.

As Fisher and I step off the bus, one of them says, "You're Fisher Leigh, aren't you?"

Fisher slaps his baseball hat on his head and says, "Yeah."

"Weren't you in Mr. Lindham's class last year?" asks a taller girl with long, red hair.

"Yeah," Fisher says again.

The girls seem to be headed to the same place we are, but they aren't dressed like they're planning to play any baseball. So either they're coming to watch, like me, or they're just following us so they can talk to Fisher.

The first girl, who is dressed fancy and wears makeup, says, "Do you know Sebastian? He's my brother."

We reach the edge of the field. A few people are already sitting on the bleachers across the grass.

"Yeah, I know him." Fisher doesn't seem to have much to say to these girls. That's okay with me. It's like they are *trying* to know him, but I *already* know him.

I feel like a stranger walking with all of them, not saying anything and not being able to talk to Fisher like normal. Fisher looks over at his coach and some other players gathering on the field. He's probably going to join them any minute now, and I'm going to have to figure this out by myself.

Fisher says to me, and not to the other girls, "I gotta go." He hands me a hat from his backpack, not his Omaha Storm Chasers hat—he's wearing that one. It's his Dodgers hat. It's one of his favorites, and he keeps it clean and new-looking. "Use this to keep the sun out of your eyes. I'll see you after we're done."

Before I can say "Thanks," the tall girl with the red hair calls to him. "Hey, Fisher! Hit a home run!"

I look at her sideways, put on Fisher's hat, and turn to walk across the field toward the bleachers without these girls. But I didn't realize the third girl was almost right behind me. I stop quickly, and she dodges out of the way, but we still smack into each other.

"Excuse me," I say, a little annoyed. When I jumped on the bus to come with Fisher, I hadn't planned on this at all.

"My fault," says the girl, rubbing her shoulder where we hit. "I was standing too close."

"Well, I wasn't looking," I say, trying to match her nice tone. "Sorry."

The other two girls have followed Fisher onto the field and are talking with another boy, who seems to know the girl with all the makeup. The odd silence between me and the third girl seems to need something to fill it. I'm not sure why.

"Are you watching the practice?" I ask, twisting a loose thread from my shirt around my finger. This is so different from talking to people in the zoo.

The wind kicks up a little dust to get my attention. *"Talk to me,"* it nags.

"I think so," the girl answers. "Anna is getting some money from her brother for snacks. We might stay awhile and then go to her house."

"Let's go, Camille," calls the one with the makeup, who is Sebastian's sister, Anna. She waves some money in the air and leads the way toward a small shaved-ice shack at the far side of the bleachers.

Camille, the girl next to me, waves at Anna and the tall girl, but she doesn't leave to join them. Instead, she walks with me to the bleachers.

"Did you used to go to Lexington Elementary?" Camille asks. She has a round face with high cheekbones that looks friendly, but I still dread her questions.

Nothing good can come from the direction this is going to take.

"A long time ago." Immediately, I regret answering her.

"What's your name?"

I'm suddenly reminded of my assignment from Mrs. Leigh—the one where I'm supposed to figure out what I can learn from Karana about myself. This situation right here is my very own version of the first time Karana tries to go after her people. She makes a canoe and sails away from the island all by herself. It's the first time she tries leaving her island, and it doesn't go well. She nearly sinks and drowns, and she has to turn back.

Coming to the ball field was a bad idea. I should've listened to the wind.

"I'm Camille," the girl adds, as though telling me her name will make me feel better about telling her mine.

We reach the bleachers, and it seems Camille is determined to follow me. I don't want to have this conversation, but I don't know where else to go. The bus probably won't return to the parking lot for a while. Fisher is about to play baseball and can't help. Camille's two friends are at the snack shack and will join her soon. I can't think of a way out.

"I'm Lex." It comes out as a whisper.

"I thought I remembered you!" Camille says, her eyes widening like marbles. "You're the girl from the zoo."

"Not exactly," says the wind, laughing as it always has whenever I've asked it where I came from.

"Lexington Willow, right?" asks Camille.

I wince. I'm not ashamed of my name. I like it. But I'm worried about what'll come next.

"I think we were in class together. Do you remember?"

I don't remember, not really, but I nod and say, "I think so."

"Where do you go to school now?"

I start climbing the bleacher steps, and Camille joins me.

"I . . . um . . . I do my schoolwork at the zoo. I have a private teacher there." I adjust Fisher's Dodgers hat to shade my eyes from the sun reflecting off the silver metal seats.

"I didn't know you could do that. I guess you still live there, huh?"

The third row has no one in it, so I pause there, wondering if Camille is planning to sit down. So far, I'd be okay with that.

"Yeah, I live there—same as Fisher." I figure mentioning Fisher will help it sound more normal. She hasn't yet looked at me like she's trying to figure out if I'm a rare breed of monkey. She hasn't yet called me—

"Elephant Girl!" cries a high-pitched voice that ends in a delighted squeal and then a giggle. It isn't Camille who said it.

I turn to see Anna and her red-haired friend holding

shaved ice with a snowcap of evaporated milk drizzled over the top. I cringe inside, wishing I hadn't turned immediately in answer to that name.

"I thought I recognized you," the red-haired girl says, still giggling.

"Tae, that isn't nice," says Camille.

"But she *is* Elephant Girl," Anna says. "I should've known when she got on the bus at the zoo stop. Her hair! It's the same as it was in first grade." She's talking about me as if I'm not even here.

And suddenly, I remember Tae. So they recognize my curly hair, huh? Well, I recognize Tae's red hair and how she used to laugh at me like she's doing now.

"You *are* the girl they found sleeping in the dirt with the elephant, aren't you?" Tae asks. "You used to talk to the wind at recess."

They're all giving me that look—like I'm an exhibit at the zoo. All of a sudden, I'm Karana from my book, and all the water is coming inside my canoe. I'm going to sink if I don't turn back to my island. I push past Camille and the other girls and start down the stairs.

"*Run,*" says the wind.

"Lex, wait," a voice calls after me. I think it's Camille, but I don't turn around. My tennis shoes hit the gravel with a crunch at the bottom of the last step. I run from the bleachers and the ball field. The slap of my feet against the earth has the familiar rhythm of a chant I wish I could forget.

Elephant Girl
With the crazy hair
Smells like the zoo
and talks to the air
Elephant Girl
Elephant Girl

I remember the words the way the kids used to chant them outside the school, and I keep running all the way to the bus stop.

26

Leaf in the Wind

I feel like a lone leaf blown from a tree. I don't know how to find my way back to the zoo. But I know that Fisher takes the bus home from the ball field every day, so I wait at the stop until a bus comes.

"*You should listen to me,*" says the wind.

"*It's all your fault,*" I say. "*It's YOUR fault they call me that name.*"

A bus pulls up to the stop. It has an electronic sign on the front that shows the number five and the words East River Road.

I climb the steps with my exact change. At least I know this much.

"Will this bus take me to the Lexington Zoo?" I ask the driver. It's a different driver and a different bus, but she nods, so I drop my $1.25 in exact change into the fare box.

I'm riding the bus back to the zoo without Fisher. I left him at the ball field after I told him I'd watch him play. I'm not sure if that makes me a liar or just . . . a really bad friend.

Fisher got in a fistfight once with some of the boys who made fun of me. It was after school, outside Lexington Elementary. He punched one of them in the stomach, a very big kid who looked too old to be at the playground. The kid threw mud clods at us. A mud ball hit me on the side of my head and stuck in my hair. The kid had put a long sock in front of his nose like an elephant trunk. Then he trumpeted the Elephant Girl chant until everyone had memorized it. Fisher got hauled into the principal's office for fighting on school grounds. It didn't matter that the big kid and his friends didn't go to our school, Fisher still got in trouble, and all the other kids learned the chant anyway. Fisher knows I quit going to school because kids were making fun of me. But he doesn't know the other reason. I also quit going because I didn't want him to keep getting into trouble for me. Turns out he still gets in trouble for me—or because of me.

Now he's playing baseball at the field, and I'm not there. And I'm still wearing his Dodgers hat.

The bus creeps its way up the hill toward the zoo.

As it drives past the long stretch of undeveloped land, I press my forehead against the window, trying to see through the trees. It's impossible to make out anything but a blur of browns and greens, with occasional bursts of wildflower clusters. I wonder if Miss Amanda notices the change in the scenery around her trailer home. Does she notice changes in the weather and seasons, even if ghosts don't get wet in the rain?

The bus takes a turn away from the zoo. I'm nervous that I've gone the wrong way, and I'm about to ask the driver when she pulls the bus into a turnaround spot on River Road. More people get on and off. I pull Fisher's hat down lower and keep looking out the window. Eventually the bus stops at the bottom of the zoo parking lot. I'm out of my seat and down the steps as if the wind blew me out the door.

"Back safe and sound," says the wind.

But it doesn't feel safe and sound. It feels like the wind wants to keep me here more than I didn't want to leave. And I don't think that's a good way to feel about home.

I trudge through the prickly weeds toward the trees and Miss Amanda's trailer.

That red-haired Tae, and the way she yelled out that awful name, as though first grade and the big mean kid with the mud and the sock were yesterday, has got my head in a whirlwind and my feet moving angry-fast. I reach the dense trees in the deeper part of the woods in record time. I take the diagonal path from the fallen log, and soon I see the first of Miss Amanda's upturned chairs. I shove my hand into my pocket and feel the letter, rubbing it between my finger and thumb like it might have some power to bring her back. But as I approach, the rest of the familiar wreckage comes into view. It seems I won't be seeing Amanda Holtz today.

I kick the dirt, sending a cloud of dust and grass bugs into the air. How can I help Miss Amanda remember anything about the treasure or Nyah's family if I can't find her? Stepping over the torn fabric awning, I move slowly toward the trailer. Now that I know Mrs. Leigh found Miss Amanda after she died, it doesn't make sense that no one cleaned up this wreckage. I'm glad they didn't, or I might never have met Miss Amanda, but did people forget about it? Did they forget about her? I wonder whether Miss Amanda's belongings are untouched inside the trailer.

The idea of walking into the abandoned home of a dead person gives me a cold and squirmy feeling, but I still want to solve the lost-treasure mystery. What if Miss Amanda is wandering as a ghost and has lost her memory of this trailer? What if she can't remember how to get home? If I can find the right clues, find Eden from the letter and return the treasure to her, Miss Amanda might be free from this wandering, memory-losing state. She might be able to go where spirits are supposed to go.

I climb the two steps to the trailer door and slowly wrap my fingers around the metal doorknob.

I turn the knob, checking. It's unlocked.

Is it really invading someone's privacy if you look through their things after they've died?

A *thump* comes from inside the trailer, like the sound of a drawer or a cupboard closing. It startles me, and I nearly fall off the steps.

In a tiny voice that sounds unfamiliar, I quaver out a soft "Hello?"

Something creaks inside the trailer.

I should run, but my feet don't obey me. This part of the zoo property isn't fenced off. They've posted Private Property and No Trespassing signs around, but that's not going to keep people out. What if someone is inside stealing stuff, and I've just stumbled upon this with no way to defend myself? Mr. Bixly installed all those security cameras and alarms in the zoo, but that's not going to help me out here. If I yell, no one will hear me all the way on the other side of Bear Country.

My feet finally move off the steps just as the door swings open to the inside of the trailer. It's darker in there than out here. My eyes aren't adjusted to the change of light, and I can't make anything out. Not even an outline or a shadow.

"Lexington Willow!" calls a cheery Southern voice. Miss Amanda moves into the daylight of the doorframe, as real-looking as any person. The sun reflects off her key necklace.

"Hi, Miss Amanda." My voice comes out with a breath of air like I've been holding it for a week. "You . . . you're here."

"Well, of course I am. Where else would I be?"

"I've been coming to see you, and you haven't been here," I say, holding on to the railing to keep my balance.

"Have you, now?" Miss Amanda is wearing a yellow-and-gray skirt with a soft-looking sweater. Fisher must be right about ghosts not being affected by the weather. Miss Amanda probably wouldn't choose to wear that sweater in June if she were alive. "Tell me," she says, "did you have any luck with the loose board in the gift shop? Did you find the treasure?"

I'm trying hard to focus on the ghost in front of me, in case she suddenly disappears or something. Since everything looked undamaged and right side up when I last saw her, I assumed that the old and broken state of everything today meant that I wouldn't be seeing the ghost.

"I found a loose board," I say. "My friend Fisher helped me. We pulled up the board, but we didn't find a treasure."

"Nothing behind the board, huh?" she asks.

It seems weird that she would say *behind* the board instead of *under* it. I shake my head no. "No treasure.

But I found a few other things I want to show you. I was hoping they might help you remember something."

"Wonderful!" she exclaims. "Come in and set a spell. We'll have some tea. You show me what you found, and I'll do my best to remember some more." Miss Amanda turns from the door and walks into the trailer.

I move to the top step and peek in at the dark interior. Miss Amanda goes to a window on the opposite side, which has a small halo of daylight framing some curtains. She pulls the curtains aside, filling the trailer with filtered sunlight from the woods behind it. The window sits above a table in a very small kitchen to the right. A teakettle rests on a turquoise stove that matches a miniature turquoise fridge. At the other end of the trailer is a wide bed topped with a thick comforter. A single shelf of books and trinkets runs around all three walls of the bedroom space.

I feel for the letter and the wrinkled train ticket in my pocket. Then, as I take one step into the trailer, the wind rustles the leaves and sends a breeze swirling around my ankles.

"She'll never remember what you need," the wind says.

I wonder whether a ghost might be able to hear the wind speak, too. But Miss Amanda sets teacups in saucers on the kitchen table and begins pouring tea from her fat teapot, as though she's heard nothing. The teacups remind me of our last visit and that I lost track of time before.

I'm going to need to get a watch.

"Miss Amanda, do you have a clock?"

"Yes darlin', and it still works!" She points at the wall in the kitchen.

Sure enough, the clock hands show ten-fifty, which seems right, and the second hand is moving at an accurate speed around the face.

"Just a minute, please," I say to her, unhooking my radio from my waistband. I press down the call button and speak clearly. "Willow to Hostler."

The radio crackles to life. "Hostler here. Go ahead, Willow."

"Just checking the time. Do you have ten-fifty?"

"Yes," he answers. "But you can have until twelve-thirty, instead of noon, if that helps."

It does help, but I realize he still thinks I'm at the ball field with Fisher. I don't want to explain all that over the radio, though. "Got it. Willow out."

I step all the way into Miss Amanda's ham-shaped, vintage trailer and take in a deep breath of lemons and mint. The extra half hour is a good buffer, but I'm going to pretend I don't have that extra time, just in case.

I can give myself one hour with Miss Amanda. One hour, and then I have to leave to meet Roger. After lunch, I'll find Fisher and explain why I left the ball field. I tell myself this because I don't want to forget what I'm doing or go missing for hours, like what happened to Mrs. Leigh when she was with her ghost friend.

Miss Amanda sets her teapot on the table. "Now then," she says, sitting and smoothing her skirt, "what did you want to show me?"

I reach into my pocket for the letter and the train ticket, and I wonder if the best chance of getting results with Miss Amanda's faded memories is to focus on one thing at a time. Maybe too many things at once is distracting. So I pull out the letter first.

Miss Amanda points at it and then clasps her hands together, as though she's keeping herself from touching the paper. "Where did you find this?"

I haven't unfolded the letter yet, so she can't see exactly what it is, but she looks like she might know. She motions at the empty kitchen chair like she wants me to sit down, so I do.

"It was in the gift shop desk—in the storeroom. Isabel, the lady who runs the shop now, said she found it after you had gone. It doesn't have your name on it, but she assumed you wrote it." I open the letter and hold it faceup for her to see the writing. "Did you?"

A bit of sunlight flickers through the window, and Miss Amanda's face lights up with it. I'm still surprised that ghosts aren't see-through. But she has a softness about her that makes her different, like an old picture that's slightly blurry.

She reaches for the paper. "May I have a look?"

I let her take it and watch how the paper seems to move a smidgen before she touches it, drawn to her like a magnet.

Her blue eyes scan the words, and then she startles like someone snuck up and surprised her. "Of course! I have a picture of Eden . . . *and* of Angus Fenn."

She lays the letter flat on the table and stabs her pointer finger at Eden's name. "The fortune is hers. We have to find that box and return it to Eden."

"Can you show me the picture, Miss Amanda? Maybe a picture will help you remember."

27

The Fenn Circus

Miss Amanda walks to the other end of the trailer and stares at the bookshelf over the bed. I run my fingers lightly over the smooth tabletop. It's not dusty like a table would be if it had been inside an abandoned trailer for seven years. Everything appears as it should when Miss Amanda is using it, like the day I first saw her and she was sitting at her outdoor table having tea. Maybe the outdoor furniture and the awning look like their previous versions when Miss Amanda is out there, and the inside of the trailer looks like it did seven years ago when she is inside. It doesn't seem possible, but it's also the only thing that can explain this.

Miss Amanda finds a brown leather photo album and brings it to the table. She sits beside me and turns the pages. The album is full of black-and-white photographs behind glossy plastic. The first ones look like family photos, but then they change to photos of animals in show costumes and people of all sizes dressed like clowns and acrobats. She pauses at a picture that I think is a young Amanda Holtz staring up at me.

"I used to work for the circus," Miss Amanda says. "And not just *any* circus, mind you—the Fenn Circus. I met the dashing Angus Fenn when his circus stopped outside my hometown."

Miss Amanda's memory certainly does work better when she talks to me. She's already told me something I learned from those internet articles. I want to tell her I looked her up and what I found, but that might interrupt her from telling me something new. Her face almost looks younger as her eyes light with what seem to be happy memories.

"Angus discovered that you couldn't get Southern cooking quite like what he found in my father's restaurant, so I saw him in there often. I found Angus's life—the traveling life and the business of acquiring animals and hiring trainers and performers—very intriguing," Miss Amanda continues. "I also found Angus . . . well . . ."

"Dashing?" I use her word. It feels round and full in my mouth and makes me think of *splash* and *clash*, which doesn't have anything to do with Angus Fenn, but I think I'll keep using this word.

She nods. I never wondered before if a ghost could

blush, but I would say Miss Amanda has managed it. She has a faraway look, and I think she's remembering Angus after a long time of forgetting him.

Miss Amanda scans the album again, dragging her finger over the pictures. "He's got to be here," she mutters. She turns the pages faster and faster until it feels almost frantic. She stands from the table and walks back to the shelf at the other end of the trailer. "Got to be here." She places one hand on her hip and the other on top of her head like she's thinking.

After a long pause, she suddenly exclaims, "I knew it!" She pulls something from the shelf and turns around, showing me another leather-bound album. "I have *two*!"

She brings the second album back to the table, opens the cover, and finds the photo she wants on the first page. "Here he is. Angus Fenn. And that's me at the desk."

I lean over the table to get a closer look at the man in the picture. He's wearing a long-coated suit. He has kind eyes and a trimmed beard. He seems to be standing in a low-ceilinged room, or a hallway, and he's leaning with one hand on the corner of a desk. The beautiful young woman sitting at the desk behind him must be Miss Amanda. She has shoulder-length hair that is mostly straight but curls up at the ends. Several piles of paper are stacked on the desk, and Miss Amanda is holding a pen, as though she stopped her work just for the photo.

"Is that an office, or a closet?" I ask.

"It's a train car."

I look again. I can see it now. It looks like the old passenger cars in Roger's train books. It has the same lantern-style lights on the walls and the same wood paneling as the antique passenger train car Roger restored for the zoo. "Isn't this a passenger car? Where are the seats?"

"Angus took them out," Miss Amanda says. "He modified several train cars to suit the needs of his circus."

Miss Amanda runs her finger over the photos. "St. Louis . . . hmm, I forgot about that." She turns the page. "Montgomery, Nashville, Chicago, Des Moines . . ." Her voice trails off. She stares at the pictures a moment, and then she smiles. "We usually stayed in one spot for a month or two, depending on ticket sales," she explains. "Then, before we'd overstayed our welcome, we'd move on. It was always changing. Angus searched for just the right towns, the wide-open spaces, and the right talent. And then we moved on to bigger cities and more acts and more ticket sales."

It seems Miss Amanda remembers things pretty well if she has a picture for reference. Maybe we just have to come across the right ones.

Every photo shows the same circus tents, performers, and animals like monkeys and lions, but each photo has a different landscape. And then, suddenly, there's a picture of elephants.

"Did you know the elephants, Miss Amanda?" I ask,

pointing to the picture. I think I can tell that one of them is Nyah. One of them could be Tendai, but I'm not sure. I count four African elephants, and they're all wearing fancy circus gear on their heads and backs. I don't think I like seeing Nyah wearing all of that.

Miss Amanda looks at the elephant picture and takes a sip of her tea. When she sets the cup back in the saucer, it looks as full as it did before.

I remember to check the clock and glance at it quickly. Eleven-ten.

It feels like it's only been five minutes since I walked in here, not twenty.

"I knew the elephants," Miss Amanda says. "I liked them and visited them a lot at the beginning. Angus knew I liked them. But then . . ."

Miss Amanda shows me a picture of a bright-eyed woman in a glittery orange costume. This picture, although faded with age, is in full color. So are the others next to it. The young woman's wavy hair almost reaches her waist.

"This is Elle," Miss Amanda says quietly.

"Not Eden?"

She shakes her head. "Elle. She was an acrobat, but she also had a talent with the elephants. She joined Angus's circus about four years after I began working for him."

She pauses, and the trailer is eerily quiet. I can't hear the wind or any sound from the clock or the low hum of

186

a normal kitchen. It's just silent. I'm beginning to wonder whether Miss Amanda has lost the direction of her thoughts or has no more memories to share. I'm about to ask about Eden again when she makes a little throat-clearing sound.

"Angus had a lot of inheritance money from his family in England. He brought his fortune to the United States and used it to create shows. He featured everything that fascinated him. Different and beautiful and wild things. But he was a bit irresponsible with his money. He'd find unusual places and things to spend it on, and people would take advantage of that. He realized he would no longer have a fortune if he didn't have someone watching out for it."

"So is that what you did for the circus? Took care of the money?" I already know it is, because the article I found said Amanda Holtz was the finance manager for the Fenn Circus. But since talking to me helps her remember, I figure asking questions is a good way to keep it rolling.

Miss Amanda nods. "Mm-hmm." She's looking at another photo of the same beautiful acrobat—Elle. In this one, the acrobat is in a fancy gown and wearing long lace over her hair. She has her arm linked through the arm of a slightly older-looking, suit-wearing Angus Fenn. Elle and Angus are standing in front of a line of train cars with signs hanging over the doors. The people around them seem to be celebrating.

"I shouldn't talk about this with you, darlin'," Miss Amanda says, slowly closing the photo album.

"Why?" I'm suddenly worried my outburst of questions ruined everything.

"You barely know me," she says, shaking her head with a hint of disgust. "What I have to say is not what I would tell a child. Matter of fact, I don't believe I've ever told anyone, child or not."

This only makes me more eager to know. This is a good story. I feel I can almost touch it. "Miss Amanda, you can tell me. If you remember it well, maybe it's something you're supposed to tell me. Maybe it will be helpful."

"You'll think less of me," Miss Amanda says, looking again at the yellow paper on the table with her letter written on it.

I look at the clock.

Eleven-thirty-five.

I should leave in fifteen minutes to meet Roger. I can't lose track of time with Miss Amanda again. Just in case forgetfulness is related to ghost food, I decide not to drink her tea this time.

I place both hands on the table and give her my best serious face. "Roger always tells me, 'Everyone makes mistakes. You prove what you are made of when you try to make it right.' Isn't that what you're doing?"

If Miss Amanda were alive right now, instead of a ghost, I think she would've taken a deep breath and sighed. Instead, she pushes the letter toward me, turning it slightly so I'm looking at it right side up. "This"—she points at the name *Eden*—"is Angus and Elle Fenn's daughter."

I feel my heart quicken, like I'm running toward something important.

Miss Amanda nods. "Angus married the beautiful acrobat, Elle, who became a caretaker for his African elephants. I loved him long before Elle joined the Fenn Circus. I thought he knew that, but he didn't love me in that way. He loved her."

Miss Amanda traces the edge of the photo album with her fingers. It's suddenly rather cold inside the trailer. I shiver and fold my arms across my chest, hugging them to me.

"Even after Angus married Elle, he asked me to safeguard the fortune he kept inside a locked metal box. He said he was less likely to waste it on the latest inventions that the salesmen were always pushing at him. Word had gotten around in the selling trade that Angus Fenn would hand over a lot of cash for something interesting. So he asked me to keep the box of his extra savings hidden away where only I could get it. He figured if he had to ask me where the money was, he'd think twice about whether it was a good idea to spend it.

"So I did as he asked. It made me feel . . ." She makes a face like the words she wants to say taste bad in her mouth. "It made me feel like I had something Elle did

189

not. I figured that if Angus was asking me to safeguard his fortune, then Elle must not know about it. I realize now that was probably wrong."

Grown-ups don't talk to me the way Miss Amanda does. They always seem to assume I can't handle things the way they are.

"I did what he asked," she continues. "I kept it somewhere Angus didn't know about, so he wouldn't spend it unreasonably. He never asked for it, and I kept it hidden. Trouble is, I can't remember where I hid it, or where it is now."

"You kept it hidden, but you didn't . . ." I'm struggling to come up with a word less harsh than *steal*. "You didn't take it?"

Miss Amanda's eyes are extra round. "Oh, heavens, no. No, I would never . . ." She sits up very straight. "At least, I don't *think* I would ever take his money."

"But you said before, when I saw you last time, you said you hid it beneath a loose board in the gift shop. So if you didn't take it, how did Angus Fenn's fortune end up at the Lexington Zoo?"

A prickly feeling washes over me like a stinging rain, and I have to get to the bottom of this. Something inside me, something deeper than my heart and my stomach, *has* to know what happened. I don't know why, but someone—or something—is depending on this.

Miss Amanda opens her photo album again, shaking her head and studying the pages. The sunlight shining through the window makes the veins in her wrinkled hands look like purplish rivers on a map. It still seems like I could touch her and she would be solid, but then again, the photo album pages still move with a tiny space between them and her hand.

I catch another glimpse of elephants in a photo. Although we need more information about the lost fortune, Nyah is also counting on me for something else. "Do you know what happened to the elephants from the circus? Do you know all their names?"

Miss Amanda keeps turning the pages. I want to make her stay with the elephant picture. She is looking for something about Angus Fenn's fortune. But she's not staying on any page long enough to notice anything. What if she's missing chances to look at a picture and remember what Nyah needs her to tell me?

"Do you know Nyah and Tendai?" I ask. Discussing memories with a ghost is mostly like running in place—it's a lot of effort to go nowhere. "Miss Amanda . . ." I place my hand on the photo album and hold it there. "Why did Nyah and Tendai come to the same zoo you did? Did you bring them here? Where are the other elephants?"

Carefully avoiding Miss Amanda's hand, because I still don't want to know if my hand will go through hers, I turn the pages back to the elephant picture. "Do you know what Angus Fenn did with all his elephants?"

She looks at the picture and then at me. Her

berry-colored lips press together, and she takes another sip of her bottomless tea.

"Nyah and Tendai. Yes. They arrived at the zoo after I had been here a few years—after I left working for Angus."

She smooths a section of her silvery hair. It's tucked neatly behind her ear on one side. "Nyah and Tendai." She repeats their names like speaking them makes the memory solid. "It was a surprise when they showed up here, that's for sure." Miss Amanda is staring at the table, and for the first time since I've met her, she seems as small as she looks. The air between us is heavy and sad. "I never saw Angus when he brought them here. I only learned Angus had arranged for the elephants to come to this zoo after Nyah and Tendai arrived. I immediately searched the news and learned his wife, Elle, had died. Angus had quit the circus life and left it all to Eden and her husband."

"Oh." I'm sorry for Angus Fenn because his wife died. I'm sorry for this man who owned Nyah and Tendai and dressed them in those circus costumes. But I'm sorry for Miss Amanda, too, because she loved the "dashing" circus man with the kind eyes and because he married Elle instead. "Do you think he left the other two elephants with Eden at the circus?"

"I never did find out where the others went, but I always thought that maybe, when Angus sent Nyah and Tendai to the zoo, he meant for me to have them back.

Perhaps he didn't know I loved him, but he knew I liked the elephants. I thought about contacting him. But when I got brave enough to try, he had died."

"Oh." I reach across the table and place my hand right next to hers. "I'm sorry, Miss Amanda."

Miss Amanda stands up from the table. "Well, haven't I poured enough vinegar on the day! Where are my manners? Would you like some biscuits or cookies?" She goes to the cupboard and pulls out a plate. "Aren't you going to drink your tea this time?"

"Tea?" And then I remember.

Lunch.

Lunch with Roger.

"Oh shoot!" I glance at the clock. It's twelve-thirty-five. "I'm sorry, Miss Amanda, but I have to go! I'm late for lunch with Roger!"

I nearly trip over the table legs getting out of my seat.

"Goodness! Well, I guess you'd better skedaddle." Miss Amanda beats me to the door and opens it for me. "Thank you for coming, Lexington. It's always a pleasure."

I hurry down the steps into the humid blast of summer heat. Miss Amanda's trailer must still have some sort of power to be so comfortably air-conditioned inside.

"Goodbye, Miss Amanda!" I call as I leap over an awning pole.

"Come again soon and we'll work some more on

that lost treasure box." Her voice has a slight echo to it as it sails through the trees.

And then I realize I never showed Miss Amanda the train ticket that I found beneath the gift shop floor. And no matter how much I like Miss Amanda Holtz or how much I believe she is telling the truth as she remembers it, it seems more than ever that either she must have left Angus Fenn's money at the circus or she really did steal it.

28

Wild Eats

My tennis shoes slap against the parking lot pavement. Scratches on my right leg sting where I brushed past a thorny weed at the woods' edge. I've avoided the worst weeds before, but this time I was in too much of a hurry and didn't see it coming. My radio thumps against my hip as I run. I yank it from my waistband and press the call button.

"Willow to Hostler." It comes out breathless and unsteady as I run right through the main gate, flashing my pass at the college student at the ticket booth.

"Hostler here," Roger answers.

I veer right at the lion pride statue. "I'm on my way down," I say into the radio. "Just came in the main gate."

The Wild Eats Café is at the bottom of the zoo hill,

just after the seals and sea lions at Harbor Reef. My throat stings, and my chest feels like it will burst. Running through the woods and up the sloping parking lot is a long way all by itself, but when you add the distance across the zoo, it's massive. I keep running, though, and pass the turnoff to the Leighs' house.

"Thanks, Willow. See you soon." It's hard to tell through the radio with the hum of people and the whir of wind whether Roger is disappointed or not. At least I had my radio and could call him this time.

I reach the sea lions, and the orange building of the Wild Eats Café comes into view as I round the Harbor Reef maintenance building. I have another pressing feeling in my chest that I don't think is related to running. It was bad enough when I didn't show up without telling Roger last time. Doing it again feels a hundred times worse. Roger doesn't ask a lot of me. I'm picturing him sitting at our outside table, the one with the best view of the birds. I think of him eating alone and watching the path for a glimpse of me coming to meet him. I can almost see his worried face in my mind, because I saw that look when Mrs. Leigh brought me to the main station in the golf cart.

And then I see him for real. He's taking his napkins to the recycling bin.

"Roger!" I call.

He sees me and waves.

I run to the outdoor seating without going through the café first. I stop a few feet away from him, clutching the pain in my side and leaning over my bent knees.

"Walk it off, walk it off." Roger chuckles, guiding me to the long path in front of the Swift Aviary. "You had quite the run, huh?"

I nod, unable to speak amid my heaving gasps.

"I thought maybe it would be a tight schedule for you to get back from Fisher's practice in time."

He's not disappointed. He's not disappointed because he thought I was stuck at Fisher's practice and that my return to the zoo depended on the bus schedule. I'm still trying to catch my breath, so I have a minute to think. Roger turns with me at the second aviary entrance, and we walk along the path the way we came.

Would it be better to let him think I was late because of the bus? Maybe I could just let him think it without correcting him. We could avoid disappointed looks, and perhaps a consequence, if I don't mention visiting Miss Amanda again. But what if Roger finds out from Fisher that I left his practice early? I'll just have to find Fisher first and talk to him.

"I've got to get back on the train soon," Roger says. "But let's find something for you to eat first."

"Okay," I say, still out of breath. "I'm sorry I missed lunch again, Roger."

We slow our walk as we reach the café seating again.

"Well, I get worried when you don't show up, but I figured you came back as soon as the bus could get you here."

His words are little rocks in my stomach. It's as if my conversation with a ghost was more important to me than Roger, but that's not at all how I feel. I'm just not sure it will sound right if I explain it. Everything is getting so messy, and I don't know how to clean it all up.

"How about I help you tomorrow morning?" I say. "I could give the speech a few times around, so J.P. can switch places with you and give you a break."

Roger often lets me give the train speech over the intercom. He says I have a better voice for it. His voice is so deep that the intercom speakers vibrate and make his words difficult to understand, but Roger is the engineer, anyway. He's usually in the cab at the throttle. J. P. Felt will often give the speech, or if they happen to have an extra employee available, they take turns.

"You know what?" Roger says with a smile. "I would like that very much."

"Okay." I'm almost breathing normally again, but I'm completely out of spit.

"You need a drink," Roger says.

He takes me through the café's employee entrance. He gets me a water bottle, a lemonade, and a deli sandwich from Lucile, the café manager. We have to pay for zoo food, but at employee discount prices, it costs almost the same as going to the grocery store for everything ourselves. I do look forward to the occasional home-cooked dinner, though. Roger is a master of marinades and barbecue.

The people are lining up behind the gates at the train stop in front of the café. Roger pulls out his engineer's watch.

"It's time for me to get going. Do you and Fisher have plans?"

"I'm going to go see him right now," I say. "We have to talk about baseball." We *really* have to talk baseball— about how I went to watch him play and then left without seeing a single bit of baseball or saying goodbye. I take a big drink of my water, but it's difficult to get it to go down.

"Well, stay out of trouble, okay? Isabel radioed me this morning and said you've worked off your debt to the gift shop." Roger keeps two radios on the train with him—one set to match my channel, and one set to the channel for the rest of the zoo.

"Oh. That's good."

"And keep that radio with you. Just like the grounds crew."

I promise, although I'm especially tired of the heavy thing hanging off my waistband after my long run. I wish Roger would just consider getting cell phones.

"Maybe you can come on a round trip later today. I've got the new speech all ready. You could try it out."

Roger's been working on the new speech for a while.

I'd like to give it a try, but it'll have to wait. "Maybe tomorrow . . ."

He smiles and says, "I know, I know. You and Fisher have plans." I walk with him to the engine, and he pulls on his engineer's hat. J. P. Felt and one of the student employees take tickets at the gate. Roger climbs the steps and waves at me from inside the cab, just as Fisher's voice comes through Roger's zoo-wide radio.

"Slugger to Willow, where are you?"

29

Sorry

Fisher is a very good listener when it's important. I return his Dodgers hat to him without a mark on it. I explain the whole thing about the ball field and about the girls and how they recognized me from school. I tell him what Tae called me, and how I felt like Karana in her canoe (which he hasn't read, but I try to explain that part of the story anyway). He doesn't say anything until I finish. As I said, he's a very good listener.

"Okay," he says.

But I can tell it's not okay. He said he missed the eleven-forty bus because he couldn't find me. He said he looked all around the ball field and in the bleachers. He asked some girls to check and see if I was in the girls' bathroom. He wasn't going to leave without me.

I've been disappointing a lot of people lately, and I'm running out of ideas for how to make it up to them.

I try, with Fisher, by helping him with his chores, but Mr. Leigh gives out a big sigh when we ask what Fisher needs to do today.

"Fisher, I'm calling it good. I'll tell Frank you've worked off your punishment." Mr. Leigh rubs his forehead with his fingertips. He hasn't shaved for a couple of days and has a sunburn on top of his tan. He looks like he did in some of his photos from Kenya. "Thomas and I have a big evaluation coming up for the elephants, and I have a meeting about that Ashby family party. They want to pay big bucks to rent the zoo for the evening and send up some paper lanterns, and my crew still has to figure out an acceptable alternative." He takes a sip of his coffee. "I don't have the mental energy to come up with one more thing."

Mr. Leigh picks up a clipboard from his desk and walks us to his office door. "But thanks for offering to help him, Lex."

Fisher mutters something under his breath as we leave Mr. Leigh's office.

"What did you say?" I ask.

"Nothing." Fisher kicks at the gravel path that leads from the Wild Kingdom Education Center to the back of the Birds of Prey Amphitheater.

"Yes, you did. You said something."

Fisher turns to look at me. His hair is pretty wild

from being sweaty in his ball cap for hours. He stuffs his hands into his pockets. "I said, 'You *should* offer to help, since you're the reason we got in trouble.'"

"I . . ." Heat floods from my neck into my face. "Wait . . . you wanted to do it. You propped open the gift shop door so we could sneak in there. I didn't make you do it."

He shrugs.

"I thought you said it was fine this morning. You weren't upset about it before. Besides, your dad said you're done. You don't have to worry about it any-more."

"Yeah, well . . ." Fisher shakes his head and looks at me like he'd rather be anywhere else than here. "I think I *was* fine about it this morning."

"Is this about the baseball practice? I told you why I left. I didn't mean to take off like that. I really did want to see you play."

"Yeah, I know," he says, and continues walking toward the amphitheater.

I follow him.

"Fisher?"

"What?" he answers softly and keeps walking. He doesn't wait for me, but he goes slow enough that I can catch up.

"Where are you going?"

"I'm going to help the keepers with the raptors. I want to learn more about falconry."

"Oh." I never knew Fisher was interested in that. I wonder if this is a new interest.

He pauses at the door. The words *Stage Door* are printed on it, but it's really the employee entrance to where they set up the raptors before a show. The Birds of Prey Amphitheater is fairly new, and I don't know the keepers who work with the birds very well. I've never gone in this door.

"Lately, it seems like everything is about you," he says. "I'm doing this right now." His voice stays calm, but the way he says it, with stress on the words *I'm* and *this,* makes it clear he doesn't want me to come along.

"Oh. Okay." The words sneak past my lips without my permission. I want to tell him I made a big effort to take care of his Dodgers hat. I want to tell Fisher that the bullies weren't the only reason I left school, but that I also stopped going so he wouldn't keep getting into trouble for me. I want to say that being called "Elephant Girl" makes me feel even more lost, and that I couldn't stay at the ballpark and feel that way. But instead, I stand there doing nothing and saying nothing. My face feels like it's painted on—like the clowns in Miss Amanda's photo album.

"See ya later," Fisher says.

I don't say sorry or anything, although I do feel sorry. Very sorry.

30

Angus Fenn's Donation

Fisher goes in the Birds of Prey stage door without me, and the only place I can think to go is to see Thomas and Nyah. But I'm pretty sure Roger hasn't talked to Mr. Bixly yet about lifting his ban on me visiting the elephant barn. I knock on the side maintenance door anyway. Thomas never comes. So I walk around to the observation path and pavilion above the Grasslands. It's full of zoo guests and strollers and voices everywhere. I'm a stranger surrounded by strangers.

I wriggle through the crowd until I find a place near the fences at the overlook. Nyah is down by a tall post and a dangling feeder. She reaches her trunk high, rears onto her hind legs, and pulls clumps of hay from the feeder.

The rest of the elephants are spread around the

habitat, doing what they do. Asha, the herd matriarch, is lying down, resting in a bit of shade and watching her daughter, Zaire. Jazz plays with a giant red ball around the perimeter fences, stopping only to investigate the puzzle feeders. The feeders are brainteasers with rewards for the elephants—tires and spinning boxes mounted on poles that release a treat as the elephants play with them. Zaire is examining a metal barrel that hangs on a tether above the barn door. Nyah has elephants around her, but to me she looks lonely—maybe because I know she misses her mother and her circus herd.

Zaire's playing is becoming almost agitated. She's walking under the hanging barrel, lifting it with her trunk, and then letting it drop on its short tether until it slams hard against the barn with a piercing steel *clang*. She does it again and again.

"Elephants should not be kept in captivity," a lady says with a hint of anger in her voice. I've heard these conversations at the zoo before, and I always listen in. "They should be sent back to their natural habitat, not put on display."

"It says here that two of the elephants were part of a group rescued from a drought in Swaziland," says another lady, reading the information posted on a sign.

The two of them are leaning on the overlook railing a few feet away from me. One of them is holding a soda and a box of popcorn from the train station. The other wears a wide-brimmed sun hat and has smeared white sunscreen on her face and bare shoulders.

"People need to let elephants alone," says the first lady. "They are incredibly smart animals. Don't you think they would migrate to find water if there was a drought and if humans didn't interfere?"

"It says their herd was going to be killed if they stayed," says the lady in the hat, still reading the sign. "Maybe human interference saved their lives from other human interference."

The first lady makes a dissatisfied grunt and sips her soda. "Too bad we can't ask the elephants what they think."

Yeah. Too bad I can see Nyah's thoughts but I can't ask her questions. And I think about how Nyah has never lived outside of captivity. Would she even know how to survive in the wild?

Asha gets up from the dirt and saunters over to Zaire, who is still banging the barrel against the barn. Zaire entwines her trunk with Asha's and then puts her trunk into her mother's mouth—something they do that seems to show affection or trust. Asha then lifts her trunk and presses the underside of it against Zaire's. It calms her. I can imagine their communication—low and long and passing simultaneously through the air and the earth at their feet. I wonder if they talk about Swaziland.

I glance back at Nyah, alone at the feeder. She reaches

with her trunk for another clump of hay, and she side-steps as she brings it to her mouth. Now she is facing my direction. She is aware of me. I feel it like a warm blanket. I wait and concentrate, hoping to feel the rumblings and see her thoughts, but nothing comes. I have to get closer to her and look into her eyes if I'm going to know any more of Nyah's thoughts.

And that's when I spot Thomas on the lower sidewalk between the Grasslands and the Wild Kingdom Education Center. I push through the crowd and hurry down the hill to catch up with him.

"Thomas!"

Thomas sees me coming and waits for me, shielding his eyes from the sun. When I reach him, he says, "Mr. Bixly said you can't go inside the barn anymore, Lex."

"I know," I say. "Roger is going to talk to him about that."

"But," Thomas continues like he didn't hear the part about Roger, "he didn't say anything about the back fences."

"Oh," I say, feeling light and sunshine in his words.

"And if my theory is correct, you only need to get close to her. Is that right?"

I swallow and nod.

Thomas takes in a big breath and sighs it all out. "She's communicating with you, isn't she?"

I nod again.

"I knew it!" Thomas smacks his leg with his hand. "How in the world? Humans can't hear those low frequencies."

"I don't know, Thomas. But I don't hear sounds. I see pictures."

"Pictures, huh? Like telepathy?"

I shrug. "If that means from her brain to mine, then yes."

"Pictures of what?"

"Of her life at the circus before she came here. Of other elephants. She wants me to find them. Thomas, you were here when Nyah and Tendai came to the zoo, right?"

Thomas nods. His forehead is wrinkled up from thinking so hard. "Yes, I was here. I'm the one who assimilated them into this herd."

"Do you know where the other circus elephants went?"

"I don't. I'm sorry. But I can certainly look into it. I have contacts with other elephant managers, and I can ask around. But we aren't set up to bring in more elephants to our herd, Lex. More elephants in the herd would require more space than we have."

"We still need to look for them," I say, even though I have no idea what we can do if we find Nyah's herd. "I feel like I've made her a promise somehow."

Thomas rubs his hand over his rough, unshaven face.

I think he knows about elephant promises. What he does every day for the elephants at this zoo is like fulfilling a promise to them. They count on him.

He checks his watch. "I have about ten minutes. I can take you to the back fences to see her, and I'll start looking into the other Fenn Circus elephants tonight, okay?"

"Thanks, Thomas," I say, following him to a locked gate in one of the perimeter fences. It leads into the Grasslands, but we are still on one side of a wooden fence and the elephants are on the other. This is the same wood fence style the zoo uses around many other habitats. Mr. Leigh says it is eucalyptus wood—a strong and fast-growing wood. The zoo uses it to support eucalyptus plantations that can be replenished, instead of cutting down other forests to make fences.

Thomas and I stand at the wooden fence for only a moment before Nyah notices us. She tosses dirt over her back and fans herself with her ears. I can feel her rumbling even stronger out here, as though it moves through open earth and sky better than it does inside the barn.

"I'm feeling that," says Thomas. "It thumps at the sides of your head."

"Yes, it does," I answer, not wanting to tell him that I feel it inside as well. Considering how much Thomas has dedicated his life to elephants, I feel a little guilty that he can't feel and see what I do. It doesn't seem fair.

Nyah takes slow, even steps toward me. The sunlight is bright without the shade of a pavilion, and my eyes are watering, but I blink away the blurriness and stare into Nyah's eyes, waiting. When she is close enough for me to follow the individual wrinkles circling her eyes, I see an image.

A young woman is standing beside an elephant with a long-handled brush and a hose. She's giving the elephant a bath, and she has a baby strapped to her back while she does it. This is certainly not at the zoo. I think the elephant is Tendai.

I'm seeing this as though I'm Nyah, and a trunk, Nyah's trunk, reaches out toward the young woman, sniffing at her hair and face and tickling the baby's cheek. The baby laughs, and I'm filled with Nyah's happy feelings about this memory. The young woman wraps her hand around the outstretched trunk, allowing it to curl over her hand and playfully lift it up and down. The trunk then reaches out for Tendai, feeling her mouth like Zaire did with Asha. I'm watching Nyah's trunk reach for her mother, and now this memory is sweet and sour—as though the happiness is never without a helping of grief. And although I don't remember my family, I understand the longing. It's possible to miss people you can't remember.

I don't want to feel this anymore. I shut my eyes tight and try to squeeze out the sadness like wringing out a drippy towel. I can't do anything for Nyah and her heartbreak. And although Thomas says he'll look for leads to the other Fenn Circus elephants, even if we find them, there's no room to bring them here. Feeling Nyah's rumblings and seeing her thoughts haven't fixed anything, and it's caused me nothing but trouble.

"Everything okay, Lex?" asks Thomas.

I open my eyes and squint at the sunlight, focusing on Thomas, the crowd beyond the Grasslands, and what is real in front of me. Nyah's rumblings have stopped. Her trunk bobs up and down, touching the earth and feeling the fence.

"We need to find out about those other elephants," I answer Thomas.

"I'll do my best," he says.

"She misses her mom. She's so sad, Thomas."

He nods and rubs his chin like he's uncomfortable, and I suddenly remember that he was here when Tendai died. He would've seen Nyah's grief up close and personal. All this sadness is like a cold virus, and everyone is catching it.

"Thank you for letting me come in here." I turn and run from the wooden fence and out the gate.

I have to dodge and weave to avoid the crowd forming at the Wild Kingdom Education Center doors. It must be time for one of Mrs. Leigh's many summer education programs. The thought makes me think of past summers with Fisher, and how this summer is turning out to be the worst. How can someone be surrounded by crowds and feel so alone? I head toward Bear Country, the quickest route from here to the main station. Right now, the sound of the engine and the smell of steam and coal are exactly what I want. Something real and something in the present. Something that isn't going to ask me to fix something I can't. I'm going to give the zoo train speech.

With each step I take away from the Grasslands, the sun beats hotter, the bug swarms are peskier, and my curly hair gets thicker on my neck. Nyah's images have made everything feel so mixed-up, and I'm angry—not at Nyah, but at something. I'm angry about being called "Elephant Girl" and that I let it get to me so much that now Fisher is angry with me. Well, maybe he isn't exactly angry, but he isn't happy. And he doesn't want to hang out with me.

"I'm here," says the wind, as though it's more important than all of that.

"Shut up," I say.

I take the path behind Bear Country and cut through the Giraffe Encounter. I nearly run into a peacock on the grass just before the turnoff to the Old County Bank when it occurs to me: I need to find out if Angus Fenn donated anything else to the zoo. If Miss Amanda didn't bring Angus Fenn's money to the zoo with her, maybe Angus Fenn brought it here without knowing it. If he was quitting the circus life, he probably got rid of lots of things. This new idea brushes away some of my grumpiness. As I near the station, the sound of the steam bursting from the engine's pop-off valves goes a long way toward blowing away the rest of my bad mood. A train ride is always a good idea.

I walk along the tracks toward Roger, who is doing his last inspection before the run. I notice how he smooths a clean cloth over the brass detail on the antique passenger car. He began restoring the car before I came to the zoo. He's very proud of it. He even has pictures in the Old County Bank of the restoration process. It was originally a passenger car, but before the zoo got it, it had been gutted and used for something else. All the seats were gone, and it was just an empty space inside—like a boxcar, except with windows.

A tingle of realization creeps up my neck, and my insides suddenly feel hollow like the pictures of that gutted train car. I know what else Angus Fenn gave to the zoo. I feel it as surely as the wind blowing my hair around my face.

"Roger!" I call, perhaps a bit too loudly.

He turns and smiles, making up the rest of the distance between us with only a few strides of his long legs.

"Nice to see you," he says. He doesn't ask about Fisher, or where he is, and I'm grateful. He pulls a folded sheet of paper from his pocket. "Want to come on the run and give the speech?"

"Yes. Roger, do you—"

"I've added a few new facts to this revised version. Take a look at it before we start, so you're familiar with it."

"Okay, I will." I take the paper from him. "Roger, how did this train car end up at the zoo?" I point at the passenger car on the tracks beside us.

Roger's forehead wrinkles up. "It came from the Fenn Circus. I wrote a bit about that in the revised zoo script. Why the sudden interest in where the train car came from?"

My brain is on rewind and fast forward all at once. I'm thinking of the pictures in Miss Amanda's album, and at the same time, I'm thinking I must read this revised script and ask Roger a lot of questions right now. But there's a station full of zoo patrons, and J.P. seems to have finished his inspections, because he's opening the gates and taking tickets.

"So . . . this passenger car belonged to the circus . . . but it didn't look like a passenger car when you got it?"

Roger smiles, but he looks past me down the tracks with a distracted expression that says he wants me to hurry. "Yes. Look, can we talk about this some more when we finish the round trip?"

My thoughts are spinning so fast. "Okay," I hear myself say.

"Great," Roger says. He takes a few steps toward the engine and stops. "Lexington, have you got this?" He motions toward the caboose, indicating I should hurry over there and get on the intercom.

I pull myself together enough to say, "Yep. Good." And I turn and run to the caboose.

I scramble up the steps, plop down on the red painted bench, and grab the intercom microphone off the hook. I hold the mic in one hand with a finger over the talk button while I spread Roger's script open in my lap with my other hand.

I scan the script, skimming over the details Roger has added about the gaur (a species of bison from Southeast Asia), the bird species housed in the Swift Aviary, and the zoo summer programs and shows. I scan for just the right words.

And I find them.

After the information about the sea lions at Harbor Reef.

Nyah and her mother, Tendai, were brought to the Lexington Zoo in 2011 by Angus Fenn of the Fenn Circus. Both elephants exhibited mild stereotypies when they first arrived, and they would rock repetitively. This was abnormal behavior they developed from not having enough room to move. However, the behavior improved as they settled into their spacious new habitat here at our African Grasslands. Tendai passed away from symptoms of old age in 2013, but you can still see Nyah on the Grasslands along with Asha, the herd matriarch; her daughter, Zaire; and Jazz.

Also in 2011, the Lexington Zoo received our antique passenger train car as a gift from the Fenn Circus. The car you are riding in was built in 1880 and used as a passenger car on the Union Pacific Railroad until it was retired in 1935. The Fenn Circus gutted the passenger car and used it as a gift shop until Angus Fenn donated it to the zoo. The passenger car has been restored to its original 1880s beauty with authentic seats, interior lighting, and décor.

Two quick, shrill whistles startle me so badly that I drop the intercom mic on the caboose's slotted wood floor. I scramble to pick it up, dropping the script.

"The train's about to leave, Lexington," says a familiar, blustery voice. "Better pull it together."

I'm kneeling on the floor, snatching up the script, and my head snaps up to see Frank Bixly in his striped button-up shirt and suspenders. As usual, his gray-streaked hair, what's left of it, is combed with a perfectly straight part on the side. It's easy to tell he combs it that way to hide some of the thin spots on top. It doesn't work, though. You can still see them.

I stand up, holding the script and mic. "I've got this, Mr. Bixly."

"Well now, I've learned I can't entirely trust what you're up to around the zoo lately, so I think I'll just ride along back here and make sure you've 'got this.'"

He climbs up the steps with considerable effort. I stay where I am as he sits on the bench on the train's left side. He brings with him the smell of soap and coffee, not an entirely unpleasant smell, but on Frank Bixly, it smells like control.

"I hear Roger has a new speech all ready to go. Are you familiar with it? You need to read it with a clear, strong voice so the guests can understand you."

I'm still standing, and my hand is sweaty around the intercom mic. I don't need Mr. Bixly to tell me how to give the train speech. He's acting like I don't know how to read or something. I've done this dozens of times.

"I'm familiar with it," I say flatly.

"Well, let's have a look," Mr. Bixly says, indicating he wants me to sit and let him see the script.

This train is Roger's domain, so I feel it's mine, too. I know more about the train and the sights along the tracks than Frank Bixly does, and when I give the zoo speech, the caboose is my space. The little hairs on the back of my neck stand up like I'm a wolf defending my territory. Then I notice J.P. waving at me to get started. He closes the gate, hurries to the first open-air car, and slides his hand up the curved railing, pulling himself onto the train.

I plop down hard on the bench, as far from Mr. Bixly as possible, press down the mic's talk button, and say, "Ladies and gentlemen, welcome aboard the Lexington Zoo Train." My voice always sounds younger than I think it should when it comes out of the speakers.

My face is stiff and stony, but I proceed with the introduction as Mr. Bixly glances over at the script.

"You're about to tour the second-largest zoo in North America, and you're riding behind one of only two genuine Union Pacific steam engines in any zoo."

"Skip this part," Mr. Bixly says, pointing at the jokes that usually come next. Roger uses the jokes to liven up the tour, and the guests always seem to like them.

I narrow my eyes, swallow down a boiling remark that would surely get me in trouble, and wait in silence as the train chuffs forward. If I skip the jokes, I'll jump right into the new facts about the gaur, the tallest of the wild cattle species, before we even reach their habitat. Mr. Bixly is so stupid. Roger had this planned out so the script would fit the timing of the tour.

The couplings between the cars clang as the metal collides and catches. The cars move forward, and I listen to the sound of the wheels clacking over the track joints beneath us.

I'm staring at the back of the antique passenger car that was once the Fenn Circus gift shop. I've wrinkled the script in my sweaty hand without noticing. My heart pounds with irritation at Mr. Bixly. But even stronger than that is the unbearable need to ask Roger if he found something hidden behind a loose board when he restored that old train car. This could be the answer to the lost money box and Miss Amanda's mystery. She didn't take the money when she left the Fenn Circus, but the money *is* here. And she *did* hide Fenn's money box in the gift shop. The *circus* gift shop.

The train rounds the first curve, sending us into the sun and the warm smell of bison. I direct everyone to look to their right and begin reading the portion about the gaur. Mr. Bixly keeps an eye on the script for a few more minutes, and then, as I go on to the part about the aviary coming up on the right, he settles back on the bench and watches the scenery with a smug expression—like he's king of it all.

We pass the lake covered by the tall aviary netting. The wind sails through the open sides of the caboose, bringing with it the smell of fish and mossy water and stirring up Mr. Bixly's lingering soap and coffee smell. I prefer the fish and moss, but the wind has mixed them up now.

The wind tugs at my hair and laughs in my ear. *"Can't do anything with him here, can you?"*

Sometimes, I wish I could rattle the wind the way it does me. Just a little.

"Why don't you help me out, for once?" I snap at the wind in my head. *"Why don't you blow at Mr. Bixly so he'll decide to get off at the café stop?"*

The wind slices the air. *"More fun to watch what you'll do."*

And with that, the breeze swirling through the caboose subsides, reminding me how quickly the wind can change. Teasing isn't always harmless, and quiet isn't always good.

I guess I'll have to deal with Mr. Bixly's presence for this one round trip, and then I'll ask Roger about the passenger car and the loose board. If he didn't find a load of money when he restored the train car, then maybe it's still there. If he *did* find something, then he must know where it is.

What Roger Keeps Hidden

As I suspected he would, Mr. Bixly takes the train's entire round trip. With only brief stops at Wild Eats Café and the Wild Kingdom Education Center to pick up and drop off passengers, I have no time to talk to Roger during the run.

"Thank you for riding the Lexington Zoo Railroad. We hope your visit to the zoo today is a wild one," I say into the intercom, finishing the script as the train slowly pulls into the main station.

I release the talk button and hang the mic over the hook, standing to do so.

"Never stand up while the train is moving, Lexington," says Frank Bixly.

"The conductor stands," I snap at him. Mr. Bixly knows nothing about the train or railroading.

"Well," he says in a smug voice that makes me want to scream, "you're not the con—"

The train hisses to a stop, and I jump from the caboose's top step to the ground before Mr. Bixly can finish. Roger is emerging from the engine cab, wiping his forehead with his handkerchief. The cab can get up to 130 degrees in the middle of the summer, and he and J.P. sweat more than they can drink sometimes.

"Nicely done," Roger says to me, referring to the train script. "You always make a great announcer." Then his gaze shifts to somewhere behind me. I turn to see for myself, and Mr. Bixly is stepping off the caboose steps. "Was Frank in the caboose with you for the entire run?"

I roll my eyes to tell Roger he was. "He told me to skip the jokes."

Roger waves his hand like skipping the jokes doesn't concern him. He motions for me to follow him to the main station food stand. He needs to rehydrate. "You okay?" he asks.

"Oh yeah," I say. "Mr. Bixly just thinks he can run everything."

"Lexington, he's the General Manager. He *does* run everything. The sooner you get that through your head, the sooner you will stop getting into a tangle with him over every little thing. You know, sometimes I think you think that *you* run the zoo." Roger pulls a jumbo bottle of a citrus-flavored sports drink from the minifridge and offers me one. "But I think there's something else on your mind. What did you want to ask me about before?"

I take the sports drink from his outstretched hand.

"The passenger car from the Fenn Circus," I say, getting right to the point because Mr. Bixly is heading this way. "When you restored it, did you find anything . . . unusual behind any loose boards?"

Roger swallows and lowers the bottle from his mouth. He tilts his head and looks at me like I've just grown antlers. "Why?" he asks, holding out the word a little longer than normal. Then he notices Mr. Bixly lumbering across the grass toward us.

Roger narrows his eyes at Mr. Bixly. I think I've started something I didn't mean to start. Roger tromps off in his work boots, straight for Mr. Bixly. He stands in front of Mr. Bixly like a wall. "It's not enough that you hound me about that box, Frank—you've taken to harassing my girl about it? I told you yesterday that I put the box in the shed a long time ago and forgot about it. Now the box is missing. What else do you want?"

I duck behind a large tandem stroller.

"I haven't said anything to Lexington about the box," Mr. Bixly answers. "No one but you and me and whoever got your letter to the Fenn Circus knows about that. How does *she* know about it?"

"He knows, she knows, who knows the wind blows," the wind chants.

"Stop trying to distract me."

Mr. Bixly and Roger turn to look in my direction, but I'm well hidden behind the stroller. I stay perfectly still. I hope the stroller's owners won't return with their kids from the train at this precise moment. My brain whirls with questions about Roger writing to the Fenn Circus. Did he find the money and try to return it? The idea that Roger could have done anything other than the right thing is absurd. But why is the box missing? Why is he angry at Mr. Bixly about it?

I want to ask Roger all these things. He'll give me a straight answer. At least . . . I think he will. But I'm not telling Frank Bixly, General Manager, how I know about the box hidden in the old train car. And Mr. Bixly knows I'm here somewhere.

I slide in between some teenagers walking away from the station and hide in the crowd, feeling like a fugitive again. When there's enough crowd between me and where Roger and Mr. Bixly are talking, I head into the trees behind the Old County Bank. I can see the engineer's residence from here, but only because I know where to look. It's far from the public paths, and its earthy brown brick and the surrounding trees hide it well.

Why would Roger get so upset about this?

"Finders keepers," the wind says.

"No," I say out loud—to myself *and* the wind. If Roger found that treasure, he wouldn't keep it. He'd try to return it, just as I'm going to do.

"But he did have it," says the wind.

"He wouldn't keep it!" I shout in my head. *"No way!"*

Sometimes, I really hate the wind.

But the nagging feeling is too hard to ignore, and I've reached the Old County Bank. It's so easy to go inside and have a look around in Roger's room—someplace, unlike the train shed, where no one else in the zoo would look.

I climb the porch steps and turn the doorknob as the wind gets in one last sneaky comment: *"Find his secrets."*

My heart pounds heavy and fast. I feel like a thief invading the Old County Bank. Everything looks a little different inside, as though I haven't been here in a long time, or I've been wrong about something. I run straight up the stairs and into Roger's room. Maybe Roger found the box, told Mr. Bixly he put it in the shed, but secretly kept it in the house. I don't want to know why he would do that, if he did. I only want to find it. I've got that tingling, stinging rain feeling on my skin again that tells me this is very important.

Roger keeps his room very tidy, with the bedspread smoothed over the top of the bed and no clutter anywhere. The room smells like a clean version of the woods—it's Roger's lingering aftershave mixed with the wood furniture as the sun warms it through the window.

I open the closet doors and find his clothes neatly hung, and a few folded blankets stuffed on the shelf near the ceiling. I can use the chair from the corner to see what's behind those blankets, but it's an armchair and not easy to move. I press my shoulder into the chair and lift it from the bottom, wriggling it from side to side to move it over the carpet. I'm sweating by the time I get the chair in front of the closet.

I've never looked through Roger's things, and it nags at me a little, but I know there's something to find here, and that feeling is stronger than the nagging. The blankets are definitely hiding something behind them. I pull the blankets down, and they fall to the floor in a heap. My breath catches when I see a brown box. But it's only a cardboard box full of random items—a pocket watch on a long silver chain, a worn-out pair of dress shoes, a soft old cardigan, some dice, a deck of cards, and a wooden cigar box with a few rings and old jewelry inside it. I wonder why Roger has these things. They look too old to be his, but they definitely aren't the things Miss Amanda hid in the antique passenger car. I put the box back and jump down from the chair.

Then I notice Roger's bed is high enough off the floor to store things beneath it. I flatten myself onto the carpet and look under the bed, finding a half-empty roll of blue wrapping paper and another box. The wrapping paper is from my "arrival day" last year. Roger gives me presents on June 9 every year, since we don't know my birthday. A scratchy lump in my throat adds to the niggling thought that I should wait and ask Roger about Angus Fenn's box. But I swallow it down, because that box under the bed is bigger than the one in the closet, and it has a lid, and that makes it seem important. I slide it out, hold my breath, and lift the lid off.

This box isn't full of money, or anything that seems related to the Fenn Circus, but it seems entirely related to me.

It's a lot of papers covered with long typed paragraphs and big words. But I'm there at the top of all of them. Not my picture, but some name that refers to me. Some of the papers have the name *Lexington Willow*. Some say *Jane Doe* at the top, the name they call a girl when they don't know who she is. Some of them say *Minor*. But they all refer to me. I've overheard Mr. and Mrs. Leigh discussing the AZA and the zoo board of directors enough to recognize some legal words, but I don't really know what these papers mean.

I pick up the one that is paper clipped to a big stack. This one has *Roger James Marsh* and *Lexington Willow* at the top.

A sudden *thump* from downstairs startles me, and I drop the paper back into the box. The front door is opening, and voices travel up the Old County Bank stairs and down the hall. I shove the box under the bed. There's no time to move the chair back to the corner. I dart across the hall to my bedroom and push the door almost closed.

I try to calm my breathing and stare at my world map on the wall as I listen for the voices below. Although Roger and I have labeled the zoo animals' homes on the map, I've never asked Roger where his sticker should go. I don't even know if he grew up in Nebraska or not. I've always been focused on *not knowing* where *my* sticker should go.

And then I notice something new in my room. Roger must've placed it here. On the nightstand next to my bed is a small frame with a picture of me and Roger. I'm young in the photo, and I'm sitting with Roger inside the engine cab. Roger is showing me the engine controls. I have my hand on his and, together, we're pushing on the throttle. I've never seen this picture before. Roger is smiling at me, and I look so safe with him. I think maybe it looks like a family, and it doesn't matter that we came from different families and different places.

Frank Bixly's blustery voice sails up the stairs from the high-ceilinged entry. "I'm telling you, Roger, she's been out at Amanda's old trailer."

"Sounds to me like *you've* been out at Amanda's old trailer yourself, Frank," Roger says calmly. "See any ghosts lately?"

Mr. Bixly snorts.

"Why didn't you have all of Amanda's things cleaned up years ago?" Roger asks.

"I have a lot of responsibilities at the zoo," Mr. Bixly says, clearing his throat. "Much to think about. I thought I'd assigned it to the grounds crew, and it got forgotten."

"Are you sure it doesn't have something to do with your sudden interest in that box I found all those years ago? I forgot about it when I found Lex and began caring for her. But you . . . you've had all these years to ask me about it. Why now, huh? And why, after I told you where I left it, did my shed get broken into?"

"That's beside the point. You need to keep Lex from venturing out where you can't keep an eye on her. I'm seriously reconsidering this arrangement of having her live here."

"What are you talking about?" Roger says. "Fisher lives here, and he and Lex are the same age."

"Well," Mr. Bixly answers, "Fisher is here because Fern and Gordon are his parents. You're not actually Lex's—"

"Stop right there," Roger says, his voice deep and commanding. "*That* is none of your business. I'm her guardian, and that should be enough for you."

Sometimes I hate Frank Bixly. Who Roger and I are to each other is not something we talk about. And I think maybe we *should* talk about it, but I don't know if Roger *wants* to talk about it anymore.

"Well, anyway," Mr. Bixly continues, "the mess is getting cleaned up as we speak, so there won't be anything luring Lex out there anymore. We won't have the entire zoo staff searching for her and congesting the radio transmissions."

Mr. Bixly's words are like scissors cutting the string of a balloon, and I can almost feel Miss Amanda sailing away from me, losing her memories and her past and her place to find answers.

I need to get to the woods. I need to get to Miss Amanda's trailer before someone takes it all away. And that's when I climb out the second-story window of the Old County Bank.

32

Miss Amanda's Memories

My shorts snag on the drainpipe when I climb off the roof and onto the overhanging tree branch. I've climbed up this tree before, but never to this height. The ground far below seems to rise and fall, going in and out of focus. So I stare at the branches, taking one at a time.

I finally reach the last branch, hang suspended for a moment, and jump down. My feet hit the ground, and I fall to my knees on the soft, shaded earth. Hearing Mr. Bixly's words over and over in my head, *The mess is getting cleaned up as we speak,* I sprint for the main gates.

As I pass Bear Country, a man's voice calls after me.

"Lex! Where are you headed in such a hurry?" Mr. Leigh is wearing a suit today, but he still looks like he belongs on safari with his hat on. He finishes a quick order to one of the keepers through his radio and returns the radio to his belt.

"I . . ." I don't know what to tell him about Miss Amanda or her things in the woods. "Mr. Leigh, do you know where Fisher is?"

Another message comes in through his radio, but he lets it go for the moment. "I believe he went to a movie with some baseball friends—someone's birthday, I think. Fern knows the details if you want to ask her."

I nod. First Fisher wants to go to the Birds of Prey Amphitheater alone. Now he's off with some other friends. It's not like he's never done that before. I know he has friends who don't live in the zoo. It's just that he's never left with them when I felt like he didn't want to be *my* friend anymore.

I take a deep breath, but the air is especially humid, or zoolike, and I choke on it a little. The zoo is choking me.

"Are you okay?" Mr. Leigh asks.

I wait for the wind to comment, but it says nothing. Maybe it stays quiet to make me nervous. It's working. Maybe something terrible is coming.

I force a smile and nod. I'm reminded of my book, and the assignment Mrs. Leigh gave me. "It's not normal to live alone on an island," I mumble to myself, not really meaning for Mr. Leigh to hear.

But he hears me, and he bends a little closer. "What do you mean?"

"Nothing," I say. "I'm fine."

Another call comes in on Mr. Leigh's radio, and he reaches for his belt, still giving me a side-eyed look. "You sure?"

"Yes." I start up the hill away from him. "But will you tell Fisher I'm looking for him?"

I run from Mr. Leigh and his radio and from Roger's secrets and from Mr. Bixly's mean words. I run out of the main gates, through the parking lot, and into the woods.

Something unfamiliar is crashing about in the trees. At first I think it might be an animal. A very big animal. Perhaps an elephant.

I wish it were an elephant.

But the closer I get to the thumping and crashing, the less it sounds like an animal and the more it sounds like equipment. Large equipment with levers and moving metal hinges. I reach the small clearing with the fallen log.

And I see it.

A tow truck.

They've hitched up Miss Amanda's trailer. A flatbed attached to another large pickup holds all of Miss Amanda's patio furniture—her outdoor table and chairs, large pots that once had plants in them, the broken awning.

They are taking it all away.

"No!" I scream, running at the tow truck and the men securing Miss Amanda's trailer. "You can't!"

One of the men turns to look at me. "What's the matter, little miss?"

"Don't call me that," I snap. "Why are you taking her stuff? Where are you taking this?"

The man removes his hat and rolls his eyes. "Look, we were hired to do a job. Clear all this away. If you have a problem with it, you'll have to take it up with the zoo."

"Please," I say. "Please just . . . wait."

This can't happen. How will I find Miss Amanda? How will I know if she gets where she needs to go . . . after I find the Fenn fortune . . . after I return it?

I knew I'd have to say goodbye to her, but it can't be now. We aren't finished. What about her stories? This is her life they're towing away. What will happen to her memories?

"Please wait," I say again, much softer this time. The wind blows through the trees, but it says nothing to me, like someone quietly listening in on a conversation that is none of their business.

A hand touches my shoulder, and I startle around.

Mrs. Leigh is here. She holds her hand up at the men with the tow truck.

"Give us a moment, please," she says to them. Then she turns to me with a look in her eyes that says she's just realized something. "Lexington, have you been spending a lot of time here—with these things? Have you seen Amanda Holtz out here?"

I swallow hard, thinking of the story Fisher told me about Fern Leigh as a little girl and her friend who was a ghost. But as I stand here, not answering, Mrs. Leigh seems to have figured out the truth.

"This . . . ," Mrs. Leigh says, gesturing to Miss Amanda's old home and her belongings heaped on the flatbed trailer, "this can be a dangerous way to spend your time. It will take too much and give nothing back. It will keep you isolated from the people who care about you."

I open my mouth to argue. I've been helping Miss Amanda . . . or Nyah. I thought I was helping them both. How can that be a bad thing? But now I can't put it all into words, and I don't know where to begin.

"You cannot hold on to a ghost."

My breath catches, and I whisper, "Did you tell them to get rid of her things?"

Mrs. Leigh sighs and puts one hand to her forehead, like she's thinking hard. "No, I didn't. But I heard Frank had called this crew, and I came to check on things. To check on you. It's really unacceptable that Frank didn't take care of this before now. I suspect this is the reason you've gone missing so much lately."

My eyes suddenly burn, like my tears have turned to acid. Mrs. Leigh and the tow truck and the trailer become a blur of brown and silver and gray, as though everyone is behind a curtain of murky water.

"I didn't know she was still here, Lexington. I'm so sorry this has affected you, but the only way I know to get out of the time-consuming life with a ghost is to stop visiting them."

"Don't let them take it away," I say, my voice airy like the wind.

"Why do you need it?" Mrs. Leigh's voice is gentle and soft. "Tell me."

I don't know why I need it. I just can't bear to have all of this disappear.

I haven't told Miss Amanda what I learned about the passenger train car that used to be the circus gift shop. I haven't told her that Roger may have found something that could be the Fenn fortune and that Mr. Bixly knows about it.

If they tow Miss Amanda's trailer away, will her misplaced spirit have to go with it?

"I don't know why I need it," I say. "I just know that I do."

And I turn and run from Mrs. Leigh toward the tow truck. I push past the men and scramble up the ramp to the trailer door.

"Hey!" yells one of them. "This is private property!"

He obviously doesn't know a single thing about this place. He doesn't know me. Miss Amanda and her things were once part of this zoo, and the zoo is my home. And I'm taking Miss Amanda's photo albums.

I yank open the trailer door.

"Lexington!" Mrs. Leigh calls.

I climb inside, with one of the tow truck guys lumbering up the ramp behind me. The inside of Miss Amanda's trailer looks nothing like it did when I visited before. The dishes have tumbled from the open cupboards, leaving broken ceramic shards on the floor. Among them, the fat little teapot is in pieces. The curtains that hung over the kitchen window now dangle off a partially unhooked curtain rod. Books are scattered everywhere from the bookshelf.

I look under the kitchen table and find the photo albums, lying facedown on the floor with the pages spread open.

"Lexington!" Mrs. Leigh calls from the ramp. "Please calm down and let's talk about this."

Then she lowers her voice. "Let me handle this." She seems to be speaking to the tow truck man and is nearing the trailer door.

Mrs. Leigh has made up her mind against befriending ghosts, or helping them, so there's nothing to talk about. Miss Amanda's photo albums are too important—too full of who she was and what mattered to her. They're too full of what happened at the circus with Angus Fenn and Elle and the elephants. I can't let these things leave on a tow truck to the dump or wherever they're taking it. Miss Amanda's life can't be forgotten like that.

I leap over the broken dishes, slam the trailer door shut, and turn the lock.

Mrs. Leigh calls to me. The tow truck men complain about how this is throwing off their schedule. I go to the kitchen window. It has a sliding pane. I slide it open silently, climb onto the table, and escape out my second window for the day. With Miss Amanda's photo albums in one arm, I hang from the window by my other hand for a second. When I let go, my fingers rake over the window runner, scraping off some skin. It stings like a hundred bee stings, but I grab the albums I dropped in my fall and run straight into the trees with the trucks behind me for cover.

Don't worry, Miss Amanda. I've got your memories.

Leaving

The wind in my face is hot and stifling. It dries the tears that have fallen down my cheeks, leaving tight salt streaks behind. Miss Amanda was already dead when I met her, but it didn't really feel that way until I saw her trailer hitched to that tow truck.

Mrs. Leigh and the tow truck men talk over each other as their voices grow faint behind me. I keep running—deeper and deeper into the wild, untended woods. My arms are wrapped around the photo albums at my chest, slowing me down. I push faster. My leg muscles burn from the effort. My fingers sting where the skin was scraped off on the windowsill.

The trees are thick here and the branches hide the sun—like Miss Amanda's pink awning, but green. Shadows loom like ghostly walls in my way, but I run through them. Each one swallows me up for a moment and then spits me out for the next one.

My foot lands on a large branch partially buried beneath the leaves. The other end of the branch sails toward me, its sharp twigs gouging my bare legs like long nails on a giant witch's hand. I drop to my knees with the photo albums at my chest and roll to my side.

Blood drips from the scratches on my legs. I gasp for air in heaving breaths and sit in the weeds and leaves, gathering Miss Amanda's albums into my lap. The wind blows a tree branch, and for a moment I think I see Miss Amanda's flowing scarf out of the corner of my eye. But it's only another shadow.

I examine my injured fingers. The skin is scraped off pretty deep on two of them, but the blood has thickened and is drying. My hand is shaking. I dab my fingers gently on my sock and open the first photo album.

I turn the pages slowly, noticing the photos Miss Amanda already showed me and taking in the ones I haven't seen yet. There are photos of circus performers dressed in feathers, in tiny costumes, in long elegant dresses, in top hats, in suits, and in muscle shirts. Other photos show animal trainers and everything from monkeys and dogs to lions and elephants. I wonder what Nyah would have said about her circus life if someone could've seen her thoughts back then.

I find a picture of the African elephants in a show inside the big circus tent. Their rear legs are on the ground, and they balance on them with their front legs in the air and their trunks reaching high. I've seen Nyah do this when she reaches for hay in the baskets hanging from tall poles. I always figured this was natural. Maybe it's what she would do in the wild to get branches from the trees. Or maybe it's a learned trick from the circus. But I've definitely seen Jazz do it, and Jazz wasn't ever in a circus.

I turn the pages and find more pictures of Angus Fenn and more pictures of the acrobat Elle. I find pictures of them together. She looks at him with big, liquid eyes. In one photo, she has her arm linked through his, and he's placed a hand on hers, like he wants to keep her close.

I keep the page open to that picture of Angus and Elle. Then I open the second album and find more photos of Miss Amanda. She was very beautiful when she was young. In every picture, she is wearing an elegant hat or a scarf, but she didn't always wear skirts and dresses. It stands out to me as strong somehow—like she didn't have to look like the fancy circus performers. She also seemed to know her work and how to do it well. And then I turn the page and find a picture that proves the gift shop was a train car.

It's a picture of Miss Amanda standing inside a passenger car gutted of its original seats. I can tell it used to be a passenger car from the 1800s, like the ones in Roger's books, because of the side windows and the raised section down the center of the wooden roof. But this car now has tables lining one side and shelves at the back. An old cash register sits on one of the tables. The tables and shelves are full of funny hats and toys and pictures of circus performers. Miss Amanda is holding up long candy twists on sticks. She's smiling and has her head tilted slightly to the side in an elegant pose. I tilt my head and try smiling just like that. Then everything goes blurry, and I have to wipe my eyes. I wonder if I'll ever see Miss Amanda's ghost again.

The photo on the opposite page shows the inside of the office train car. Miss Amanda's desk is on the left, with a pile of papers and envelopes and pens. It isn't the desk that catches my eye, though. It's what's sitting on the seat of the desk chair.

It looks like a metal box with a lock on it, and it has two letters etched on top. I raise the album closer to my nose to get a better look. The letters are A.F.

Angus Fenn.

I think this is the box Miss Amanda hid for Angus. This is the box with his fortune in it.

I wish Fisher were here, discovering all this with me. The zoo is sort of an island for him, too. Except Fisher chooses to leave.

I stand up and brush myself off. The zoo doesn't feel like my island anymore. It feels like a cage, and I'm one of the exhibits under Mr. Bixly's rules. It's Mr. Bixly's island now. He's the one who had Miss Amanda's things taken away so I couldn't visit her anymore. Why would he do that? Why would he care where I go outside the zoo? I don't think it has to do with radio chatter clogging up the zoo-wide channel to find me.

I think Mr. Bixly has talked to Miss Amanda's ghost. She did say she had business to discuss with Frank Bixly. She must've told him the missing box had a fortune in it. Maybe Mr. Bixly broke into Roger's shed to get it, and he doesn't want to risk anyone else talking to Miss Amanda and finding out the money belongs to Eden Fenn. And the best way to keep the fortune's secret is to get rid of Miss Amanda's ghost.

The only reason someone would do that is if they planned to keep the money for themselves.

I tuck the photo albums under my arm. I need to find Frank Bixly. If he took that box from the train shed, I'm going to find it.

I survey the surrounding trees, trying to get some sense of where I am, but the tall zoo structures are hidden by the thick canopy of branches. Maybe I've run away from the perimeter fences instead of parallel to them. I take a few steps, listening to the constant vibrating buzz of the cicadas in the trees. After a moment, the wind shifts and carries with it the distant whirring of tires on pavement. If I follow the sounds, I'll eventually reach the road.

Leaves and sticks crunch beneath my tennis shoes, and the cicada buzz feels electric. The most logical place to look for Mr. Bixly, or someplace he would hide the box, is his office above the gift shop. If I head back through the woods, though, I might run into Mrs. Leigh. If I follow the road, I might actually see the tow truck and the pickup with the flatbed trailer driving off with Miss Amanda's things. I'm not sure which is worse, but walking along the road is definitely easier than slogging through the grass that stings the scrapes on my leg. So I trudge in the direction of the whirring tire sounds.

The humidity presses down on me until it seems I will shrink under it. The gnat swarms are difficult to see in the shade, and they appear without warning. I swat at them, but some get in my mouth and nose anyway. I finally reach a clearing, yet even without the tree branches overhead, I'm still under a large shadow. A great blanket of gray clouds has rolled across the sky and covered the sun. With a wide-open space now in front of me, I can see the road clearly in the distance.

My sweaty palms stick to the photo albums. I rearrange my hold on them to keep my bleeding fingers off the leather, and as I hold them against my chest, I think I can feel warmth spread through me from the memories inside. I imagine the people and animals in the pictures, including Miss Amanda, all hoping for me to succeed.

Find the Fenn fortune.

Find it.

The faces in the pictures fill my head and are more real to me than any words the wind has ever whispered.

I reach the end of the clearing and step onto the sidewalk. A bus is coming up the road on the other side of the street. It growls its way up the hill toward the turnaround point at River Road. Then, it'll come back the other way, stopping at the corner of the zoo parking lot, where Fisher always catches it. Maybe Fisher is on that bus, coming home from his baseball friend's party. I wonder what it would be like to go to a birthday party. I wonder what it would be like to be invited.

A bright blue car speeds down the road toward me. Feeling a little exposed outside the zoo and alone, but not too much like I will blow away, I step back from the sidewalk. The car takes the curves too fast, and I step back even more, concealing myself in the trees. I recognize the car from the zoo, even though the car and the driver are a blur as they pass. The rear license plate is personalized.

ZOOMNGR

Zoo Monger.
Zoo Manager.
Frank Bixly.

34

Trailing Mr. Bixly

The only way to follow a car when you are too young to drive is if someone else will drive you. My only option at this moment is the bus. I'm too far from the zoo parking lot to make it to the stop in time, so I run away from the zoo, farther down the street toward the intersection. I remember seeing another bus stop there when I rode with Fisher to the ball field.

I'm almost to the intersection, but not close enough to reach the bus stop in time, when the squeal and sigh of the bus brakes announce its approach behind me. I shift the albums to one arm and wave my other arm at the driver. It doesn't look like he's slowing down at all.

I wave my arm as hard as I can and yell, "Stop!" But the wind gusts and snatches my voice. I can't even hear it coming out of my mouth.

The bus is my ship off the island. I have to catch it. I wave and yell again. The bus driver sees me this time. He turns on his flashers and pulls over to the curb.

The door squeaks open, and the driver calls out to me, "Getting on?"

"Yes," I pant. "Thank you for stopping."

I clamber up the steps like I've forgotten how to walk and dig into my pocket for money to pay the fare. "Is this bus going *that* way?" I point to the right, the direction Mr. Bixly's bright blue car turned at the intersection.

The bus driver nods very big, like he's holding back an eye roll and is tired of explaining the bus route to kids like me. But then he looks me up and down and says, "Hey."

"Yeah?" I still have a handful of change from the first bus I took today—which feels like years ago. I shove $1.25 into the fare box. "Please hurry," I say to the driver. I've lost sight of Mr. Bixly's car, and I can only hope that he's been stopped at a few red lights, or by a police car for speeding.

"Are you okay?" the bus driver asks.

I nod, closing a fist around my bloody fingers and holding my head high. "I'm fine."

I walk down the aisle toward an empty row, nearly choking on the heavy tire smell and musty air-conditioning. The passengers on the bus stare at me with those looks that people save for unusual things. I run my hand through my hair and try to smooth the wild curls. It feels like I have some leaves and dirt in there, probably from when I tripped on the branch. I slide into the empty row and sit next to the window so I can watch for Mr. Bixly's car. I can feel all the eyes on me, watching me from every angle.

The bus starts forward and turns right at the light.

"Excuse me?" I say to the bus driver. Some girls in front of me turn around and stare when I speak.

"Yes?" He keeps his eyes straight forward on the enormous windshield and the road. The bus steering wheel is bigger around than the tires on the keepers' work jeeps.

"Do you have to stop at that bus stop there? It looks like there's no one waiting."

"No, I don't have to stop if there's no one waiting," he says. "It's not a main stop." He says it nicely enough, but with a little edge of tired.

"Okay. Thank you," I say. "I'm in a bit of a hurry."

"Oh, really?" the driver asks. I can see part of his face in the mirror above his head, and this time he does roll his eyes.

Chills take over my arms and legs. The bus's air-conditioning is too cold down my neck, and my injured hand is shaking like the helicopter seed pods that fall from the maple trees. I hold my shaking hand in my lap with my other hand, trying to calm the injured trembling as I watch out the giant windshield, looking for the ZOOMNGR car. Each time we pass a side street, I look down the street both ways, in case Mr. Bixly turned a corner.

The bus picks up speed, its engine revving like a hungry beast. My heartbeat revs up with it. I have to find Mr. Bixly.

Find the Fenn fortune.

Find it.

Cars are everywhere, but none of them are bright blue or have license plates that say ZOOMNGR. All the cars look unusually small from way up here inside a bus. They're like minnows compared to one of those fat koi in the zoo pond. And that makes me think of the zoo. And that makes me think of Roger. And I realize that I've left the zoo without calling him on the radio.

My radio is lost. I haven't noticed its weight hanging from my waistband for a long time. I remember how my shorts snagged on the gutter when I climbed out of the Old County Bank window. Roger's going to hear his own voice coming out of the rain gutter when he tries to call me on the radio—when no one knows where I am or that I've left my island on a city bus.

And suddenly, I see the bright blue car. It's stopped at the traffic light up ahead, but it is inching forward slowly in the very right lane—a turn lane. Mr. Bixly is going to turn right.

"Hey, mister?" I ask the bus driver, leaning forward so he can hear me better.

"Yeah?"

"I really need to follow that blue car right up there." I point at Mr. Bixly's car. "It's about to turn right."

The bus driver laughs and then stops himself. "This isn't a police stakeout. I can't just follow a car because you say so."

"Okay, well . . . can you drop me off wherever he goes, then?"

"This isn't a taxi either. It's a bus with a route and a schedule, so I have to take you where this bus stops. Nowhere else."

"Oh." I keep an eye on the ZOOMNGR license plate. "Are you turning right at the light?"

"No. I'm going straight."

"Well, where's the nearest scheduled stop?" I gather up the photo albums and lean forward on the seat.

"In two more blocks."

I keep watching Mr. Bixly's car as it turns right at the red light. The bus is stopped. "Well, you're stopped, now. Can't I just get off here?"

"No, you have to wait for the next stop."

Mr. Bixly's car has passed a business building, and I can no longer see it. I stand up and walk forward in the aisle until I'm almost next to the bus driver.

"You have to get behind the yellow line before I can start driving," he says, sounding annoyed.

"I'm not sitting down," I say. "This is where I need to get off."

"I told you—"

"I'm not sitting down." I shift the photo albums to get a better grip. "So you might as well open the door and let me off."

The light turns green, but the bus driver doesn't push on the gas.

"Let her get off," yells a guy from the back of the bus. "We all have places to be!"

The bus driver looks at me. Not just one of those annoyed, up-and-down glances that grown-ups sometimes do. He looks at my face and right in my eyes.

"Are you sure you're okay, kid?"

Cars are honking behind the bus, and more passengers are grumbling at the driver and at me. For the first time, I don't care what some rude stranger says, even outside the zoo. This is more important than what they say. This is for Miss Amanda. And something I felt when I was looking at Miss Amanda's pictures tells me it might be for Nyah, too.

"I'm okay," I say. "I just need to follow that car."

He shrugs his shoulders and shakes his head, but I notice a hint of a smile starting at the corners of his mouth. He flips a switch that turns on flashing hazard lights on both sides of the bus. He turns the enormous steering wheel to the right, edges the bus closer to the curb, and pulls the large, hinged lever to open the doors.

"Thanks." I grab the railing to steady my wobbly legs and grip Miss Amanda's photo albums tightly before jumping to the curb.

More cars honk at me and the bus. The driver smiles a little and waves as he closes the door and the bus pulls away.

My legs are shaky and tired, but I push myself forward. Mr. Bixly's car is nowhere in sight, but I know he went down this street. I run past an antiques shop, a clock repair shop with grandfather clocks in the window, and El Toro Mexican Restaurant.

The loud sounds of the street are so different from the zoo. A food truck beeps as it backs into an alley, and another truck pours concrete on the opposite side of the street. Construction workers yell to be heard over the noise.

My leg muscles burn with exhaustion. Suddenly, I realize what I've done. I've left the zoo. Alone. I've left the bus and I have no radio. But I'm not turning around. My aching legs are firmly pounding the pavement and going where I want them to go.

Find the Fenn fortune.

Find it.

I chant the words in my head with my running rhythm.

The next few buildings are an insurance office and a boutique. The radio plays loudly through the open door of the boutique, and large industrial fans blow air through the windows. The air-conditioning must be broken. The fans aren't going to help much in this humid heat.

I can't keep running. My legs don't even feel solid anymore. I slow to a walk, which becomes a shuffle, and I think I've lost Mr. Bixly and my chance to find out what he's up to. Every building has either a driveway or a parking lot in back. I look for the bright blue ZOOMNGR car in every single one. But no luck.

Suddenly, someone gasping behind me taps me on the shoulder. I wheel around. It's Fisher, heat flush in his cheeks and sweat dripping down his forehead.

"Lex . . . ," he says between breaths, "I've been calling your name for two blocks!"

"You've been behind me this whole time? How?"

Fisher rests his hands on his knees, catching his breath. "I . . . I saw you on the sidewalk by the woods."

"Wait . . . really?"

"Yeah, I was coming back from Sebastian's birthday party."

"You *were* on that bus on the way back to the zoo!"

Fisher nods and wipes his forehead with the back of his arm. "Man, I need a drink. You don't have any water do you?" He looks at my hands, which are holding Miss Amanda's photo albums. And then his eyes widen as he notices the rest of me. "Lex! What happened to you? Your leg is bleeding, and your hair . . ." He stops, clearly embarrassed that there is no good way to finish that sentence.

"I know." I run my hand over my hair real quick and

try to smooth it. I have never cared how I look in front of Fisher, but right now, I care a little. It's a weird feeling. I'm still not sure why Fisher is talking to me again all of a sudden, or why he would care enough to follow me after I ditched him at the baseball field.

"Are you okay?" he asks. "What are you doing all the way out here by yourself?"

"I'm okay." I stick my leg out and turn sideways to examine the streaks of dried blood. "*This* is from a nasty stick in the woods." I hold out my scraped fingers. "And *this* is from climbing out of Miss Amanda's trailer window with *these*." I show him the albums. "They're full of pictures from her circus life—her memories. Stupid Bixly had her trailer towed away."

"Bixly did that? Today?"

I nod.

"Wow."

"And I figured out that Miss Amanda hid the fortune in a box inside the old passenger train car, and Roger found it. Then I overheard Roger talking to Mr. Bixly, and I think Mr. Bixly may have taken the treasure."

Fisher coughs a little in surprise. "You figured out all that?"

"Yeah, and so I've been trailing Mr. Bixly. He was driving his car all wild and crazy, and I think maybe he's going to a bank or something."

"You mean with the treasure?"

"I don't know exactly, but I think he has it, so I followed him." I let out a sigh. "But I couldn't run fast enough, and I lost him. You wanna help me look?"

"Of course," Fisher says. And things finally feel like they were between us before all the gift shop trouble and the baseball misunderstanding and the extra chores. I still have some fixing to do, though, I think.

"Are you going to be in trouble for being out like this?" I ask. "Does your mom or dad know where you are?"

Fisher shrugs. "Does Roger?"

"No. I dropped my radio when I climbed out of the window at the Old County Bank."

"You what?" Fisher's enthusiastic responses to everything I say are sending little sprays of spit. I make a face at him and wipe my cheek.

"Yeah. After I heard Mr. Bixly say he was getting rid of Miss Amanda's things."

"Oh." Fisher looks like he wishes he hadn't missed out on all this.

A car door slams, and I turn to look. It's a white convertible leaving the insurance office.

"Mr. Bixly's car is blue and it has personalized license plates," I say.

"Zoo Manager," Fisher says.

"Yes! Well, the last time I saw him, he turned down this street. I checked all those businesses back there and the alleys. I guess maybe we should keep heading this way."

Fisher and I walk past a few old houses where people seem to be living in the middle of all these businesses, and I realize this part of town seems old. And that means the EF5 tornado probably didn't hit this side of town.

"Maybe we could ask someone for a drink," Fisher says, looking at the houses as we walk past.

"Fisher, if we find Mr. Bixly, I'll buy you frozen lemonades for life."

"I'll hold you to that," Fisher says.

"By the way, how did you follow me here?" I ask. "There couldn't have been another bus that fast."

Fisher takes a few steps up one of the driveways and looks in the back. He shakes his head to tell me there's no blue car back there. "When I saw you come out of the woods near the road, I thought maybe you needed help. So I caught up with that guy Cory from the gift shop as he was getting in his car to go home, and I asked him to drive me down the road to find you. We saw you get on the bus, and I convinced Cory to follow it."

"Oh. That was pretty clever."

"Thanks. And when you got off the bus, Cory's car was held up in the traffic, so I got out of his car and followed you. I kept calling your name, but you didn't hear me. Those trucks were too loud."

"Well, thanks for chasing me while I was chasing Mr. Bixly," I say. "It's nice to have you here."

The next building is an old home converted into a cupcake bakery. The vanilla sugar smell reaches all the way to the sidewalk. Fisher notices a parking area be-hind the building, so we follow the driveway to the back.

"Um . . . Fisher?"

"Yeah."

"I'm sorry again for leaving you at the ball field . . . and for getting you in trouble before."

"I know. And you didn't get me in trouble. You didn't get me in trouble when we used to go to school together either. You've got to give me more credit. I get in trouble all on my own." He smiles and nods like that's an ac-complishment.

"I worried about that. I didn't know you knew."

"Yeah. I think the wind has taught you to worry. You shouldn't let it do that."

"Oh," I say. "Well, if it makes you feel any better, the wind and I aren't speaking at the moment."

The clouds overhead have darkened the air so that it feels more like nighttime than afternoon. I need to keep an eye on that. Although I haven't missed it that much, the wind has been too quiet. You'd think that after years of having it constantly with me, I'd appreciate the si-lence, but the wind can change in a flash, and I'm wor-ried it's up to something.

Fisher and I reach the end of the long, thin driveway between the bakery and an auto supply. I doubt this is where Mr. Bixly was headed in such a hurry, and if he was, it doesn't seem likely to have anything to do with the Fenn fortune, but we check to be sure. Five cars are parked on a small concrete pad at the back of the bakery. The ZOOMNGR car isn't one of them.

Just as I'm about to turn around, I notice an exit driveway out of the parking area. The exit driveway connects with the parking lot of another business on the next street. A sliver of blue pokes out from behind another car.

"Fisher, look!" I run down the connecting driveway, and my breath catches.

ZOOMNGR

Fisher cups his hands around his eyes and peers into Mr. Bixly's car windows.

"Nothing in here but some old newspapers and soda cans," Fisher says.

The back door of the building where Mr. Bixly's car is parked has a small window in it.

"Over there," I whisper. I listen near the porch first to be sure it doesn't sound like someone is about to come out the door. When it seems that all is quiet except my raging heartbeat, I climb the concrete steps and peek in the window.

It's the back room of a store. Both sides are lined with work counters and shelves. Straight ahead, a guy stands at a counter with his back to me. Frank Bixly is on the other side of the counter, talking to the guy, but he's facing the door and the window where I've made myself incredibly visible. I duck down fast.

"What is it?" Fisher whispers, joining me on the porch.

"He's in there—facing this window." I motion for Fisher to get down, and he does. "I'm not sure what this place is. It looks like a workshop. There are a bunch of small metal tools on the counters."

"Hmm. Did you see what he's doing?"

"Not yet. I don't know if he saw me out here."

We wait on the step, crouching by the door, listening for any sign that Mr. Bixly saw me. But nothing happens, so I stretch myself up to the window again, this time keeping my face as low as possible and stopping when my eyes are just over the window's edge.

The man at the counter has moved away from Mr. Bixly. He brings something over to one of the work counters. He sets it down. His arm is in the way, so I can't see what it is. He reaches across his worktable for the tools on the shelf above. When he selects a tool and brings it up to his eye level to examine it, I can see what he's placed on the table.

It's an old metal box.

And it has the initials A.F. on top.

35

On the Run

"Mr. Bixly has Angus Fenn's box in there," I say. "I think this is a locksmith's."

Fisher's eyes are wide with adventure. "Wait . . . how do you know it's Angus Fenn's box?"

"I have a picture of it in Miss Amanda's photo album. The box has the letters A.F. on it."

Fisher peeks in the window and slides back to the ground. "Yep. And Bixly needs an expert to open it, because *he* doesn't have the key. It's not *his* box."

My shirt is stuck to me with sweat. My hair is like a wool blanket on my neck, and sections of it are plastered to my damp face. Despite the cloud cover that has blocked the sun, it's still sweltering hot and off-the-charts humid.

"We have to get that box before the locksmith opens it and Mr. Bixly takes Angus Fenn's fortune," I say.

"I can cause a distraction," Fisher suggests.

"Maybe we should call the police."

"What will they do? You have to prove he stole the box."

"I have a photo of the box, but that doesn't prove anything—only that it was at a circus and that it's an old box."

The air is getting darker directly in front of my face. I look up at the sky, and it has that soupy-storm look with clouds in varying shades of gray to darker gray to nearly black, mixing together like a poison brew. I know this sort of sky all too well. I know it better than most people. Just as I suspected, the wind has been quiet because it was up to something. June is peak tornado season in Nebraska.

"Looks like a big one," Fisher says, referring to the clouds.

"Yeah. I hope it's only bluffing." But I think I know better.

I rest my hand on the warm metal doorknob and peek through the bottom corner of the window again. The locksmith is talking to Mr. Bixly, and the box is still sitting on the back room counter. It seems like the locksmith hasn't found the right tool yet.

"I'm going to go in there," I whisper, glancing at Fisher.

"I'll go around the front and distract them," he says. "Then you can sneak in and take the box." A smile breaks through at the corners of his mouth.

I make a quick promise to myself to watch his next baseball game and stay the whole time, no matter what.

"Thank you," I whisper.

He stands up and takes off running around the front of the building. I watch through the bottom corner of the window. Fisher enters the shop's front doors.

Mr. Bixly turns when the bell above the door jingles.

"I've got a problem!" Fisher says super loud. The locksmith sets down his tool.

"Fisher? What are you doing here?" Mr. Bixly sounds both surprised and annoyed.

"I've got this lock I can't open," Fisher almost yells.

Mr. Bixly turns all the way to face Fisher. Both Mr. Bixly and the locksmith have their backs to Angus Fenn's box. I try turning the doorknob to sneak in there, but it's locked. I stand upright and wave frantically at Fisher through the window. I point at the door and shrug.

Fisher wrinkles up his face at me and keeps talking very loudly. "I can't open it because it's not my box. Someone else has the key. What would you suggest?"

"Well, I can't help you open something that doesn't belong to you," says the locksmith.

Fisher gives Mr. Bixly a wicked look, and with Fisher's wild hair and excellent smirk, he's good at it. He leans over the customer counter and points at the box in the back. "Then," he says to the locksmith, "you can't open that!"

The locksmith turns around to look at the box, and he sees me peering in the window. He comes over to the door and opens it. "Can I help you?"

Without pausing to think, I slip under his arm and through the open door.

"Hey!" says the locksmith.

Mr. Bixly is blustering like the wind at Fisher, who has opened a swinging half door at the end of the customer counter.

"Over here, Lex!" Fisher calls.

I run to the worktable and grab hold of the metal box, but it's heavier than I expected. I drop Miss Amanda's albums on the table, heft the box down, and slide it across the tile floor to Fisher's waiting hands. He catches it.

"Don't take my tools!" says the locksmith.

"We won't!" I grab the photo albums and run after Fisher and the box, through the swinging half door, past Mr. Bixly, who isn't nearly as fast as we are, and out the front doors of the shop.

We are two doors down the street when we hear Mr. Bixly's voice explode out of the shop doors.

"He'll be after us in his car as soon as he can get to it," I call to Fisher as we run down the sidewalk. "This way!" I point to an alley between two stores. I don't even notice what the stores are anymore. I only know we have to get to a bus stop before Mr. Bixly gets into his car. The sky is even darker now, and the air has turned an eerie hint of green.

"Fisher!" I point at the sky.

Fisher nods.

He knows it, too.

A twister is coming.

We tear out of the alley onto another street and turn left toward the traffic light. We angle across the street and cut through the grass. There's a bus stop sign on the next corner, and Fisher and I bolt straight for it.

The buses run regularly through the city, but that doesn't mean one will arrive just when we need it. We might be running to the next stop and the next one, moving in little segments closer to the zoo, hoping for luck with the bus's schedule. My feet barely touch the ground anymore. Maybe it's all the running I've been doing lately, and I'm getting used to it. Maybe it's the exhilaration of finding the metal box with A.F. stamped on top. Maybe it's that I feel more powerful *without* the wind speaking to me.

We reach the bus stop, and Fisher sets the box in the grass at his feet. I can tell he's trying to be careful with it, but it almost tumbles from his hands.

"What . . . do you think . . . is in that?" he gasps out between breaths.

"I don't know. Miss Amanda just said it's what's left of Angus Fenn's fortune." I look up and down the street for signs of an approaching bus.

The air is very still. If a bus doesn't come soon, Mr. Bixly will be the least of our worries. We'll have to find shelter from the storm out here, away from the zoo.

"Maybe we should head to the next—"

Suddenly, Mr. Bixly's bright blue car appears at the corner. He spots us. He's waiting for a break in the traffic so he can turn left, and then he'll catch up to us.

"Fisher!"

"Yeah, I see him." Fisher picks up the box, and we start running.

Just then, I see the top of a city bus towering above the cars on the road. It's driving toward us on the other side of the street—away from the zoo. If we can get across the street and wave down the bus, maybe it will stop for us. I grab Fisher's arm and point across the street. We're watching for a way through the traffic when the blue car pulls up to the curb.

"Run!" I yell to Fisher.

But Mr. Bixly rolls down the passenger window and says, "This phone call is for the two of you." He holds his cell phone out, facing us. He has a call in progress, and the phone is on speaker.

"Fisher and Lexington"—Mrs. Leigh's voice sails out of the phone—"one of Isabel's sales clerks called to say he lost track of the two of you downtown. What are you thinking? There's a storm coming!"

"You both need to get into Mr. Bixly's car right now," says Mr. Leigh's stern voice. "He's going to bring you home. Do you understand?"

Fisher and I glance at each other, and I grab onto Angus Fenn's box with my free hand. After all I've done to find the Fenn fortune, we have to put it right back in the car with Mr. Bixly?

"Please come home with Frank, Lex," says Roger's voice. I picture him huddled around a phone with the Leighs. "It's going to be okay."

How can he possibly know that? I don't think he knows that the box he found inside the old passenger car has a fortune in it, or that Fisher and I have it right now.

"Lex?" He sounds nervous.

"Yes?" I yell so I don't have to get close to Mr. Bixly.

"You need to outrun this storm. That's more important than anything else right now, okay?"

I bite my lip. Roger's right, and he's worried about me. It's for this reason only that I decide to get into Mr. Bixly's car. Not because Mr. Bixly points at us and then points at the seats inside the car, as though he's commanding us to get in and sit.

A burning, pinching sensation at the corners of my eyes signals the tears I don't want to fall.

Mr. Bixly puts the phone to his mouth and says, "They're getting into the car. See you in a few minutes."

I yank open the rear car door and slide across the seat, clutching Miss Amanda's albums. Fisher stumbles in with the heavy box, gives me a look that says he's not giving up, and shuts the door.

Mr. Bixly places his wide arm across the front seat and turns to talk to us. "I'll take that box right up here, Fisher."

Fisher scowls. "It's too heavy for me to lift it over the seat," he says. "You got us to get in the car, Mr. Bixly. Now drive. Storm's coming."

My mouth drops open. I've never heard Fisher talk like that.

Mr. Bixly checks his mirrors and talks as he pulls into traffic. "You kids don't seem to understand something."

I glare at Mr. Bixly, wishing I had some superpower to make him be quiet.

"It's my job to oversee all aspects of the zoo," Mr. Bixly says. "That's what it means to be General Manager."

"Does it mean you can steal things?" My words tumble out. I don't care that he's the General Manager. He's wrong, and he should know it.

"I have responsibilities for all the zoo's resources," Mr. Bixly says calmly. He talks to me like I'm either five years old or stupid. I hate that. "And that includes donations to the zoo."

"This box wasn't a donation," I say. "And I think you know that, or you wouldn't have towed away Miss Amanda's trailer."

Mr. Bixly stops for a minute when I say that. Maybe I have a superpower to make him be quiet after all. Fisher looks at me with raised eyebrows, but gives me a little nod.

"Well, we will see what your . . . ahem," Mr. Bixly clears his throat and looks at me in the rearview mirror. "We'll see what Roger has to say about all this."

Anger boils inside me. He was going to say "your dad," but he stopped himself. I'm sure that's what he was going to say. Mr. Bixly is awkward when he talks about Roger and me, because Roger isn't my dad and I'm not Roger's daughter. Years ago, I cried when Roger brought up adoption because it made everything so final, and I didn't want to believe my family was definitely gone. But now I think my family is gone no matter what. And Roger hasn't asked me about it again. Whenever Mr. Bixly stumbles over his words, it makes me think of that feeling of missing people you can't remember—and now I'm thinking of Roger framing that photo of us in the train cab. Mr. Bixly shouldn't be the one to make me think of these things.

I grit my teeth and refuse to look at the back of Mr. Bixly's head or his rearview mirror anymore. I keep turning pages in the album for Fisher to see, pointing out the young Miss Amanda and finding pictures of

Angus Fenn and his wife, Elle. And then I find a page in the photo album I haven't seen before. But it's still very familiar. It's the image I saw in my head this afternoon when I looked into Nyah's eyes at the Grasslands.

It's Tendai getting a bath. The young woman with the baby strapped to her back sprays Tendai with a hose. Nyah showed me this memory of her mother with this woman who looks as comfortable with Tendai as I am with Nyah. The woman isn't Fenn's wife, the beautiful acrobat Elle, but she looks a little bit like her. All of a sudden, I can't see the pictures very well anymore. It's too dark.

Mr. Bixly's car has turned onto the road that curves along the woods outside the zoo fences. We'll reach the zoo parking lot soon, but maybe not soon enough. The greenish haze in the air has given way to darkness beneath heavy storm clouds that refuse to let the daylight through. The wind slams the side of the car, and it swerves from the force. Mr. Bixly keeps driving up the hill, but the wind thrashes like how I imagine ocean waves beat against the side of a ship. And I wish that Karana from my book and I were not alike in this one thing. Because the wind had it in for her, too.

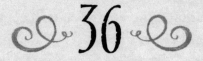

When Earth and Sky Speak

The tornado-warning sirens start wailing, and Mr. Bixly drives his car right up over the zoo's front curb, screeching to a halt before he hits the entrance gates. Fisher and I scramble out of the car with Miss Amanda's albums and Angus Fenn's box before Mr. Bixly opens his door.

"Get into the cart!" Mr. Bixly hollers over the sirens, walking faster than I've ever seen him move as he points to the lone golf cart parked outside the gift shop. There are often two or three golf carts parked there, but Isabel and her staff probably left in the larger ones. The remaining one has a front seat and two rear-facing seats.

"Hurry!" Mr. Bixly yells, motioning to us with frantic arms. And for the first time ever, I think Mr. Bixly looks worried instead of bossy.

Fisher and I slide into the rear seats of the golf cart as Mr. Bixly starts it up.

He zips around the lion pride statue and down the zoo hill toward Fisher's house. The paved path is empty except for two keepers who dart out of a maintenance door and across the grass toward the Wild Kingdom Education Center.

The Education Center's basement is the gathering place for storms like this. All guests still in the zoo would have been herded into the big room used for ambassador animal presentations, where rehabilitated animals educate people about their species. I know about the gathering place from Mr. Bixly's zoo procedures training, but I've only had to go down to that room for storms twice in my life. This storm feels bigger than those did.

The wind whips my hair around my face and stings my neck and cheeks. I hold tight to the photo albums as leaves and small branches fly at the golf cart from the trees. The air is thick with the stormy smell of soil and wet concrete. Fisher holds on to the box with one hand and the bar at the rear of the golf cart with the other.

I glance at Mr. Bixly in the forward-facing seat as he speeds us toward the Wild Kingdom Education Center. He hasn't even looked for Angus Fenn's box since we left the car at the gates. I'm sure he'll remember about the fortune once the danger is over, but by then I can tell

Roger the truth about everything. Roger will help me find Eden Fenn and return her father's fortune.

Suddenly, I want to see Roger so badly. I think of his strong arms and how safe they are, and I hope I don't have to face this storm without him. It's like the feeling I get when I'm with the elephants—like I belong to something bigger than myself and bigger than the zoo. Even bigger than the wind and everything the wind touches. And I think about Mr. Bixly not being able to say Roger is my dad and why that bothers me now.

And then I see him. Roger is coming out of the elephant barn door.

Mr. Bixly turns the golf cart sharply onto the path before the African Grasslands, and Fisher slides into me as I slam into the sidebar on my seat. Mr. Bixly hasn't seen Roger. At least I don't think he has, because he keeps driving crazy to outrun the storm.

"Roger!" I yell, waving at him frantically. I want him to know I'm all right. That I'm back in the zoo.

Roger holds the metal door open as he walks out, but the enormous gusts snatch it open and slam it against the building. Just as quickly as it bangs open, the door rebounds and hits Roger hard. His face wrenches, and he grabs the side of his head as he falls to his knees. My tall, strong Roger.

And suddenly I'm seeing Miss Amanda in my imagination, as the storm rips her awning poles from the ground and slams them down hard.

"Roger!" I scream, smacking Mr. Bixly on the shoulder. "Mr. Bixly, stop!"

He stops, and I'm off the golf cart and scrambling to Roger before I know how I got there.

"I'm all right," Roger says, just loud enough for me to hear over the bellowing storm. But he's not all right. He looks dazed, and he's holding his head and wrinkling up his face like the pain is splitting him open.

And then the sky really does split open, and a funnel snakes down from the clouds just beyond the trees behind Fisher's house. I watch it descend lower and lower, from thick to thin, a wide mouth down to a deadly finger that will destroy everything it touches.

I try to help Roger stand, but I'm not strong enough.

"Leave the box!" Mr. Bixly is yelling at Fisher, "Leave it! We have to get you all inside!" Mr. Bixly gets on the other side of Roger and helps him to his feet. Fisher grabs the swinging door, and we hurry inside the elephant barn.

Thomas is by the side wall, throwing buckets of grooming tools and target poles into a closet and securing the door. The elephants have gathered behind the barrier fence inside the barn—their indoor refuge from the weather. They look like they've been here awhile. Animals know when a storm is coming.

"What happened?" Thomas asks, running over to us. Roger tries to speak, but all he can manage is a soft groan.

"The door hit Roger on the head!" I shout above the

roar of the storm. The approaching wind sounds like a freight train about to burst through the barn wall.

"The tornado is here!" Fisher yells.

Roger's arm presses down on me until I feel like my legs will buckle. Mr. Bixly has the other side of him, but I'm far too short for this. Thomas rushes to my side and ducks under Roger's arm, supporting him.

"Where's the safest place?" Mr. Bixly hollers, as though he's never been in this part of the zoo.

"Lex knows," says Thomas, looking at me like I know something more than he does. "Don't you?"

With Roger supported by Thomas and Mr. Bixly, I run to the barrier fence. "Over here!" The barrier fence stands beneath the strongest beams of the building. All the fence poles run deep into the ground. Everything about the barrier fence must support and withstand the processes of elephant training.

The fence must support and withstand elephants.

Let's see how it does with a tornado.

We help Roger sit on the floor by the fence. He leans against it and holds his head as the tornado roars outside the elephant barn. The building creaks and groans, and suddenly, with the sound of screeching metal and splintering wood, a section of the roof lifts away, and I'm looking straight into the black, swirling storm.

"*Stop!*" I yell in my mind at the wind. "*Get back!*"

The wind pulls on me and sucks my hair straight in front of my face.

"You haven't been listening to me," says the wind. *"Pay attention now."*

I grab onto the fence behind us. I grab onto Roger.

"Nothing you say helps me!" My thoughts are screaming so hard that my head aches.

The twister roars louder.

"Done talking," the wind growls.

The elephants trumpet and stamp their large feet—maybe they're telling the wind to stop, too. Everyone is lined up against the fence, but I can hardly see them with the haze of flying debris and my hair blowing in my face. I think they're holding on to the fence as tightly as I am.

Something new pulls at my hair. It feels different than the wind's wildness. It's coming from behind me. I turn and see the end of a trunk, the two fingers feeling for me. The brown and gold eyes peering at me from the face above belong to Nyah. This is what Thomas meant a moment ago. This is something I know from experience that no one else knows. I risk the tornado's suction for a moment as I loosen my grip on the fence and turn myself around.

"Lex! Hold tight!" shouts Thomas.

Roger grabs on to me, his strong arm keeping me from losing my footing against the powerful wind.

"Open the gates!" I yell to Thomas, and reach for the latch on the nearest training gate. I unhook it and swing the door open. Nyah can reach her trunk through the opening more freely than through the barrier fence when the gates are closed. She wraps her trunk over my shoulder, feels my hair, my head. She does the same to Roger.

Somewhere in the commotion, Mr. Bixly is protesting. Thomas looks me in the eyes, watches Nyah wrap her trunk over me and Roger, and nods in understanding. "Open the training gates!" he yells to Mr. Bixly. "The small gates in the barrier fence! Open them!"

"But . . . they can reach through them!" yells Mr. Bixly.

"Exactly!" Thomas answers.

"They're dangerous and they're scared!" Mr. Bixly protests.

"You wanna take your chances against *that*"— Thomas jerks his head at the black twister outside the open roof—"all by yourself?"

Hoses fly from their hooks and boxes hurtle into the air as the twister pulls them from inside the barn. The elephants trumpet in alarm. Fisher manages to get a training gate open, and Zaire lowers herself to reach her trunk toward him. The twister's suction is fierce, but I hold on to the barrier rails, and Nyah holds on to me and Roger, all 40,000 muscles in her trunk keeping us safe. Right next to us, Zaire has entwined her trunk under Fisher's arms, and he's gripping her tightly. Thomas must've yanked the other gates open, because Asha and Jazz have reached their trunks through, keeping Thomas and Mr. Bixly grounded as the building groans beneath the twister's fury, and more of the roof is pulled away.

Just then, something appears in the barn doorway, moving into the training area from the hallway on the left. Completely unaffected by the force of the tornado, Miss Amanda walks calmly toward us.

"Roger!" I nod in Miss Amanda's direction.

Roger and Fisher both see her. Fisher's eyes are like large brown marbles, but I think his surprise is the same as mine. Even those of us who believe in ghosts don't expect to see one in the middle of a twister.

I had hoped to see Miss Amanda again, but not this way. I can't talk to her. I can't tell her I found the Fenn fortune and saved her albums, but that it's all surely lost again. We left it all behind at the golf cart.

Miss Amanda moves gracefully like always. Her wide-brimmed hat is tilted slightly on her head, as though she is walking in the woods on a clear, still day. Even the power of a tornado is not strong enough to deter a ghost. She's standing in front of me now and bends toward me with her hand out. She wants to give me something. But first she looks intently at my face and then at the swirling mass of wind above the gaping hole in the roof.

Nyah hugs her trunk more firmly around me, and even through the force of the wind and the gnawing, raging sound of the twister it has become, I can feel the thumping pulse of her rumblings in my head.

I see brown earth beneath the blue-and-white sky. Elephant feet slog through mud and hold up their massive weight like solid tree trunks rooted into the earth. Elephant trunks reach high into the sky, reaching for branches, smelling and touching the wind. The rumbling in the earth and the voice of the wind speak at once, and they speak to each other. And I see myself, looking very much like the pictures Roger has of me when I first came to live with him. It's my same face, my same curly hair. The young woman from Miss Amanda's photo albums, the one in the picture giving Tendai a bath, is holding me. She kisses me on the cheek, and the man who is with us lifts me onto his shoulders. We're at the African Grasslands in this zoo. This zoo. We're visiting Nyah, and Nyah knows who we are. She knows us all—from the circus. And we're a family. She touches the man and woman with her trunk, smelling them, recognizing them.

And suddenly I remember them, too. Not everything. Not much. But enough. The feel of his hair in my hands and the smell of her soap as she kissed my cheek.

And as I notice again the similarities between the young woman's face and the face of Elle the acrobat, as my past and my place in Nyah's life are finally becoming clear to me, the wind roars and pulls harder, threatening to take away everything I love.

Nyah makes a trumpeting sound that startles me out of the warm images that are both her memories and mine. Miss Amanda looks between me and Nyah and says something I can't hear.

"What?" I yell, but it's swallowed up by the deafening storm.

Nyah trumpets again, and I believe she is showing me what I need to do. But it's the warmth in Roger's hand and the sight of Fisher wrapped up in Zaire's trunk that opens my mouth.

"GET BACK!" I yell at the wind, staring down the sky above the open roof. Every time I've ever spoken to the wind or it has spoken to me is now like a jolt of electricity through me, and although my voice is no match for the twister's destructive strength, my words have never felt more powerful. "You took one family from me, and you're not taking another one! Leave. Them. Alone!"

Another rumbling vibration, like an overhead thunderclap you feel inside your own heartbeat, moves from Nyah into me. It's an energy flowing through the earth and through Nyah, like it's connecting elephants to it and to each other. I think this is how elephants communicate across long distances. Maybe it's how they know when someone they love has died. It's beyond anything human, but it's about animals and people and life. This energy is too strong to stay in just the two of us, so it fills the air.

For a moment, the earth and the sky are speaking.

Something whips through the dark cloud above us, tossed violently by the funnel. It's a large chunk of metal debris—a piece of a vehicle or a building, and it's sailing toward us with dangerous speed.

"Look out!" Fisher yells. Roger leans over me, shielding me with his upper body.

"No!" I scream. A large chunk of metal flying at Roger's body from a tornado might kill him. Tears squeeze from my eyes, and I hold Roger tight, smelling steam train and aftershave and feeling him breathe.

I wait for something awful.

But it doesn't come. No painful impact or crashing blow. And Roger and I are still breathing the same air, huddled together, afraid to move because of the crash that hasn't come. Why hasn't it come?

And I realize that the wind's roar is quieting down. It weakens. It retreats, like it's no longer interested in destruction, or in me. Debris falls around us and comes to rest as the building creaks and settles. Roger exhales in relief, his breath warm. Fisher, Thomas, and Mr. Bixly stir against the fence nearby. Elephant feet shuffle and trunks drag in the dirt behind us. Nyah's trunk lifts from my shoulders, bobbing between me and Roger, touching our heads and leaving a little slime behind.

Roger breathes deep, holding me in his arms. He slowly moves away and sits up. Miss Amanda is still standing directly in front of us, holding Angus Fenn's box in her outstretched arms. A thin sliver of light frames the box where Miss Amanda is not quite touching it.

"The wind let go of it, and I caught it for you," she says.

I'm too surprised to answer. Surprised that a ghost could catch a metal box hurled through the air by a tornado, but then, I suppose I've noticed that Miss Amanda has been able to move the things she touched when she was alive. And who knows the strength of a ghost? Apparently, they can be quite strong.

Maybe it helps when the ghost is trying to set things right.

"Amanda," Roger says, holding his head and wincing, "we owe you our lives."

"Yeah," Fisher breathes in relief. He stares at the box in Miss Amanda's hands. "Thanks for catching that."

"A-Amanda?" Thomas wipes his eyes with the back of his hand, and it smears mud across his face. "Is that you? How?"

And I realize Thomas knows her. And it makes so much sense that he would. After Angus Fenn brought Nyah and Tendai to the Lexington Zoo, Amanda would have spent a lot of time at the elephant barn. She did say she liked the elephants.

"Have you never seen me visiting Nyah, Thomas?" Miss Amanda asks. "I've been here a lot lately. But you have to pay close attention to notice the presence of a misplaced spirit."

Thomas's mouth is hanging open, and he nudges Mr. Bixly, who just nods.

"It's all right, Thomas," Mr. Bixly says. "You pay such close attention to those elephants, no one would expect you'd be able to divide your attention with a ghost."

"Frank Bixly!" Miss Amanda scolds. "I'm a misplaced—"

"You're a misplaced spirit, I know," Mr. Bixly says, as though he's heard this from Miss Amanda as many times as I have. His white button-up shirt is stained with mud and soaked with rain. What little hair he has on his head has blown loose from his usual carefully combed style. And I realize Mr. Bixly chose to get Fisher and Roger and me to safety instead of saving Angus Fenn's box for himself. And that thing he said to Thomas about paying attention to the elephants. That was actually kind of . . . nice.

Miss Amanda sets Angus Fenn's box in front of me. Her face looks much younger. Like in her photos. "Well, now . . . it seems I had to do the right thing to get my faded memories back, and now I can see it all clear as a mountain spring. I didn't recognize you that night I saw you alone with Nyah, but maybe misplaced spirits get a boost of intuition. I knew Roger would take good care of you. But with my memories back, I recognize you now. You know, darlin', you were just a little thing when I last saw you at the circus, but now you're the spitting image of your mama Eden sitting there with Nyah. And you've got your daddy's touch with the animals. His name was Russell Palmer. He was one of the keepers."

Roger startles beside me, and Fisher gasps in surprise. I'm grateful to Miss Amanda for saying what she did. My heart fills up fuller than it's ever been—happy to know, not just to wonder, that I look like my mom and that I got some of my connection with animals from my dad. I stroke Nyah's trunk with my hand. I'm holding the trunk of an elephant who knew my family.

"You must've understood the clue I left under the floorboard," she says. "You found the train ticket, right?"

"I, uh . . ." The train ticket was a clue from Miss Amanda? "I noticed the date. *You* put the ticket under the gift shop floor?"

"Well, don't look so surprised. You figured out the treasure was hidden in that train car, didn't you? I rolled up that ticket and shoved it under the floor as soon as I realized I might not remember the gift shop was a train car. I was running out of time, and Roger never noticed me when I tried to get his attention. Once he had you to care for, you were his world."

I feel Roger's warmth next to me, and my heart fills up even more.

Nyah's trunk bobs over my head and shoulders and then stretches long toward Miss Amanda. Miss Amanda moves closer to the fence. The tiny gap between Miss Amanda's hand and Nyah's trunk doesn't seem to matter to either of them, and Nyah wraps the end of her trunk around that space like she's holding Miss Amanda just a little.

"Thank you for bringing me Angus Fenn's box," I say.

Miss Amanda smiles, and her blue eyes shine in a way that looks both happy and sad. "It's the least I could do for his granddaughter."

Her words aren't a surprise to me, but it's strange to hear them out loud. They are the very tip of a mountain of things I've begun to realize. But they are a surprise to everyone else. I can feel Fisher and Roger staring at me. I look around at Thomas and Mr. Bixly. Thomas smiles behind all the mud.

"Angus Fenn, huh?" He looks delighted. Maybe even relieved. "Well, that explains a lot."

Mr. Bixly's expression is one I've never seen on his face before. He looks almost . . . lost. What do General Managers do when they learn they can't manage everything? I think, maybe, I've been a little wrong about

Frank Bixly. The way he runs the zoo—the rules and the meetings and telling everyone what to do—he's always trying to make things right and comply with AZA guidelines. And that means we really want the same things. We want what's best for the animals.

Miss Amanda steps slowly away from Nyah, as if they've said goodbye, and she extends one hand toward me like before. She wants to give me something. I hold out my hand, and she drops her key necklace into my open palm.

"The key," I whisper.

"It's yours," she says with a smile. "Your mama understood elephants, too."

I heft the box into my lap and squeeze its key. The pictures I remember from Miss Amanda's photo albums and the images from Nyah match up in my head like color filling black-and-white drawings. It's a beautiful story—a sad story. But I think it ends happier than I expected. It's the story that's mine, and it makes me whole.

I'm Angus Fenn's granddaughter. Eden was his daughter and my mother. And this box has been returned to its rightful owner.

"It's not what they call you," Miss Amanda says to me. "It's what you answer to. You keep that in mind, you hear?"

"I will." I wipe my eyes as tears fill them up. "Do you think you can get to where you're supposed to be now?"

Miss Amanda smiles and nods. "It seems we've both found our way, darlin'."

She turns and walks away from us, no longer "misplaced." Like a mist evaporating in the sun, one minute she's there, and the next—somewhere between the blink of my eyes—Amanda Holtz is gone.

The Unspoken Words

Time knows how to slow down when you need a few extra moments to take everything in. Roger tries to insist I open the box right away, but I'm too worried about the blood that has trickled down the side of his face and the swollen lump on his head from the barn door. He seems dazed and in a lot of pain.

Mr. Bixly says nothing about Miss Amanda, my identity, or the box. Instead, he hands Roger a handkerchief and encourages him and me to put pressure on Roger's wound. Then he puffs out his chest and announces he will call an ambulance for Roger and then check on the guests and zoo staff in the Wild Kingdom Education Center. I'm surprised by the change in Mr. Bixly as I watch him lumber out of the barn in his muddy clothes. Maybe he's not the only one who has changed.

Thomas moves quietly through the barn, watching the elephants and checking the barrier fence. Then he says, "Do you want me to stay with you and Lex, Roger?"

"No, Thomas. I'll be fine," Roger says softly. He's leaning against the fence, and Nyah keeps snaking her trunk over him and touching his head.

Thomas hesitates a moment. He looks back and forth between me and Nyah. He closes all the training gates except the one I opened.

"I'm going to inspect the Grasslands' fences," Thomas says on his way out. "You never know what that twister might've done. Holler if you need anything, Lex. I'll be back to check on Roger in a few minutes."

Fisher wants to go with Mr. Bixly to find his parents, but first he has something to show me. "I grabbed those photo albums when you jumped out of the cart to help Roger," he says.

"You did? Fisher! You're the best!" I yell, a little too loud because Roger groans and holds his head.

Fisher's face falls, and he hands me one album. "I sat on them to keep them from blowing away, but the wind got one from me. I hope the pictures you want most are here."

I stand up and take it. "Thank you." I really do want to hug him, but instead, I say, "You were right, you know."

"Of course I was." He smiles his million-dollar-baseball-contract smile. "What about?"

"Concentrated orange juice . . . wind immersion . . . that I needed to learn to get out of the zoo sometimes."

Fisher nods and folds his arms all satisfied with himself. "Good thing we're friends, then."

"Why? Because you're right all the time?"

"No. Because it's always good to have a friend who can find a treasure and tell off a twister, and because *I* can show you around *outside* the zoo." He glances at Roger, who gives us both an approving nod and smiles weakly.

"*And* you can show me the world of baseball," I say.

Fisher grins, and I think he knows I mean it.

"I'll go find my parents, so they know I'm okay," he says. "And maybe they can come take a look at Roger's head, in case the ambulance is slow to get here."

"Thanks, Fisher." I hold up the photo album.

"My pleasure, Lex from the Fenn Circus." Fisher takes off toward the side doors and leaves the barn.

I kneel beside Roger, who reaches for my hand. "Let's look at those pictures while we wait," he says softly. "Or you could open that box."

I swallow and look at Roger's strong engineer arms and his gentle eyes. I'm not sure I want to know what's in the box right now. It's enough to know something of who I am, and who I was before I came to the zoo. But now that there's a possibility of finding some family somewhere, I know I don't want to leave Roger and the

Old County Bank. I don't want to leave home. This is my home, and Roger is my family. I had this home and family all along, but somehow I missed it.

Nyah snorts and bobs her trunk over the ground behind the fence. She finds some stray fruit that was tossed around when the supply closet doors went flying off their hinges. She lifts the fruit to her mouth, her bottom lip flopping open as she chews.

"Roger?" I say.

"Yes."

"I snooped around in your room when I thought you might be hiding Angus Fenn's box from Mr. Bixly."

"Hmm. I saw that my chair was moved and my closet had been opened. I wondered what you'd been up to."

"Yes, well, I found a box of old things in your closet, and a bunch of papers with our names on them under your bed."

Roger nods again. Maybe I should help him lie down.

"Sorry," I say. "Don't talk if it hurts your head. I shouldn't bother you about this right now."

"I'm all right, Lex," Roger says. "I want to tell you this." He shifts his position on the floor and looks straight into my eyes. "Fern and Gordon suggested I should've told you this a long time ago. I'm not very good at this sort of thing."

"Okay." My heart pounds a little harder, and I think of the picture of the two of us in the engine cab and how he framed it and set it on my nightstand. I think of the map of the world on my wall and how there are no stickers on it for me or for Roger.

"I've never talked to you about my family. And I think it would have been better for you, growing up here with me, if I had. Maybe you would have felt better about your own place in the world.

"I never knew my mom. But my dad—he was a great dad. I'll tell you more about him sometime soon. Those were his things you found in my closet."

I nod, feeling his words enter my heart and stay there.

"My dad got sick, and a few years before I found you, the sickness made him completely forget me. He didn't know my face when I went to visit him." Roger looks like he's hurting again, but it isn't the bump on his head this time. "I guess, after he died, it was just too hard for me to talk about dying. With anyone. So I didn't tell you about him, and I didn't tell you about Amanda, and I didn't talk to you the way you needed me to—about your parents being missing from your life."

"And that's why you never wanted to talk about it when I asked about my family . . . and dying."

He nods. "I'm sorry, Lexington. I could've done a better job of talking to you about your parents and helping you with grief. I don't know what happened to them. We tried everything to find them, but they weren't reported missing from anywhere. It makes a lot more sense now." He taps his fingers on the box. "If they were with the circus, they never settled down in one place. And if they closed the circus down and sold everything off, which I believe they did, no one from the circus would've reported them missing either.

"I've tried to be a good . . ." He pauses and swallows. The vein in his forehead that sometimes swells up when he's working or thinking hard is pulsing now. He takes my hand in his and squeezes it gently. His eyes are glistening, but he smiles as a single tear spills out. "I asked you this a long time ago, but the way I said it, or because I couldn't talk about death to you, it made the timing all wrong. I guess I've been afraid to bring it up again."

Roger was afraid? I can't imagine that. But now I think all this has something to do with that psychology book he's been reading.

"Ask me what?"

"Well, now that you have some new information about yourself and who your family is"—he tilts his head toward the box and the photo album—"this may be the wrong thing to say."

"It's okay," I say, thinking of what Mr. Bixly couldn't say and how it bothered me, and how I've been aching to have this conversation more than I knew. "Tell me."

"Those papers you found under my bed—they're the legal papers from when you first came to the zoo. It's everything that was required for me to take care of you. But some of them are about . . . adopting you. If you want. I mean, unless you find that you have a family to go to"—he nods at the box again—"I'd be very happy if I could adopt you and be your dad . . . if you want."

I hug Roger right there on the floor of the elephant barn. I feel his heartbeat and breathe in his aftershave, and he holds me. And we stay there, just like that, until the paramedics arrive with their equipment and bandages, and I only let go of him so they can lift him onto the stretcher and take him to the hospital. And I sit next to him in the ambulance, holding his hand all the way there.

38

What Friends Do

An unexpected phenomenon followed that second tornado over the Lexington Zoo. Cleanup crews and zoo staff found interesting old photographs littered throughout the exhibits, the trees, the rooftops, and the flower beds. The twister scattered the black-and-white photos and color photos of circus people and animals from the album it snatched away from Fisher. We haven't found them all, but anytime someone brings me a few more pictures, I add them to the growing display on the wall of my room.

Roger's head injury kept him in the hospital for two days, but he's home now on doctor's orders to rest and sleep a lot. The train isn't running while he heals, but the zoo isn't open to the public yet anyway. Repairs to the elephant barn, the Leighs' house, and some of the nearby maintenance buildings will take a while, and those areas have been blocked off. The zoo will open again next week. In the meantime, the Leighs are sleeping in the living room of the Old County Bank and keeping Roger from doing too much.

Mrs. Leigh's kitchen is under repair, so she cooks in ours. She's already stocked the Old County Bank with things Roger never buys, like fish sauce and four different kinds of curry paste, and she's teaching me to make khao pad moo, which is pork fried rice. She also brought her two wooden elephants and set them by our door. I asked her to do that. The Leighs' living room, where the elephants sat, was undamaged in the storm. So I think those elephants really are good luck.

All of us living under the same roof means Mrs. Leigh gets more opportunities to remind me I have a paper to write. But I don't mind. After the week I had with the twister, and Nyah, and finding out who I am, I have a lot to write about.

My grandfather's box was *not* full of money, as I thought it would be. It was full of things Roger says are *worth* money. Apparently, certificates for something called stocks dating back to 1959, for some company called General Telephone and Electrics, means that Angus Fenn's family, which is me, owns part of a major cell phone company. I guess I don't have to use a radio to call Roger anymore . . . but we have to talk about that, he says. Apparently, my grandfather didn't entirely trust his stocks, though, because he also had some gold in his locked box. That's why it was so heavy.

The most interesting thing from the box that now belongs to me is Angus Fenn's will, which named his descendants the owners of all his property, including the elephants he sent to the zoo from his circus. And that includes Nyah. So Nyah and Tendai were technically on loan to the zoo, an arrangement Mr. Bixly had on file in his office. But except for my parents, who one day showed up at the Grasslands and then disappeared, no one ever came forward to claim the elephants.

Roger and I have a lot to discuss when he feels better. Mostly, it involves him and me and some African elephants. But today I'm watching a baseball game.

"Okay," I say to Fisher, "so the batter can technically have more than three tries to hit the ball?"

Fisher is standing in the dirt at the bottom of the bleacher steps. He's wearing his Omaha Storm Chasers ball cap and looks pretty official. His worn leather glove forms to his hand when he slips it on, and he's wearing baseball pants instead of his usual shorts. He's getting ready for that baseball camp in Kansas City, and I think it looks like he's doing a good job.

"Right," he says. "If the batter has two strikes and then hits foul balls—that's if the ball goes out of bounds—they keep batting until they either hit the ball within bounds or get a third strike."

"Oh." I think I understand.

Fisher glances back at the rest of the players wearing blue jerseys. The coach has called them over, and they're gathering on a bench to listen to him.

"Well, it's time for me to go," Fisher says with a look of excitement that makes me happy. "I'll see you after it's over?"

I smile to reassure him. I'm not going anywhere today. "Absolutely. I'll be in these bleachers, cheering you on the whole time."

"Thanks." He smiles back, tugs on the bill of his hat, adjusts it a little. He starts toward the blue-jersey bench but then hurries back to say something else. "Oh, um, you know about the pitcher, right?"

I've seen bits and pieces of baseball games at the Leighs' house and in the back kitchen at the Wild Eats Café. I never paid much attention to the rules, but I've seen enough on TV and listened to Fisher talk about the game and his baseball cards enough to know this.

"Of course. It's the guy who throws the ball to the batter from the hill."

"Well . . ." Fisher smiles a little like I said something funny. "From the mound. But yes. Great!" Fisher's smile keeps growing. He takes a deep breath. "The pitcher is really important to the game. And it's hard to do it well."

"Got it," I say.

"Okay . . . see ya." Fisher turns again and runs to meet the other blue-jersey players and his coach.

I climb the steps to an empty section on the fifth row of bleachers. Fisher said the ball can come into the bleachers sometimes, if a batter hits a foul, so I want a little buffer. As I walk to the spot I've selected, I see a familiar face. I take a deep breath. If I can tell off the wind in tornado form, I can do this. I approach her.

"Hi, Camille," I say. It's the nice girl from the last time I was here.

Camille looks around and sees me. I brave a smile, wondering what she thinks of me after I ran away from her and her friends. I don't see them here with her this time.

"It's Lexington," I say.

"Yes," she says, smiling. "I remember."

"Sorry I took off so suddenly the other day."

Camille slides down on her bench, offering me space to sit. So I do.

"Tae and Anna can be a little much sometimes," she says. "I really think I would have done the same thing."

"Really?" I laugh unexpectedly. It's a kind of happy relief spilling out of me.

Camille laughs, too. She has her hair in braids, and I wish I knew how to do that with my hair. It wouldn't be so hot on my neck.

I glance at the players on the field and look for Fisher. The coach is finished talking to them, and Fisher and another boy are throwing the ball back and forth to each other for practice. Fisher throws it hard, and the ball slams into the other boy's glove with a slapping thud. I didn't know Fisher could throw the ball like that. It's so fast I can hardly follow it with my eyes. It reminds me of those baseball games on TV, and I can tell that Fisher definitely knows what he's doing. He looks like the pros when he throws the ball like that. And then I think I know why Fisher asked me if I knew about the pitcher.

The blue jerseys spread out across the field, and Fisher stays where he is while his coach talks to him.

"I heard about the tornado hitting the zoo last week," Camille says. "Is everyone all right? Did you see it?"

"I definitely saw it. It took the roof off the building I was in with my family and friends."

Camille gasps, and her eyes go wide. "I bet that was terrifying."

"It was scary," I say, but I keep my voice matter-of-fact. I don't want to make a big deal about it, because this time the tornado won't live on as the thing that describes who I am. I get to do that. "But everyone is going to be okay."

"Oh, that's good," Camille says. She smiles at me. She has braces with pink bands on them. "You know, I love going to the zoo and seeing the animals. I think it's so cool that you get to live there."

Fisher is walking to the small dirt hill in the middle of the field—the mound. He looks so sure of himself. So confident. And I realize how much he wanted me to know what his hard work is all about, and how pleased he is to have me see this. My heart squeezes with pride for my best friend.

"You should come for a visit," I say to Camille, glancing at her briefly but watching Fisher so I don't miss a thing.

"Really?"

"Yeah," I say. I've never had someone visit me at the zoo before. There must be some way for me to have a visitor without her having to pay to come into the zoo. "I'll talk to the customer service manager and get you some free passes."

"Cool," she says. "I'd like that."

Fisher stands on the pitcher's mound, his hands together in front of him, holding the baseball in his glove.

"The pitcher is my friend," I say to Camille.

"Friend," whispers the wind. It hasn't spoken to me much since Nyah and I told off the twister. But this version of the wind, when it shows up, is a changed wind. Many things have changed since the twister.

"Yes," I answer. *"Friend."*

The umpire yells, "Play ball!" and the batter from the white-jersey team walks to the plate. He shoulders the bat. He swings it over home plate a few times, waiting for Fisher's pitch.

Fisher winds up like a pro, and I hold my breath. Maybe he's done this hundreds of times, but it's the first time I've seen it, and my arms prickle with goose bumps.

The ball leaves his hand so fast, it hits the catcher's

glove with a thud before I can spot it. The batter swings and misses.

"Strike one!" yells the umpire.

And I don't care whether this is what people do or not, but I'm on my feet cheering for Fisher and his fast pitch.

39

Found

The repairs to the elephant barn are going to take longer than a few weeks. The roof still isn't finished, but we have even bigger construction plans underway.

It's been almost two months since the tornado and my discovery of the Fenn fortune. Fisher left a month after the big storm to visit his grandparents in Omaha, and then he had three whole weeks at his Kansas City baseball camp. He's due back on a fancy bus this afternoon.

"Lex!" Camille and some of Fisher's school friends are heading toward the construction trailer at the edge of the woods. They've been helping with our new project. They arrive at the construction trailer with a pile of papers and a cooler full of sports drinks and ice cream sandwiches.

Camille hands me the papers. "We came up with a bunch of different flyers to take to all the downtown businesses. Our teacher from last year wants to help, and he said he can help us create a website for the sanctuary if Fisher's mom is too busy."

"Always good to have more people on your team who can handle the internet," Roger says from his swivel chair. He is sitting at the desk, going over the latest plans the architect delivered this morning.

According to the accountant and the attorney Roger hired to help me, my family fortune and the money my parents had in an account from selling off the circus property, plus the donations we've had rolling in after all the news coverage, is going to be more than enough to get the Amanda Holtz Elephant Sanctuary ready for Nyah and five other elephants.

Yes, five others.

We still have Asha, Zaire, and Jazz.

But with some excellent news coverage (thanks to Mrs. Leigh and her press releases), and thanks to Thomas's and Mr. Leigh's connections with other zoos, we've been able to find the rest of Nyah's circus herd—the two remaining elephants that my grandfather loaned to a zoo in Ohio. Two females named Gypsy and Star. I have their pictures taped to the wall of the construction trailer.

With our plans for an elephant sanctuary, and my grandfather's will that was in his metal box, both zoos agreed to send Gypsy and Star to join Nyah. Herds should always stay together.

"Thanks for all your help, Camille." I spread the flyers out on the desk and show them to Roger. They have various pictures of the elephants, artist drawings of the planned sanctuary, and information about how to donate to the project.

"My pleasure," Camille says with a smile. "This is the best summer we've ever had. Thanks for letting us be a part of this."

"Of course," I say, handing her an ice cream sandwich from the cooler.

I think of the time I first saw Camille and Anna and Tae on the bus, and then again at the ball field. Camille doesn't hang out with them as much anymore. The other two girls aren't interested in what we're doing here. I'm glad to have found some friends who enjoy animals and the outdoors as much as Fisher and I do.

Although Mrs. Leigh was super impressed with the paper I wrote about myself and Karana and learning to leave my island, I'm considering going to school with my friends in the fall. But I'm still not sure. I'll miss how active the animals are in the mornings, and lunch with Roger every day, but Roger says we will have the weekends for that. I still have time to decide.

"It looks like Fern has something to tell us," Roger says, motioning at the window. I look out and see Mrs. Leigh waving her arms. She's wearing one of her business suits with a lavender blouse. That color almost lights up on her. She dresses like this on days when she meets with zoo donors and the press, but today she has layered a cooking apron on top. She notices the apron and laughs as I wave out the window at her.

I open the trailer door and jump off the top step.

"Is he here?"

"I just got a call from my mom," Mrs. Leigh says. "They'll be here in a few minutes! I was so excited that I didn't even notice I was still wearing this!" She laughs again and takes off her apron.

On top of all her zoo and sanctuary work, Mrs. Leigh has been cooking a lot of food, preparing a feast for Fisher's homecoming and a special occasion we have later today. Her newly remodeled kitchen is full to the brim, so she's been using the refrigerators and stoves at the Wild Eats Café. We even have papaya salad and the pork fried rice I made at the Old County Bank. Fisher's Thai grandma is riding with him from Kansas City, and I think Mrs. Leigh's excitement might have to do with that a little.

Camille and the others leave the cooler and flyers in the trailer and follow Mrs. Leigh to the bus stop. I hurry back inside, and Roger hands me the welcome-home banner Camille helped me make.

"Maybe we planned too much at once," Roger says. "Are you going to be okay to do all this today?"

I give him my biggest smile.

Fisher is finally coming home and planning to go with us and the Leighs to the courthouse this afternoon. We have an appointment with the judge. To settle the matter of Roger Marsh and his guardianship of a girl with the given name of Autumn Palmer.

Once we knew I was Angus Fenn's granddaughter and my mother's name was Eden, it didn't take long to locate a birth certificate. But after all those years of wondering about my last name and my birthday (which is October 23, by the way, and that means I'm older than Fisher by about eight months), I've decided to keep Lexington Willow. I'm adding two names today, though, and after the adoption, I'll be legally Lexington Willow Palmer Marsh. I'll have the names of my two dads—the circus animal keeper and the zoo train engineer.

"It's not too much," I say to Roger. "I wouldn't change a thing."

Roger nods. He has a tiny pink scar on the right side of his forehead from his head injury. I'm so grateful I didn't lose him.

"Well," he says, "it's about time, right?"

I hug him, and my arms can't reach all the way around his middle, but I squeeze tight. He hugs me back with those strong arms that survived the twister right alongside me.

Roger and I join the crowd waiting at the bus stop for Fisher. There's Isabel and some of her gift shop staff, Cory, DaLoris, Thomas, Camille, Fisher's school friends, and of course Mr. and Mrs. Leigh. The surprise person in the crowd is Mr. Bixly, who warmed up to the idea of my elephant sanctuary and how it's putting the

Lexington Zoo in the news with good publicity and increased crowds. He agreed to close the zoo early today for our special celebration. And he's here now, waiting at the bus stop with all of us instead of sitting in his office or the General Manager's residence all alone. Between Roger and me, we think Mr. Bixly is on his way to learning what family means, just like we all are.

Camille and I stretch out the welcome-home banner and cheer when Fisher steps off the bus with his Kansas City Royals hat on backward.

His skin has darkened from all his time in the sun, and he looks strong. Most of all, he smiles like a kid who just spent three weeks doing something he loves. His grandma joins him on the steps, looking even prouder than Fisher does. She resembles Mrs. Leigh, pretty with smiling eyes, but she's just a little shorter and rounder. Fisher waves his baseball star wave as if he's on one of those floats in the Thanksgiving Day parade. Then, with his travel-worn, sun-worn backpack over his shoulder and a baseball in one hand, he hops off the last step.

Mrs. Leigh grabs Fisher in a hug. I think Fisher grew taller. How did he grow taller in three weeks? Mr. Leigh hurries over to Fisher's grandma and helps with her bags. She has brought a lot with her.

"Hello, Fern." Fisher's grandma hugs Mrs. Leigh and then pulls a pot and a woven basket from one of her bags. "To replace the one you lost in the storm."

"Thank you, Mom," Mrs. Leigh says.

"What do you use that for?" I ask.

"It's a steamer pot and basket," Fisher's grandma says. "The authentic way to make Thai sticky rice."

"Yum," I say to Fisher's grandma. "Mrs. Leigh has been teaching me to cook."

"Well, maybe I can teach you some more while I'm here. I understand Fern is quite busy these days."

Mrs. Leigh nods at that. "Mom, you remember Lexington?"

"Yes, I do," Fisher's grandma says, taking my hand and squeezing it gently. "Nice to see you again."

"Nice to see you, too," I say.

"Fisher has been telling me about your adventures, *and* your ghost friend." She smiles like someone who knows about ghosts.

"Oh, well," I say, thinking she may want to know this, "my ghost friend has found her way. . . . She's not lost anymore."

Fisher's grandma glances at Mrs. Leigh. "Well, that is *very* good to hear."

"Hey there, Slugger," I say to Fisher. "We missed you around here. Looks like you had fun at that camp, though. Are you gonna be Lexington's famous major league player in a few years?"

He shrugs, but if I know Fisher, he'll never stop working until he gets where he wants to go. "Well," he says, presenting a signed baseball to me and his parents, "look who I got to meet."

We all lean forward to examine the signatures. I don't know the names, but Mr. Leigh does. He claps Fisher on the back and spouts out the names, adding more excitement to his voice with each one until finally, he says a name I do know, just as I see the writing next to Fisher's thumb.

"Johnny Damon!" Mr. Leigh exclaims.

"He met his hero," Fisher's grandma says, laughing. I can see where Mrs. Leigh gets her laugh. It's the kind that isn't about being funny. It's about being so happy that joy spills out of you. And I know Mrs. Leigh has had plenty of things to be sad about, yet she laughs like this. Like her mom.

"You met him?" I say.

"Well, he used to play for the Royals a long time ago, so he came to say hi to us at the camp. He asked me about my pitching and signed this for me."

Fisher's grandma wraps her arm around Fisher's shoulders. "Fisher's going to be just like that. He's very talented. I'm bragging to all the cousins. My talented grandson is going to be a big American baseball star."

Fisher blushes a little. His grandma always makes a big deal out of him, and it's never subtle.

"How are the sanctuary plans coming?" Fisher asks me.

"Amazing," I say. Because they are. And I hand him a folded piece of paper, a color printout of Mrs. Leigh's design for the sanctuary logo that I've been carrying in my pocket. It's an outline of Nyah and Tendai, surrounded by a rich variety of trees, and the words "Amanda Holtz Elephant Sanctuary" in an arc above them.

Fisher opens the paper and studies it. "You've been busy," he says to his mom.

"Oh, you have no idea," Mrs. Leigh answers. She's right. She's the reason so many people know about me, and Nyah, and my plans for the Fenn fortune to fund research and education about elephants once the sanctuary is up and running. She's the reason we've had so many donations.

"She got me two more spots on the news, too," I say. "And wait till you see the food she made for this afternoon."

Fisher's eyes widen at the mention of food, but then he says, "Ooh! What time do we have to be there?" He means the courthouse. He didn't forget.

"We should leave in an hour," Roger says.

"Then . . ." Fisher gives me that sideways look with a smile that says he's missed the zoo. "Do we have time to go see her?"

"Of course," Roger says.

And Fisher and I, along with Roger and Camille, take off for Nyah's habitat. Thomas and Mr. Leigh come along, because although Angus Fenn's will left Nyah to me, while she's in the zoo, we still have AZA rules.

Thomas and Mr. Leigh let us in through the locked gate at the African Grasslands perimeter. Nyah sees me on the other side of the eucalyptus wood fence. She leaves the large truck tire she's been playing with and saunters over to me. I've found the part of the fence where I think I was visiting Nyah with my parents. This is what it looked like in Nyah's memory anyway. And Thomas says he remembers bringing a young couple to visit Nyah. They wanted to take her to a sanctuary. They said they were going to talk with the zoo manager and the board. But they never returned.

Thomas and Mr. Leigh watch as Nyah reaches her trunk over the fence, and I hold out my hands to her. I hug her trunk with one arm and stroke it gently with my other hand. She lets out a gentle snort, sniffs me, and bobs her head slightly in what looks like a nod. I look into her eyes and feel the rumbling of her silent words.

I see the images of Tendai and Gypsy and Star in my head.

Although I can't communicate the way she does in my thoughts, I know she understands me when I whisper, "We've found them, girl. We found your family for you."

Nyah's trunk feels my head and drapes over my shoulder, snuffling and tickling my neck.

"Thank you," I tell her again, as I've said many times since the storm. Because of Nyah, I survived another twister. Because of her, I went to the woods and I found myself.

Roger, who has been watching silently next to Thomas and Mr. Leigh, steps forward and hands me a small wrapped present. "I was going to wait until after we go to the courthouse, but I want to give it to you now," he says. He's not wearing his engineer overalls today, but is dressed in nice, freshly ironed pants, and he's wearing a tie.

I take the present and open it slowly. I recognize the blue corner of the book before I've fully unwrapped it.

It's a new copy of *Island of the Blue Dolphins*. My own copy.

"Roger! Thank you!" I run my fingertips over the dolphins swimming in the ocean and the profile of Karana.

"Look inside," he says.

I open the front cover, and on the title page, Roger has pasted another picture of us on the Lexington Zoo train. Beneath the picture, he's written:

This book belongs to:
Lexington Willow Palmer Marsh

In blue skies or wind,
and whether you sail
or ride the rails,
you'll always be my brave daughter.

Love,
Dad

I wrap my arms around Roger, my dad, and hold him tight. And the wind, with a gentle breeze in my hair, says something so soft I can barely make it out.

"Home."

"Yes," I answer as Roger kisses the top of my head. *"Home."*

Author's Note

I never expected a book about a girl and an elephant to teach me so much. Although Lexington Willow's ability to "see" Nyah's thoughts and memories is fiction, the complexities of elephant communication are very real.

When I first heard about seismic communication among elephants, I had to know more. Research shows that an elephant's rumble is the ideal frequency to travel as a signal through the ground. Caitlin O'Connell, a renowned elephant expert and author, has carried out experiments showing that elephants can detect seismic signals, or vibrations that travel through the earth. They can even determine where the signal came from and respond to it. Katy Payne, an elephant communication expert and author of the book *Silent Thunder: In the Presence of Elephants,* reported that she and other researchers sensed a silent thumping feeling from a nearby elephant herd communicating with infrasonic sound (sound too low for human ears to detect).

This "secret language" of an intelligent species sparked my imagination and inspired me to add elements of magical realism to my novel—taking elephant communication even further. What if elephants really could communicate more clearly to humans? What would they tell us? And what are they trying to tell us now?

As I researched elephants for this story, I learned things that forever changed my perspective about how these amazing and complex creatures are treated. What I discovered made me sad and angry. At times, I saw things that made me want to look away. Instead, I chose to face the truth and learn what could be done to help.

At the age of fourteen, Juliette West became so concerned about elephant exploitation that she raised enough money to travel to Thailand on a mission to help. In Southeast Asia, many elephants are trained using violent methods to get them to do tricks, paint pictures, and give tourist rides up and down mountains with heavy wooden saddles strapped to their backs. In Thailand, Juliette worked with Lek Chailert, founder of the Save Elephant Foundation, to use the money she raised to rescue a sick and aging elephant and send her to the Elephant Nature Park, a sanctuary for exploited Asian elephants.

Juliette's efforts were documented in the award-winning film *How I Became an Elephant*. But she didn't stop there. She founded a nonprofit organization called JulietteSpeaks and travels to schools and conferences to encourage other young people to learn all they can and find ways to help elephants, too.

One person, one girl, one boy, can make a difference.

As I developed the idea for Lex's friendship with Nyah, I knew elephants were sometimes mistreated or living in inhumane conditions in the United States, and I was especially concerned about the treatment of elephants in circuses. I chose to write about Nyah, who came from a circus, where she had been forced to perform for audiences and live in confined spaces. But I also wanted Nyah's circus to have been run by people with a conscience, who came to understand her need for space and family and freedom. I wanted to show the evolution of her "rescue." Part of my research came from the documentary *One Lucky Elephant,* which shows a circus producer's relationship with an African elephant in his care, and his journey to find this elephant a safe and appropriate home away from circus life. This true story shows that not all circus stories are horrible, but they will always be complicated.

After the circus, Nyah went to live in a zoo, which also is a complicated situation for creatures as large and intelligent as elephants. Still, zoos are not the same as circuses, and not all zoos are equal. I mention the Association of Zoos and Aquariums (AZA) in the book and have made Nyah's zoo—like many zoos—accredited through the AZA. This means that it meets specific high standards and provides excellent care and environments for the elephants. AZA zoos also support elephant conservation projects, and many assist with research for a vaccine to prevent an incurable disease that kills young elephants both in human care and in the wild. Zoos often work to preserve threatened and endangered species through breeding programs, too. Check the AZA website to find out whether a zoo you are thinking of visiting is accredited. If not, decide whether you want to support it with a visit.

Elephants are complex creatures, especially in their social interactions and communications. Observing their behavior in person—hearing them, smelling them, sensing their infrasonic rumbling—can teach us their importance and make us feel connected to them in a way that watching them on a screen cannot. This can inspire more people to get involved in conservation efforts. I know this has been true for me. But not everyone agrees that our desire to observe elephants in person at zoos is more important than their need to be in the wild. I chose to end Nyah's story with the promise of being reunited with her "family" in a sanctuary. But as Lex discovered, these questions and answers are complicated.

Since *The Elephant's Girl* uses magical realism in its storytelling, I was able to make some plot choices that would not likely happen the way I've described them. A zoo with AZA accreditation would most likely not have two twelve-year-old children involved in elephant care and training—though elephant training is open for the public to observe. And most Nebraska winters would be too harsh and extreme for an elephant sanctuary, which usually provides an outdoor environment more closely matched to an elephant's natural habitat. Still, I chose to set this story in Nebraska because it has a history of frequent tornadoes, an AZA-accredited zoo where I once worked as a teenager—Omaha's Henry Doorly Zoo and Aquarium—and a city named Lexington, which makes a great name for Nyah's girl.

On behalf of Nyah, and all elephants, I hope *The Elephant's Girl* inspires you to learn more about these intelligent and majestic animals and to get involved in helping them, so that elephants will share our Earth for a long, long time.

*   *   *

Here are some books to get you started:

Downer, Ann. *Elephant Talk: The Surprising Science of Elephant Communication*. Minneapolis: Twenty-First Century Books, 2011.

Laidlaw, Rob. *Elephant Journey: The True Story of Three Zoo Elephants and Their Rescue from Captivity*. Toronto: Pajama Press, 2015.

O'Connell, Caitlin. *A Baby Elephant in the Wild*. New York: Houghton Mifflin Harcourt, 2014.

O'Connell, Caitlin, and Donna M. Jackson. *The Elephant Scientist*. Scientists in the Field. Boston: Houghton Mifflin Harcourt Books for Children, 2011.

Ruurs, Margriet. *The Elephant Keeper: Caring for Orphaned Elephants in Zambia*. Toronto: Kids Can Press, 2017.

These websites can help you learn more about elephant research, organizations that help elephants, and how you can adopt an elephant. Don't worry—if you adopt an elephant, they won't come to live with you! Donated money helps provide food, medicine, and care for elephants in orphanages and sanctuaries.

Cambodia Wildlife Sanctuary: cambodiawildlifesanctuary.com

Elephant Listening Project at the Cornell Lab: birds.cornell.edu/brp/elephant

Elephant Nature Park: elephantnaturepark.org

Elephant Voices: elephantvoices.org

International Elephant Foundation:
    elephantconservation.org

JulietteSpeaks: juliettespeaks.org

Performing Animal Welfare Society (PAWS): pawsweb.org

Save Elephant Foundation: saveelephant.org

Sheldrick Wildlife Trust: sheldrickwildlifetrust.org

Wildlife SOS: wildlifesos.org

World Wildlife Fund: worldwildlife.org

Acknowledgments

I'm eternally grateful to my brilliant superhero agent, Danielle Burby of Nelson Literary Agency. Your unflagging enthusiasm for this story is the reason readers can hold it in their hands today. Thank you for phone conversations that leave me smiling and for your vision. It's a gift to have found both a champion agent and a friend in the same person. I promise to write more casts of characters you'll love and worlds you'll want to live in.

Thank you to Kristin Nelson and everyone at Nelson Literary who works tirelessly on behalf of the NLA clients and their books. You're kind, conscientious professionals and true advocates.

A truly delighted thank-you to Emily Easton, my editor and the publisher of Crown Books for Young Readers, for loving Lex and Nyah as much as I do. Thank you for your passion, for understanding "the beating heart of this story," and for knowing how to strengthen it. Thank you to Ramona Kaulitzki for the gorgeous cover art that captures Lex's strength and Nyah's beauty and makes me want to hold them close. And thank you to Bob Bianchini for finding and working on the cover with Ramona. Thank you also to Samantha Gentry, Claire Nist, and all the talented people at Crown and Penguin Random House who worked tirelessly to bring this book to readers.

To my mom, who made library visits a priority of my childhood and who challenged me to read 100 books. You gave me Narnia and Green Gables and books that expanded my understanding of the world. Thank you for handing me books over and over again and for encouraging me when I wanted to write my own stories.

To my insightful and unfailingly loyal critique partners: Kate Coursey and Melanie Jex. I know you will always ask me the hard questions. You make me a better writer, and more importantly, a better person. I can trust you with my most vulnerable words. I'm blessed to be surrounded by such selfless, talented, and strong women.

Thank you to the people who told me I was a writer many years before I wrote this book—Rogene Boyd, Ardath Junge, Terry Foster, Kendra Rollins, Kirsten Honaker-Carter, and Christina Hilton Hall. Thank you to all my English teachers at Mission Junior High and Bellevue East High School in Nebraska. Dedicated teachers make all the difference.

I owe a debt of gratitude to the Utah writing community; the Writing and Illustrating for Young Readers conference, where I met my critique partners; and the Storymakers conference, where I met my agent. Thank you to all the writers who have sacrificed their time to teach or give critiques at those conferences. A special thanks to Rick Walton, Carol Lynch Williams, Ann Dee Ellis, Courtney Alameda, Ilima Todd, Amy White, Rebecca Leach, Rachel Coleman, Olivia

Carter, Brook Andreoli, Meagan Brooks, Chersti Nieveen, Steven Bohls, and Nan Marie Swapp.

Holly Black, thank you for teaching at the WIFYR conference, for the generous gift of your time and talents, and for showing me that even fictional worlds require research and even magic has rules.

To June, Tyson, and Amy Williamson, thank you for sharing your perspectives on family, food, and culture.

A big hats-off thank-you to Eric Peterson of Utah's Hogle Zoo, a veteran elephant trainer and advocate for worldwide elephant welfare in zoos and in the wild. Thank you for sharing with me your heartfelt experiences with these gentle giants and your belief in their irreplaceable importance in our world.

Thank you to Lawrence Anthony, a conservationist who put his life at risk to protect a dangerous herd of African elephants on a game reserve. He wrote about his experiences in his book *The Elephant Whisperer*. Mr. Anthony has moved on from this life, but his work remains to inspire and teach us all.

To my husband, Paul, my expert on steam trains and antique train restoration—you didn't know when you married this dancer that she would one day take up writing again and that it would shape and change our lives. Thank you for being my steadfast supporter, for listening to me go on for hours about plot and characters and story structure, and for always providing a safe place to land when I fall. It's your opinion that matters most.

To my daughter, Victoria, and my son, Maxwell—you inspire me and give me reasons to write. Thank you for being my first readers and for begging me to finish this book. Thank you for your patience when I've been unavailable and unmoving from my desk to meet a deadline. Always remember that you can change the world by doing what you love. Just be sure to change it for the better.

My thanks would not be complete without acknowledging my God, who answers my prayers in unexpected ways and teaches me that light will always chase away the storms.

And to Roald Dahl, Mildred D. Taylor, Judy Blume, Beverly Cleary, Ellen Raskin, Scott O'Dell, Irene Hunt, and Frances Hodgson Burnett: my child-reader heart thanks you. Your books were my friends and taught me empathy. Your books made me want to write in the first place.

About the Author

Celesta Rimington is the author of *The Elephant's Girl* and *Tips for Magicians*. She holds a degree in social psychology from Brigham Young University and has a background in the performing arts. She has lived in nearly every region of the United States, and although she can't actually talk to the wind, she's had several close encounters with tornadoes. Celesta is an elephant advocate, an enthusiastic supporter of the Performing Animal Welfare Society (PAWS) wildlife sanctuaries, and a member of the Society of Children's Book Writers and Illustrators. She now lives in the Rocky Mountains with her husband and children, where they have a miniature railroad with a rideable steam train. Follow her online at celestarimington.com.

TURN THE PAGE FOR A SNEAK PEEK
AT MORE MAGIC!

TIPS FOR MAGICIANS

CELESTA RIMINGTON

TIP ONE:
NEVER REPEAT A TRICK

You never really know if you're ready to perform a magic trick until you give it a try. I shuffle the cards and think through the steps of this new trick one more time. The sunlight shines through the living room windows, creating boxes of light on the blue carpet. I remember Mom wanted to replace that blue carpet.

Kennedy, who isn't my babysitter, pours what's left in her cup of water into the soil of Mom's withering houseplant. I have been watering it, and I put it in the sun every morning. I've done that for a year, but right now it's not doing well.

"Maybe we should pick up some plant food from the garden store," she says, giving the plant a look of pity. People look at me that way sometimes. It makes me want to change the subject.

"Maybe we should go to the pool," I say, shuffling my cards again. I use the overhand technique.

Kennedy smiles. "Harrison, your skin is still sunburned from the last time I took you and your friends swimming."

I look from her dark-brown skin to the bright-pink tint all over my white arms. "I'll wear more sunscreen."

Kennedy is starting college at the end of the summer. She's practically a grown-up. She has a car and a job working for her mom's talent agency. But even though Kennedy is like six years older than me, she's one of my best friends. And she's been hanging out with me a lot since Mom died last year.

"Mmm," she says, sitting on the couch and checking her phone. "Maybe I'll just put my feet in." She glances up and gives me a serious expression. "But you and the guys have to promise not to splash me."

"Okay," I say. Kennedy's black hair is smooth and much straighter than it was the last time we went to the pool. She's told me that it takes a long time to get her hair done that way. "Are you ready for this one?" I hold up my deck of cards.

She sets her phone down. "Ready. What is this trick called?"

"Topsy Turvy Cards."

I use the coffee table, and Kennedy watches as I

spread out the cards, to show they're all facing the same direction. She looks at the cards and then at me. I think she's wondering if I'll give away the secret.

I follow the steps as I remember them, turning the cards over in my hand like the video showed. I make it seem like I've turned half of the stack faceup and half of the stack facedown. But by passing a "magic" card through the center of the deck, suddenly the cards are all the same direction again.

Kennedy grins. "Wow, Harrison. I totally didn't see how you did that," she says.

"Is that sarcasm?" I let out an awkward laugh.

"No, not at all. I don't know how you did it." She leans forward. "Lemme see it again."

I gather up my cards in one hand. "No way."

"Pleeeease."

This is a test. I'm sure of it.

"A magician never repeats a trick," I say.

"Because?" She raises one eyebrow.

Yeah, she was testing me. Kennedy knows what happened last time I showed a card trick to Creed and a few of the other kids at karate.

"Because someone will figure out your secret and ruin the mystery."

Kennedy pumps her open hands toward the ceiling. "I think he's got it!"

The air-conditioning clicks on and blows the curtains

by the sliding glass doors. Sometimes, when the air is blowing from the vents, I still smell whispers of Mom's hairspray and perfume.

"But can I make one suggestion?" Kennedy pulls out her phone again and motions for me to come closer.

"Sure," I say.

Kennedy types the words *magician persona* in a search on her phone. I've been watching YouTube tutorials for how to do these card tricks, but I've never seen those words together before.

"You and I know a lot about show business because of our moms, right?" Kennedy's mom was my mom's talent agent and friend. I like how Kennedy brings up my mom in regular conversation, like it's no big deal. When Dad talks about Mom—or I mention her in front of him—it feels like a big deal.

"Well . . . you know about show business from *both* of your parents," she says, waving her hand like that wasn't her point. "What I'm saying is, to be a good magician, you've got to bring in some performance quality to your tricks."

"Okaaay," I say. "Like what?"

"Look here." Kennedy shows me the website for a stage magician named Leo Abbott. "This says, 'A magician persona is a character you play as the magician. Your audience might be impressed by how well you do the magic tricks, but you add to the wonder by the way you present yourself.'"

I read the list on her screen. "'Magicians can be mysterious, scary, funny . . .'"

"'Decide on your style, and then perform *with* the trick,'" Kennedy says. She drops her phone on the couch and points across the room toward the fireplace. "Go over there like you've just walked onstage in front of a huge audience. They are waiting. A completely silent crowd, holding their breath in anticipation. Waiting for *your* magic."

I've learned not to argue with Kennedy. She's usually right anyway.

I take my deck of cards and stand in front of the fireplace, facing her.

"Now, who are you? You feel those stage lights warm your face. The music is quiet. It's just you: a magician and your cards."

I take a deep breath. I can't imagine I would ever be in front of a huge audience. Kennedy widens her eyes at me, and I start laughing.

"You're making this too serious," I say.

She smiles. "Okay, so maybe you're a comedic magician. You make people laugh with your tricks."

"I don't think so. I just feel weird standing here like this."

"Face the other way, then. Pretend I'm not here. Imagine performing as a magician. How will you act?"

I turn toward the fireplace. The hearth still has a clay sculpture on it that Mom made. She thought it was terrible, and only made it because her sister, Maggie, was visiting, and Aunt Maggie gets everyone to try art projects. The sculpture is supposed to be me and Mom together. I asked to keep it, even though she didn't think it was very good. The memory feels heavy enough to make my shoulders slump. It makes me feel like I don't want to go swimming or see my karate friends today.

Suddenly, I know what my magician person-thing will be. It'll be mysterious and keep my audience from knowing too much. It will be impressive and confident. It will push away this sad feeling.

"Harrison?" Kennedy says. "Don't make it too hard. You can try out some different ways."

I think of all the times I saw Mom perform onstage. Even when I watched her from the wings, I noticed what Kennedy is talking about. Mom had a way of being bigger and braver than her usual self when she was in front of an audience.

I can be like that.

I turn back toward Kennedy and give her a smile.

"What will you call your magician self?" she asks.

That one is easy. "Harrison"—I pause for effect— "the Magnificent."

TIP TWO: CHOOSE A GOOD MAGICIAN NAME

"*Lavender's blue, dilly dilly, lavender's green . . .*" Mom sat on the edge of my bed and sang.

"*Mom?*" I lifted my head from my pillow and interrupted her. "*How can lavender be blue and green? Isn't lavender light purple?*"

"*It's referring to the lavender plant, Harry.*"

"*Oh.*"

She continued the song. "*When you are king, dilly dilly, I shall be queen . . .*"

Mom's voice was what the reviewers called "*a clean, clear soprano that rises from the stage and takes audiences to the heavens with it.*" Or something like that. Some people said her voice was magical. To me, though, Mom's voice was the sound of home.

"Who told you so, dilly dilly," she sang, "who told you so?"

I joined her on the last part, my voice able to match her notes.

"'Twas my own heart, dilly dilly, that told me so."

Mom leaned over and kissed my forehead. She smelled like peaches and lime-flavored lip balm. She hadn't washed off her stage makeup, and her long eyelashes tickled my face.

She tucked the sheets around me and whispered, "Never stop singing, Harry. It's a gift."

I sighed and nodded, too sleepy to answer. I'd waited up for her, something I always did on her show nights, so we could have a good-night song before bed. She always met with her audiences and signed autographs after her shows, but she kept the meet and greets short and hurried home to sing me to sleep. That was our thing. That was Mom.

She sang one more song—one from her show. It was called "You Are." I closed my eyes and listened, happy to have her home.

"I sang that at the Red Cliffs Amphitheater the summer we lived in Muse," she said. "Do you remember?"

I was only five when we were there, but I still remembered a few things about that summer in the Utah art village. I remembered walls of red rocks and the buzz-

ing of bugs in the desert. I had made a friend named Chloe, and I remembered that, too.

I was getting sleepy. "Yes," I whispered.

"That place is full of magic, Harrison. We'll go back to visit again sometime."

"Okay," I mumbled.

"Good night, Harrison the Magnificent."

Mom often called people names that sounded like magicians. So I was Harrison the Magnificent, and Dad was Calvin the Incredible.

"Good night, Mom."

+ +

Kennedy drops me off at home after karate, like she does every Tuesday and Thursday. I wave at her from the porch as she backs her car out of the driveway.

"Put some ice on that elbow!" she calls out the car window.

My elbow got bent back a little too far in a move called Breaking Twigs today. I didn't want to make a big deal about it in front of Creed and the rest of the class, but now, it's pretty sore.

I wave at Kennedy with my good arm. "I will!"

"And tell your dad!" she adds.

I nod at that one. Kennedy keeps nudging that Dad and I need to "communicate." Dad doesn't say much, so I guess I don't, either. But we used to have a lot of fun together.

I push the front door open and lug my karate bag inside.

"How was class?" Dad asks from behind his laptop on the living room couch. He's home a little early from his job at the National Theatre in Washington, DC.

"It was fine," I say, not wanting to bother him about my elbow. "How was work?"

Dad runs his hand over his unshaven face. He sometimes goes days without shaving—just one of many things that's changed since Mom died. "We need to have a talk as soon as I finish this."

"Okay." I can't tell if this is good or bad news. I leave my bag by the door, holding my throbbing elbow. Dad didn't used to work all the time. We used to go hiking along the Potomac in the fall. In the hot summer months, he always found time to take me kayaking at Lake Ridge Marina. But not this summer. I've missed time with Dad. It's weird to miss someone who is still here.

I grab my deck of cards off the top of the dusty piano and practice my one-handed cut. My hands are still a bit too small to cut the deck, spin the top section, and put it back together with only one hand. But I'm getting better at it.

"I'll be back," I say as I head to the kitchen.

I pocket my cards and grab a bag of peas from the

freezer. I return to the living room with the frozen peas on my sore elbow and sink into the orange armchair. Dad closes his laptop.

"I wanted to ask you . . ." He leans forward, resting his elbows on his knees. He stares at the glass coffee table as though he might develop superpowers and cut through it with his laser vision. "What would you think about going to visit Aunt Maggie?"

"Aunt Maggie? *Really?*" Of all the things to follow the words "We need to have a talk," I didn't expect something this great.

My aunt owns an art gallery in a town called Muse, where we lived that summer Mom had a performing contract there. It's in the southern Utah desert, and people come from all over the world to tour the national parks and hike the red cliffs. Aunt Maggie has come to visit us a few times, too. The last time we saw her was at Mom's funeral, but even then, it was comforting to have her around.

"Yes! Dad, that would be awesome!" If we went to Utah, Dad and I could go on those amazing hikes, and he'd have time to do things with me again.

Dad doesn't seem as excited as he should be. I'm about to remind him about the parks and the hikes when he says, "Well . . . there's an opening in the Dorian Striker show, and they've asked me to stage-manage."

"In Utah?"

Dorian Striker is a performer that Mom and Dad

knew before I was born, when Mom was touring as a professional singer and Dad was her stage manager. Dorian Striker plays guitar and sings. He has a full band and big sets and special effects. I saw ads for his show on TV just last month.

Dad still stares at the smudged, dusty glass of the coffee table. I don't remember the last time we used a cleaner on that glass. "It's a national tour, Harrison."

I know right away what this means. Mom used to tour before I was born. It wasn't a life like I have, with a colonial-style house and Christmas wreaths in the windows and a backyard forest. It was a life of different cities every week, sometimes terrible food, hotel beds, lots of vitamin C, and lots of travel.

"Oh." My fingers are icy from holding the bag of peas. My skin burns with the cold, but it gives me something else to feel besides the thumping in my chest. Dad didn't mean he would be coming to visit Aunt Maggie *with* me.

"Life on tour isn't something I want for you. But I also don't want you to be alone so much."

I wonder how much Kennedy tells him.

"I'm not alone that much," I say, lying.

Dad looks up, finally. "I think it would be good for you to be with family and to meet new people. And if you went to live with Maggie, I could take this stage-managing job and know you were okay while I was on the road."

I let the peas drop to the floor.

"Wait . . . I'm going to *live* in Utah?"

"Did you hurt yourself at karate?" He's noticed the peas.

"I'm going to live in Utah *without you?*"

"What happened to your arm?" Dad says, concerned, and stands up from the couch.

I shake my head. "It's fine." I bend and straighten my elbow a few times. "See?" It feels like it's creaking, from being frozen.

Dad relaxes a little and walks to the front window, looking out at the cherry tree in the golden sunset. It's nearly the end of summer, so the pink blossoms are long gone.

"I think we should sell the house, Harrison." The spring in the old clock clunks as it unwinds. I feel the noise in my chest, almost as if it's hitting my heart.

"I need a fresh start," he says. "And I think you do, too."

"But what if I don't want a fresh start?"

"This place reminds me of your mom." Dad looks darkly at the room, like he can't stand it here. It hits me like a kick to the stomach.

"Can't we have a fresh start *together?*" I suddenly feel like I'm sitting in a stranger's living room. I take the cards from my pocket, fumble, and drop half the deck.

Dad turns at the sound, his expression stiff. I can't

tell if he's mad at me for dropping cards, or if it's my card tricks in general that irritate him.

His face relaxes after a minute. He steps over my spilled cards and helps me pick them up, and I catch a glimpse of what Dad was like before Mom died. Calvin the Incredible who needs a shave.

"You still working on that new trick?" he asks. "What do you call it?"

"I have two I'm working on," I say quietly. Harrison the Magnificent should be bolder, but I can't do it right now. "The Ambitious Card and the Four Burglars. I'm not quite ready to show them yet."

"You'll get it," he says. "Keep practicing. I'd love for you to show them to me before we leave. Production meetings start in Las Vegas in six weeks. And I want to get you to Aunt Maggie's in time to start school there."

"Isn't there a job you can do in her town?" I think of Dad and me in another place, in a house I imagine from my aunt's description—adobe-style, with cactus and rocks in the yard and red cliffs rising behind it. I imagine us exploring desert caves. Following a different plan. I imagine Harrison the Magnificent performing a spectacular trick to make all the dusty sadness disappear. Like a bright light shoving out a heavy fog.

"In Muse?" Dad stands and paces the room. "Not the kind of work I'm good at, Harrison. That theater where your mom performed used to have a professional crew and stage management, but Maggie said it closed down a few years ago."

"Maybe you could get it running again."

"Harrison . . ."

"Or I could go on tour with you!"

Dad shakes his head.

"But I don't see why it's better to split up. We used to be three of us. Now we're two. And if you leave me in Utah, we're not really like a family. It's me by myself, and you by yourself, and that's not any better."

"The tour is only for six months," Dad says, using *his* new trick of not showing emotion. He's worked hard on that talent—almost as hard as I've worked on my card tricks. One of the ways he stays emotionless is to never play Mom's recordings. I haven't heard her sing for over a year. "I need the work, and it'll be good for you to live with Aunt Maggie."

I can tell I'm not going to win this discussion right now. I notice that Dad is standing directly in front of the fireplace. On the hearth behind him is the clay sculpture Mom made of her and me. I think about how Muse is a place Mom has been, a place she's performed. It's a place I've been with her, even though I don't really remember it. Maybe I could feel close to Mom there, but I won't have those painful aches that creep up and take your breath away when you round the ice cream aisle in the Food Lion.

I try the one-handed cut again. For the first time ever, I split the deck with my fingers, spin the top section, flip it over, and combine the deck together again in one piece. With one hand. Without dropping a single card.

That has to mean something important.

And I decide right then. If Dad is sending me to live in Muse with Aunt Maggie, then I have to figure out a way for Dad to be there with me. A fresh start in a place Mom has been.